To Live or Die in Arizona

An Abby Taylor Mystery

Elizabeth B. Lewis

D1022473

Elizabeth Bruening Lewis

Dromedary Press

Dromedary Press
4350 East Camelback Road
Suite 260-E
Phoenix, AZ 85018-2757

This is a work of fiction. All characters and their
actions are a product of the author's imagination.
Any resemblance to actual events or persons, living
or dead, is entirely coincidental. Most settings are
equally imaginary, including the Pycenium Mine.
However, the magnificent San Francisco Peaks are
very real. Also in the world of reality is the Copper
State 1000, a colorful and much enjoyed annual
event sponsored by the Phoenix Men's Art Council
for the benefit of the Phoenix Art Museum. But no
car has ever gone missing, most especially not a
vintage Alfa Romeo.

Cover by Mark Mohlenbrock
Book Design by Hal Sandy

ISBN 0-9717325-0-7
Manufactured in the United States of America.

For Allene Ragan Bruening,
Erma Bombeck and
Elle Bergstrom

and for all those, too numerous to
mention here, who gave of their
time and talents to this book

In their honor, all proceeds from this book,
both author's and publisher's, will go to the
Polycystic Kidney Disease Foundation
and the Arizona Kidney Foundation.

INTRODUCTION

To Live or Die in Arizona is a work of fiction, but the threats to the fragile environment of Arizona woven through the fast-paced narrative are very real. The 1872 Mining Law is no figment of the author's fertile imagination. It does indeed allow mining companies free access to *our* national forests to explore for minerals, no permits or other permission needed. If they discover valuable minerals, they can stake a claim to the land on which the minerals are found, then proceed to mine them, incidentally paying no royalties to the government for the privilege.

Not even the San Francisco Peaks, sacred to Navajo, Hopi, and eleven other tribes, have proved exempt. One of the great challenges I faced as Secretary of the Interior was to negotiate the closure of a pumice mine operating on the Peaks and to effect the beginning of the return of the land to its natural state.

However, there are still thousands of claims scattered about the region of the San Francisco Peaks. This is a situation which does not bode well for the future, since the Mining Law has a provision whereby a mining entity, having done a stated amount of work on a claim or claims, can patent them. This means, in effect, that they can buy the land, at a song, even in a national forest. There has been a moratorium on patenting since 1994. But that could change, allowing inappropriate development in areas that the public mistakenly thinks of as being theirs forever for recreation, the enjoyment of scenic beauty, and spiritual refreshment.

Against this background of a challenged Arizona, Elizabeth Lewis has skillfully told the tale of a challenged heroine. She is a woman running for her life—from the demons within and, it soon becomes apparent, from murderous forces from without. The author has used the Arizona setting to mirror and enhance the protagonist's personal drama as the central question ominously looms larger and larger: To Live or Die in Arizona?

THE HONORABLE BRUCE BABBITT,
Former Secretary of the Interior
and Former Governor of Arizona

To Live or Die in Arizona

An Abby Taylor Mystery

She came back to the present in darkness. Panic swept over her like a cold wind. Once, long ago, she had been born from darkness into light, joining the world as a howling baby. Now she felt she was slipping inexorably back into darkness again. Not a gentle journey. Her head ached violently, her body was an alien thing—violated by the now useless mechanisms of life. Her abdomen was distended, the pressure of unexcreted fluids pressing heavily upon her. She was trapped. Trapped by the sickness of her body, trapped by the lightless, almost airless place of confinement. Perhaps after all death would be a blessed release.

Desperately she fought the panic as well as the waves of nausea that assailed her. Where was she? The only light was a muted one from some sort of aperture with horizontal slats close to the ceiling. An air duct? She was lying on a rough concrete slab, but she could tell nothing more about the materials or structure of the place, except that she sensed it wasn't large. Perhaps the size of one of those big walk-in closets she had encountered on a Scottsdale house tour she had taken with her sister. But this was no closet. The place was empty except for a few piles of something that looked like shallow boxes in the faint light, and something alive and breathing beside her. She reached out a hand. Something soft and warm and furry.

Then it all came back. She knew where she was. She knew who had put her here. She knew for certain that her friend had been murdered and who had murdered him. Even more important, she knew *why* he had been murdered. But would she, could she, live long enough to tell anyone else?

CHAPTER 1

She flashed her lights and the Ford Explorer that had been hogging the fast lane reluctantly pulled right. The way ahead clear, she zipped past a camper with a couple of kids' bikes strapped to the back, a Qwest service truck, and a white van boldly announcing in bright blue letters the New Christian Church, Mesa, AZ. Abby Taylor wasn't usually an aggressive driver. But now she was running; in a sense she was running for her life.

I'm running all right, but from the past or toward the future? she wondered. She gripped the steering wheel even tighter, maneuvering around an eighteen wheeler, like her accelerating rapidly up the highway toward Flagstaff, Arizona. The past, for all its pain and heartaches, had certainly had its compensations. *The future?* Not an inviting proposition. No, she decided, she wasn't running from the one or toward the other. She was running as any wounded, startled animal ran, the deer from the mountain lion, the rabbit from the coyote, the elk from the hunter. A blind reaction triggered by an atavistic instinct for survival.

Great ponderosa pines whipped by, their black shadows slicing across the interstate. The shadows cleaved the bright ribbon of sunlit pavement into disjointed segments and increased still further her sense of speed. Through no volition of her own the insistent rhythms of Respighi's *Pines of Rome* pounded in her head. Yet in spite of the velocity at which the traffic moved along I-17, she noted with surprise that this last stretch up from Phoenix had an unexpected air of tranquility which even in her present fragmented state of mind she couldn't fail to appreciate. It was the gift of the three enormous peaks looming directly ahead—massive, commanding, eerily beautiful. The peaks dominated their environs by the sheer weight of their presence. Huge and aloof, they seemed to belong to this world, yet also to another; to be part of this time, but also part of all

3

times past, present, and future.

For a tenuous moment Abby ardently wished her soul could soar, free and unencumbered, off to those distant mountains, leaving the weary body that had betrayed her behind. A quick jerk of the wheel. . . . But no, she countered, feeling a hot wave of shame and anger for ever having had such a thought. Whatever else she might have become, she was still no quitter. Expressing her exasperation at herself and at life in general, she stomped down harder on the accelerator.

Traffic slowed to a crawl as she passed under I-40 and into the city of Flagstaff. It was a bottleneck that abruptly constrained the vehicles that had bounded so freely along the highway. Not at all like the brochure from the Chamber of Commerce, was her first impression. Too much crammed into too small a space. Not enough breathing room. Certainly too much frenetic activity for someone seeking R&R. Perhaps renting a house for the summer here without first checking out the situation had been a mistake. It wasn't that Flagstaff was so far distant from Phoenix. In theory she could have driven up for the day. But as her disease progressed she'd discovered that even small things required a disproportionate effort.

"Damn!" she cursed and hit the horn as a teenage boy driving an aging, sun-blistered red Chevy truck shot out of a side street without stopping. At the last minute the sound of her horn penetrated the miasma of country western music that spewed forth from the truck's cab. The pimply, gum-chomping adolescent swerved, missing her Volvo by inches. Then unconcernedly he drove on, snapping his fingers to a song about a cold, cold-hearted lover who'd done his woman wrong. Abby, swearing at the boy, his gum, and his appalling music, again laid hard on the horn. *Damned inconsiderate, self-absorbed idiot. Damned uncaring little bastard.*

Still shaking, she turned into the side street the kid had exited and pulled over to the curb to regain her composure. Her heart was beating double-time. With effort she unpeeled her clenched fingers from the steering wheel, stretched her rigid hands, and tried to breathe deeply.

Looking about she suddenly realized that in avoiding her the boy had sideswiped a small dog. A sudden bolt of anger seared her flesh, leaving her shaken and trembling. How could anyone treat life so casually, especially the life of an innocent little animal? That one thoughtless act seemed to sum up everything wrong in the world, the blind unfairness of it all.

Hastily she put the car in park, turned off the motor, and ran over to the side of the street where the dog lay curled up, whimpering softly.

"Easy does it, little fellow," she told him while looking for a collar and tags. *Nothing. So what now? Pick up a strange, wounded animal? Insanity.* She reflected that if she were in the dog's present plight she'd probably bite anyone who so much as touched her, even a friend. "But I can't just abandon you," she told the soft brown eyes which gazed trustingly up at her. Abby looked around. Plenty of vehicular traffic on the main drag, but nothing on the small side street and not a pedestrian in sight.

The little creature solved the problem. A rough pink tongue emerged and caressed her arm as she knelt before him. Taking that as a sign of trust and acceptance, Abby, although still wary, gently lifted the wounded animal. He continued whimpering but made no move to harm her.

She found him heavier, more solidly built than she'd first assumed. His reddish-brown pelt was soft as a teddy bear's. But underneath was solid muscle. She carried him carefully to her car, where she was confronted with the problem of opening the passenger door. She could, of course, set him down on the asphalt while she opened the door. But to lose physical contact with him at this point seemed a breach of trust. She hesitated a moment, then tucked him firmly under her left arm, pinning him to her body, and hoped he wouldn't wiggle. Yes, much heavier than he looked. Yet, except for a small whine, he remained utterly passive, perhaps sensing the delicacy of the operation. She pulled the door open and settled him on the passenger seat.

Abby got in and turned on the motor. For a moment she sat there assessing the situation, her heart still pounding from the shock of the truck's near miss and the sight of the injured animal. Surely someplace in the snarl of commercial development along the main drag she could find an intact yellow pages, or perhaps a filling-station attendant who could direct her to an animal hospital. As it happened, neither alternative was necessary. A block or so down the way she spotted a sign for a veterinarian.

* * *

"Here, drink this."

Abby took a sip of the proffered glass of water to buy time to regain her composure. How embarrassing! A mature woman who had recently passed the big four-o, a college professor, albeit on indefinite leave of absence for health reasons, a sensible and presumably competent human being behaving as if she were a giddy school girl or a menopausal matron with the vapors.

"It's probably the shock of that crazy kid almost hitting her and then finding he had hit the dog instead," she heard one veterinary assistant whisper to the other.

"She said something about blood, only there isn't any," the second assistant whispered back. Of course the woman was right, Abby thought. No blood at all, only the tubing for the dog's IV. But that had brought up a sudden, stark image of other tubes through which blood had run, the blood of her father. Her heart started pounding frantically again. The room did a slow spin. She remembered with undiminished horror the years of dialysis. She could never forget her father's blood flowing from his body into an artificial kidney. The kidney cleansed it and removed the excess liquid, yet also seemed to filter out a little bit of his vitality with every treatment. And now she herself faced a similar fate. Abby concentrated on breathing slowly and evenly, thus restoring some semblance of balance and calm. Gradually the dizziness began to ebb.

"Could be the altitude," the first assistant quietly told her companion. "Seven thousand feet affects some people that way."

"I'm sorry," Abby said, and put down the glass of water. "It's been a rather long day." A very long day, she reflected, stretching from the stunning heat of Phoenix to a veterinarian's clinic in

Flagstaff 150 miles north and some 6,000 feet higher. Moreover, the day wasn't half over yet. She hoped that at least it would contain no more traumas. One long, hard drive, one close call, an injured animal, and a near fainting spell—enough already! And all that against the backdrop of trying to adjust to her illness, trying to make something of her shattered life. *Would she, could she, ever adjust to what life had flung her way?* A numbing wave of helplessness engulfed her. She craved peace and quiet. She only hoped the rental house wouldn't be too hard to find.

A small, brisk woman with pressed Levis under her white lab coat, jogging shoes, and a friendly smile trotted into the examining room as the two assistants departed to care for other patients. A name tag identified her as the vet.

"Is the dog going to make it?" Abby asked right off, surprising herself with the level of her concern.

"Yes, indeed, he's basically a hearty little thing," the vet assured her. "A bone's cracked and he's suffering from malnutrition and dehydration. But he'll weather that. No sign of an owner?"

"None."

"It's a darned shame. All too often some university student will adopt a pet, then abandon it at the end of the semester. Considering that the spring semester finished up not long ago that's probably what happened to this fellow. Only you rarely see that problem with a pure bred."

"A pure bred?" Abby looked again at the animal: reddish-brown fur with white on the chest and at the paws, black at the end of a long muzzle; large pointed ears, a long thick body, short legs, no tail. To her mind, a most unusual combination of parts. "He's not a Heinz 57 variety?"

"No," the vet laughed, "he's not a mutt. He's a Welsh corgi, specifically a Pembroke Welsh corgi. They're two sorts of corgis, but it's easy enough to tell them apart. The Pembrokes don't have tails."

"Can we find him an owner? I'm happy to pay you for all you've done," Abby added quickly so there would be no misunderstanding, "but he's going to need a permanent home. I'll advertise for his former owner and do whatever you suggest. However, if you're right about someone abandoning him, then it's probably a wasted effort."

"Probably. And finding a new owner wouldn't be much of a problem if only he were a puppy. People want puppies, not older dogs." The vet shook her head. "Although I'd guess that this guy is still under two years. Young and lots of life there. Couldn't you adopt him?"

"Oh, I don't think so," Abby replied quickly. "I'm renting, you see. Just for the summer. It's so hot in Phoenix that I couldn't take it any longer," she explained ruefully. "I haven't even seen the house yet, but I really doubt whether the landlord would allow an animal."

And I don't want an animal either, she added to herself, reflecting bitterly that through no fault of her own her kidneys were going to hell and there was nothing she could do about it. She had abandoned a teaching position she loved because she didn't have the energy to perform any longer in what she considered a satisfactory fashion. Along with her job she'd left friends, colleagues, and an entire pretty darned satisfactory way of life. She'd come to Phoenix to be near her younger sister, her only living relative, and her sister's family. But the onset of summer had assaulted the desert with such intense heat that she'd scurried away like a lizard making for the shadow of a boulder. Up to Flagstaff, where in the first ten minutes some demented kid had almost crashed into her with his ratty truck and mowed down a poor dog instead. Then at the sight of the IV tubes she'd become faint and had come damned close to passing out in the vet's office. This just wasn't a very good batting average! *My life is out of control, my energy is fading fast, and my health is on a steady downward spiral*, she screamed inside herself. *Take care of a dog? I can just barely manage to take care of myself.*

"At least consider it." The vet looked around as if just remembering that she had a waiting room full of other patients. "In any case, we'll need to keep him overnight for observation. Come see us tomorrow."

Yeah, sure, Abby thought, *if I can keep my life from totally unraveling that long.*

* * *

Thankfully Abby found the place she had rented without too much trouble, a modest, one-story, forest-green bungalow on a quiet residential street well away from congestion and traffic. Flagstaff was looking better. She had picked up a sack of groceries and brought them in, along with an overnight case. Her legs still felt a little shaky and her heart had not yet entirely reestablished its natural rhythm. She decided that everything else could wait.

The key she had been given worked smoothly. Inside, a quick glance around assured her that all was in order. Off the small entryway was a nice-sized living room with a wood-burning fireplace and a dining area at the back. With approval she noted the extensive, built-in book cases, not surprising since she understood that her landlord was a university professor. With equal approval she took in the large chairs, good reading lamps, and what looked to be a superior music system. Except for an inexplicable overabundance of red plaid (did the professor see himself as a Scottish laird?), she doubted that she could have found anything more suitable.

A quick walk through the house revealed a small but apparently exceptionally well organized kitchen at the back. Two bedrooms opened off a hall which paralleled the living room. The front one was set up as a study with a computer, more books, and other expected academic paraphernalia. The couch looked like the sort that opened into a bed. Good if for any reason her sister came up and spent the night. Between the bedrooms she discovered an adequate though not luxurious bathroom in a shade of Pepto-Bismol pink that shrieked 1950s, or, this being Flagstaff, Arizona, maybe 1960s. Anyway, the house had everything that she really needed. Best of all, no constant whir of air conditioning, no claustrophobic sense of being trapped indefinitely in a refrigerated space, and no fear that if she went out of doors she might start to melt like the gooey asphalt on the Phoenix streets.

She fixed herself a bite of lunch in the tiny kitchen–though no smaller, she reminded herself, than the one in her digs in Poughkeepsie, New York. Certainly someone had worked a lot harder at making it functional: instead of being tossed haphazardly into drawers small items were hung on a wall of pegboard, along with pots and pans, colanders, and all the other basics. Even the spices in their racks were alphabetically arranged. Cutting knives filled a knife rack beside a substantial chopping board. Mixing spoons, cooking forks, and spatulas waited ready at hand in large, bright ceramic beer steins.

After lunch she called the Humane Society to report finding the dog. She also placed a notice in the newspaper, noting down the number so that if the owner didn't respond, she could call back and place an ad for adoption. These tasks having been accomplished she left a message on her sister Becky's answering machine to let her know she'd arrived safely and would call back later. Then with great pleasure she selected some of her landlord's classical CDs—a bit of Mozart, Grieg and Shostakovich—and curled up in one of the big armchairs with a juicy, tell-all biography of Clare Boothe Luce. She took a deep breath of lightly pine-scented air and felt herself begin to unwind. The tension in her neck and shoulders from the hours at the wheel started to loosen, her heart calming to something approximating its natural rhythm.

The clarinet entwined sensuously with the violins as the strains of Mozart's *Concerto in A* came over the sound system. She cuddled further down in the armchair. At long last the peace and quiet for which she had yearned! Maybe Flagstaff wasn't going to be so bad after all.

And yet the issue of the dog remained to nag at her, worming itself in among Clare Boothe Luce's truly amazing escapades like a needle tripping over a slight scratch on an old Mozart LP, the tick interfering with the lush, soothing sound. Abby found herself balking at the thought of consigning the creature to the animal shelter. The little animal didn't deserve what fate had dished up for him any more than she deserved some strange disease she'd never heard of a year ago.

Autosomal dominant polycystic kidney disease. What a tongue-twisting, heartbreaking, polysyllabic diagnosis. All those syllables just to say that her kidneys were giving out, and not because of anything she'd done or failed to do.   Simply born that way. Specifically, cysts filled with matter she would normally excrete were forming in her kidneys, blocking their usual function.   And not a damn thing she could do about it.

"Am I going to die?" she'd asked the doctor in a voice as flat as the line on a heart monitor when the patient has expired.

Abby knew that people who received such dire news were supposed to feel anger, fear, helplessness.   She felt the fear all right. It coursed through her body like some vicious, painful cancer attacking all her vital organs.   And she felt the helplessness.   But beyond fear and helplessness, the shock was so great that she had no sensation whatsoever.   No emotions at all.   It was as if part of her had been buried under an icy avalanche never to reappear, or at least not until this very morning when a ratty Chevy truck had sideswiped a little dog.

"Don't think so negatively," answered the doctor who was trying to explain what those many syllables meant.   "Yes, polycystic kidney disease can be fatal.   In fact, it's by far the most common of all life-threatening hereditary diseases.   But you are a strong, vital woman with a healthy lifestyle.   In some instances the cysts develop so slowly they don't constitute a major health problem during a normal life span.   Unfortunately, however, not in your case; the disease is progressing at a steady rate.   On the other hand, there is dialysis and perhaps eventual transplant, although I don't want to get your hopes up on that score because the increasing demand for organs makes the waiting list stretch out to years.   But with dialysis. . ."

Christ almighty, Abby had thought, *has this kind, well-meaning general practitioner ever spent time with someone on dialysis? Well, I have. My father. And I cannot even imagine enduring what he did.*   In the recesses of her mind she could still see the tubes— those life-giving, life-taking tubes—the same image that had caused her to come close to fainting earlier today in the vet's office.

As the doctor in Poughkeepsie who had first diagnosed the disease and later the specialist in New York had made clear, there was no cure for the many-syllabled monster; no treatment except for keeping blood pressure under control and some slight dietary modifications. Abby had denied the reality as long as possible, as long as she could reasonably function as an English professor at Vassar College. But the nausea, vomiting, headaches, and above all the crushing fatigue finally had put an end to that. And so she had started running, running first to her sister in Phoenix and then from the dreadful summer heat of Phoenix to the relative cool of Flagstaff. When would she, or even *could* she, stop? She shook her head. She felt disgusted at her own inability to deal with the situation.

Well, her own life might be spinning out of control, but at least she could temper what seemed to be fate's malicious scenario for the dog, she thought with a sudden spasm of anger at life in general and a careless kid in a Chevy truck in particular. Should she board the little animal or keep him here until someone, owner or potential new owner, appeared? And could she keep him here for a short while even if she decided to? How did her absent landlord really feel about dogs? Unfortunately she hadn't read the lease all that carefully. Was there some clause prohibiting animals? To find that out she would need to consult Sorrell Lawrence, the Realtor who had found her the rental. But that, thank heavens, along with all other significant actions, could wait for tomorrow.

* * *

Abby reached her sister, Becky, in Phoenix that evening to give her an account of the day beginning with the near fender-bender or worse.

"What is it about cars and Flagstaff?" Becky wailed.

Abby reminded her sister that this morning's foe had been a truck, not a car. She could picture Becky, cordless phone tucked between shoulder and small, determined chin, moving deftly around the large, bright kitchen of her home, her short, dark curls bouncing with every light step. Although the sisters bore some resemblance to one another, Becky was shorter, softer, and, without being the slightest bit overweight except by a model's skeletal standards, more well rounded. Her curves—from the bouncing dark curls to her small, dainty feet—contrasted with the vertical lines that distinguished her taller, longer-limbed older sister. Even before illness had started to make its subtle alterations to her appearance, Abby often found that new acquaintances, swept away by her sister's genuine prettiness and infectious animation, might initially ignore her. It was a state of affairs that had always amused rather than annoyed Abby, especially since it gave her more latitude for observation. She enjoyed watching people, or at least she had until their vitality contrasted with her own increasing lethargy began to annoy and depress her.

"Speaking about cars. . . ." Abby had been going to make a cutting comment about the volume of traffic in central Flagstaff, when her sister interrupted her.

"Oh, Abby, things are getting worse, not better! The Alfa Romeo. . . ."

Becky did not have to explain what Alfa Romeo. In April everyone in Arizona if not the entire country had been speculating on the fate of the fabulous antique car stolen the last night of the Copper State 1000, a four-day classic car rally along the scenic, less-traveled roads of Arizona sponsored by the MACs, members of the Men's Art Council of the Phoenix Art Museum. And, if at that time anyone had been in a coma or fishing on some far northern Canadian lake and thus detached from the rest of the world, the continuing furor stirred up by Albert Foster Richmond, the car's irate owner, would subsequently have brought the story to his or her attention.

"So what's happening now?" Abby asked as she settled herself further into one of her landlord's lusciously oversized armchairs.

"That pompous ass Foster Richmond is threatening to sue Charles along with the Copper State 1000, and the Men's Art Council, and the Phoenix Art Museum, and the city of Flagstaff, and probably the whole state of Arizona."

"He's *been* threatening to sue the Copper State, the Men's Art Council and all the rest ever since his car was stolen. Adding Charles to the list seems like gilding the lily, but then I don't really see what Foster can do about him anyway," Abby replied, referring to her sister's tall, blond, solid husband, the perfect foil, Abby had always thought, for the petite, vivacious brunette he had married.

"So the car disappeared on his watch, but no one has ever criticized Charles for the arrangements he made for the machines that last night in Flagstaff. And if push should ever come to shove, as a member of the Men's Art Council he's undoubtedly covered by their insurance policy," she added reassuringly.

Charles, the conservative, methodical banker type, who rarely if ever made waves, being sued? Poor Charles, Abby mused as she aligned the neatly sharpened pencils next to the message pad by the telephone which her landlord, or perhaps the Realtor, had so thoughtfully provided. He would hate the ensuing publicity, but Charles would manage to survive.

"It's the bank, not a law suit, that has me worried," Becky snapped uncharacteristically at her sister. "With Foster's connections he could *skewer* Charles's future at the bank and skewer it but good."

"Oh, Becky, you don't think. . . ."

"I *know* what he could do. The bank probably wouldn't fire Charles, but no promotions, no future, a dead end. In effect Charles would be through in banking in Phoenix."

This put the matter in a different light. It sounded as if her sister really might have cause for concern, Abby reluctantly admitted to herself. She picked up one of the pencils and started doodling on the fresh memo pad.

"Foster Richmond's *vindictive* and he's *ruthless*." Abby pictured Becky's curls bouncing like Mexican jumping beans as her sister paced around her large blue, white and yellow Country French kitchen, pausing beside the wrought-iron étagère to yank a dead leaf off one of the assorted houseplants in their terra cotta pots or slamming down hand-painted earthenware plates on the table. Sounds echoing down the telephone line suggested the latter. Abby feared for the majolica. "He wants someone to pay, and pay *big time* for his loss," her sister spat into the phone.

"Foster's an ass," Abby agreed soothingly. "I'm not arguing that a 1929 Alfa Romeo 6C 1750 SS isn't something very special. Every man at the send-off for the Copper State couldn't have been more thoroughly mesmerized by that car if it had been cast in solid gold and filled with gorgeous, half-naked bimbos. You'd think they'd found the Holy Grail. But aside from the opinion of some salivating males, a car is a car is a car no matter how unique, costly, or beautiful. Now if someone had been injured or killed. . ." On the message pad a long, low-slung racing car began to emerge, but instead of bimbos it held a figure that looked to be of the canine persuasion. The car with its passenger aboard was racing up the road toward the San Francisco Peaks.

"To you and me a car may just be a car and all that sort of thing. But *not* to Foster Richmond. That car's a symbol. It makes him important in a way that all his money and connections can't."

"So, tough. Now Foster's just a spoiled, overfed, overaged kid again." Casting her mind back to the send-off for the Copper State which she had attended with Becky and Charles, Abby could see the Alfa Romeo, an elegant machine: sleek, aristocratic, a glowing red-orange. Standing beside it was a man wearing a sport shirt whose prominent logo proclaimed it to be expensive but which didn't quite fit over his soft belly, khakis that could have come from any mid-price mail order catalogue, and scuffed, rundown loafers worn without socks. Foster's jolly, round, moon-like face gave him a decidedly boyish appearance, although he must have been somewhere in his mid-fifties. Plump pink cheeks and chubby little hands added to the youthful impression, an impression that was not entirely dispelled by his wispy, graying blond hair or the grooves of sullen discontent that bracketed his rosy, cherubic mouth when he wasn't smiling.

"Too bad about the car, but he'll find another expensive toy," Abby reassured Becky.

"You may think I'm overreacting," her sister replied tartly. "But that Foster's bad news."

The clink of silverware told Abby that the plates were temporarily out of danger. Their mother's sterling. She was glad that Becky and Charles used it on a regular basis. After their parents died Abby had insisted that her sister take the sterling. Then she had quite happily gone out and bought herself a quality set of stainless which had the inestimable advantage of requiring no polishing. She liked to keep things streamlined, simple. Definitely no strange diseases popping up out of the blue to create havoc in her life. No pets either.

As for Foster, Abby had to admit that her sister had a point there. What she had learned about the man during the send-off suggested that he did not view ethics as a high priority. This clearly did not bode well for Charles, who, for reasons she still did not entirely understand, seemed to have become a target. And, given the ultra conservatism of the bank for which he worked, perhaps a vulnerable one. "So what can be done?" she asked, questioning herself as much as her sister.

"Well, Abby, you're there in Flagstaff for the summer," Becky answered tentatively.

"Yes?"

"The car disappeared in Flagstaff. Maybe you could ask around about the theft of the Alfa Romeo."

Wow, Abby thought. Becky must have hit rock bottom. Only desperation would have made her suggest such a ploy to her older sister, who had never shown any flair for detective work in her life. Well, Abby backpedaled, outside of the academic world. She had found some forgotten fragments of Anglo-Saxon poetry in a manuscript in a British library, but that had been basically serendipitous.

"But the police, the Department of Public Safety, and every law enforcement agency in northern Arizona have been over the same ground!" Abby protested. She looked again at her doodle. Definitely a dog in the car, a corgi. What *was* her subconscious trying to tell her?

"I know. I know! I don't expect you to *find* the car because it's undoubtedly long gone by now. I realize that's totally unrealistic. But if you could only come across something to divert Foster's attention, sic him on someone other than Charles. That would be enough, believe me."

Yes, Becky was seriously worried about her husband's future, and undoubtedly would do almost anything to protect him. As for herself? It occurred to Abby that the idea of focusing on a vintage

Alfa Romeo rather than the impending dialysis did have a certain appeal. Maybe it was merely another form of running, but at least it was running with a purpose. And what harm would there be in asking around?

Abby considered Becky's request in light of her own situation. Although there were plenty of annoyances—vomiting, diarrhea, itching, ankle swelling, coughing and other similar plagues—from her perspective the biggest problem with end stage renal disease, however caused, was the constant fatigue. In fact it had been the fatigue that had originally led her to undergo a series of medical tests that had eventually produced her diagnosis. On the other hand, it wasn't as if she were bedridden. And she refused, absolutely refused, to give any more quarter than absolutely necessary to the polysyllabic monster that was making hash of her life. As for the Alfa Romeo, well, she could do a little at a time. A whole summer stretched before her. A summer to make something of the shambles of her life? *Yeah, sure.* In any case, the only other thing on the immediate agenda was finding a home for the little dog.

"I can try, Becky," she agreed reluctantly, crumpling the paper on which she'd doodled. "But I'm sure not promising anything."

* * *

Under other circumstances Abby would have phoned Sorrell Lawrence, the Realtor who had arranged for her to rent the house, to ask about the homeowner's policy on animals. However, Sorrell's office was on her way to the veterinarian's, and she wanted to return an already-read stack of materials on Flagstaff and the environs that Sorrell had assembled for her.

A secretary ushered Abby into a beautifully paneled room with a large Oriental rug covering a goodly portion of the polished parquet floor. Only a detailed map of the Flagstaff area suggested Sorrell's profession. Otherwise the wall decorations consisted of oil paintings in heavy gold frames, mostly English country scenes reminiscent of the nineteenth century. Two almost floor to ceiling windows opened on a small grove of firs that effectively cut out the urban sights and sounds. Having her own forest glen within the confines of the crowded city center, where they probably sold land by the square inch, spoke volumes about this woman's success, Abby reflected.

"So how do you like the professor's place?" Sorrell asked with the self-confidence of someone who knows she's achieved perfection.

The Realtor's cocksureness irritated Abby, but she wasn't about to show it. "It's just what I wanted," she replied evenly.

Sorrell smiled graciously at the acknowledgment of accomplishment. She had big, straight white teeth which stood out against smooth, unblemished skin just tan enough to look healthy, without foreshadowing a leathery look in later years. Abby had to admit that she was a handsome woman—tall, broad shouldered, long limbed, with outstanding posture and carriage, and a thick, shiny mane of hair. Did Sorrell's mother have horses on the mind when she was born, Abby wondered? If so, the mother really should have called her child Palomino, because her hair was exactly the platinum shade of palomino mane and tail, not the reddish brown of sorrel. But it wasn't horses that concerned Abby. Only the fate of one small dog.

Sorrell sat behind an executive-sized desk covered in black leather with gold studs decorating the perimeter, bare except for a flat panel monitor and a sleek, voice-activated telephone. She looked perfectly turned out in a rust-colored silk suit and elegant gold jewelry: a thin, expensive-looking watch, small earrings that resembled cleverly tied little golden knots, and several beautifully worked necklaces of varying lengths. Perhaps a little overdressed for northern Arizona, but the majority of her clients, so Abby had heard, were the same ones she worked with in Paradise Valley and Scottsdale, a wealthy, discriminating clientele with a palatial permanent residence in the Valley and a summer getaway, probably as large as their permanent residence, in the mountains. Over the last decade or so, a lot of money had been attracted to Flagstaff.

"Our firm prides itself on our personal service," Sorrell said with a toss of her thick, gleaming palomino mane.

Damn it, she bugs me, Abby admitted, gritting her teeth. *Health*, she thought, *Sorrell simply radiates health along with that inflated self-confidence. Healthy hair, healthy teeth, healthy skin.*

Even healthy hands, she noted as she admired the large, strong hands stretched out on the uncluttered desk with their long, white fingers culminating in oval nails lacquered to match the silk suit. *All that vitality and animal energy while I've felt better when recuperating from the flu. Probably looked a lot better, too.*

A glance that morning in the professor's mirror had shown her that her own chestnut hair had lost much of its bounce and shine. She already knew that her oval face, in spite of sufficient exposure to the sun, had taken on a somewhat grayish cast, an unwelcome development that for the first time in her life caused her to use foundation and blush on a regular basis. Her hazel eyes alone hinted at the vital woman she had seemed to be even a year before. But dark smudges underlined them, as if someone inexperienced in the ways of makeup had experimented with kohl.

"My sister was right. You do have a knack for matching the house with the person." Actually what Abby's sister had said was that Sorrell Lawrence was sure that she was always right and actually was right enough of the time so that her high opinion of herself was not altogether misplaced. Sorrell sized up a person and found just "the thing," even if it wasn't necessarily what her client had originally intended. Abby had taken Becky at her word and had not even tried to make the tiring drive up I-17 to check out the territory and confirm Sorrell's selection. After all, she had rationalized, it was only for a summer. About any decent place in the Flagstaff area, out of the heat of Phoenix, would have suited.

"We do try." A broad man—or woman—eating smile. *And granny, what big teeth you have, said Little Red Riding Hood.*

"Of course I love being surrounded by books. The chairs and lamps are great for reading, and what a superb music system!" Abby smiled, or at least she tried to. Successful professor takes on predatory Realtor, she coached herself. Be charming and *never* show hesitation or self-doubt. She knew how to play the game; at the Modern Language Association conferences she'd practiced against some real pros who loved nothing better than trying to intimidate their younger colleagues.

It was strange. She admired strong women and usually dealt

19

well with them. But there was something about Sorrell, something beyond the health issue, that galled her. The Realtor was just too full of herself, as if she and she alone had the answers to life.

"Yes, I'm delighted with the house," Abby affirmed. "I have just one question. Do you have any way to contact the owner?"

"Professor Neale's a member of the College of Forestry at NAU, that's Northern Arizona University, and has gone to the Yellowstone area to do some research on the aftereffects of the fires there a few years back. I gather that he's camping out. Of course, I do have some numbers in case of an emergency. . . ." Sorrell's voice hung in a question mark.

"I want to know if he would permit a dog, a small dog that is." Abby had checked with the animal hospital that morning. They did have boarding facilities and she found the cost quite reasonable. But, no matter how well run, it wouldn't be like being in a home, she'd reasoned, remembering the hurt, bewildered look in the dog's eyes and the long, pink tongue that had caressed her arm. Also, she reassured herself, she would only have the dog for a short while, just until she found him a new owner.

"Oh, that's answered easily enough. If we're dealing with a rental—a bit unusual since our firm specializes in development and sales, as you know—we have the renter fill out an extensive form covering everything that might normally come up. I just need to consult the computer."

Abby steeled herself for disappointment as Sorrell pulled out a drawer with a keyboard, tapped it expertly with her perfectly manicured nails, and the monitor on the desk came alive.

"Yes, here it is. And no, Professor Neale has no objection to house-trained pets."

Was the dog house-trained, Abby wondered?

* * *

"Yes, he's housebroken," the vet informed her with a warm smile.

Well that answered that, Abby thought. She wasn't sure whether she was more delighted with the news or appalled at what she was getting herself into, if only temporarily. So far no one had called the Humane Society to ask about the dog and there had been no response to her found-dog notice. But it was early days. Maybe his rightful owner would still claim him.

"I'm delighted that you're going to keep him."

Abby held her tongue, not wanting to disabuse the kindly vet of the idea that this arrangement would be permanent.

"Too many good animals have to go to the shelter because there just aren't the homes for them. It's one of the hardest things we have to deal with. Here at the hospital we try to keep a few, hoping they'll be adopted, but only a few because of space considerations." The perky little woman sighed. "In any case, you're going to love your corgi. They're such smart little dogs and very brave. I've seen a female, smaller than this male, herd range cattle, and they're enormous beasts."

"But the dog has such short legs!"

"They nip the Achilles' tendon, then drop down. The animal kicks right over them."

The vet gave the little dog several sorts of shots together with a clean bill of health except for his leg, which would take a while to heal. On a borrowed leash he trotted, toenails clicking the linoleum, in a rather hip-hop fashion thanks to the injured leg, beside Abby as she went out to the desk to pay the bill. She glanced down at the dog, who seemed to be handling the situation with aplomb. At least he wasn't tugging on the leash or barking at the other animals. As she awaited her turn, she swept her eyes over the room. Instinctively her glance stopped at the figure of a small, wiry man, probably around fifty, whose bright green eyes peered out between a bush of long hair and a thick beard, in both of which strands of gray and white intertwined with traces of the original red. Now where had she seen him before, she wondered?

Until yesterday she had been to Flagstaff only twice, the first time, a couple of years earlier, simply driving through with Becky, Becky's husband, Charles, and their two young children on the way to the Grand Canyon. The second time, really the only one that counted, had been this spring when she had come up with Becky to meet Charles for the final festive night of the Copper State 1000.

Then they had stayed in a resort on the edge of the city, not in the city proper.

"Here's what we did, the shots your dog received, and the fee for overnight boarding," the receptionist said, handing Abby the bill. Pointing to the computerized printout she explained the charges, and Abby brought out her Visa. When the transaction had been completed, Abby looked over at the man again, hoping that she would remember where she'd seen him, and even more under what circumstances. She sensed that whatever her association with him, it was not a happy one. However, further than that she could not go.

At that moment a veterinary assistant emerged from the back area which contained the examining rooms and boarding facilities. She brought the small man a cage from which a long beak suddenly protruded, the beak of some sort of raptor, probably a hawk.

"You did a good job with the wing," she told the man. "Give him a few days to recuperate and then he can go back into the wild."

Noting the surprised expression on Abby's face, the receptionist chuckled. "We deal mostly with small, domestic animals here, but we're willing to treat the wild ones too—free of charge. That fellow over there loves the forest. I think he hikes a lot. Every now and then he brings us a wounded bird or animal."

Abby was about to ask the man's name when the woman next in line showed definite signs of impatience, shifting from one foot to another and fiddling with her purse as if she couldn't wait to pull out her credit card. Abby turned away. If the association was an important one, sooner or later she'd remember the identity of the hawk man, or at least where she'd previously come across him.

The answer came to her just as she was going out the door. She hesitated momentarily, to the consternation of the man behind her toting a large, vocal tiger cat in an undersized carrier. She had seen the hawk man on TV. He belonged to some environmental group that had tried to make hay with the theft of the Alfa Romeo, claiming that people should be a lot more concerned with species going extinct than the loss of one vintage car. One Universe, that was it. She wondered if they really knew anything about the disappearance of the Alfa Romeo.

CHAPTER 2

"*What dog?*" The words ricocheted down the telephone line.

"The dog that crazy gum-snapping kid almost ran over," Abby reminded her sister as she squirmed further down into the armchair by the phone. After only a few days the armchair was already becoming something of an old friend.

"I thought you were advertising for the owner—or trying to find it a new home." Becky's voice came to her puzzled, questioning.

"I *did* try to find the owner," Abby defended herself. "No luck. I think the vet was right about some college student abandoning him." Part one of her plan, trying to find the owner, had been put into action, but part two, advertising the dog for adoption, had somehow fallen by the wayside. No, she admitted, she had rudely shoved it aside.

No wonder Becky sounded taken aback, confused. How could Abby explain why anyone who was having problems enough just coping would take an animal into her life? How could she explain what she didn't understand herself? If not her sanity, then her sister must at least doubt her rationality. The disease. She could only blame it on the damned disease. She grabbed a pencil and the message pad and started doodling.

Anger, fear, and helplessness—she considered again that these were what a person was *supposed* to feel on being confronted with an incurable, life-altering disease. Yet of the three, anger had hitherto been lacking, replaced instead by a strange, unsettling absence of emotion into which even the fear and sense of helplessness had gradually been absorbed. A sort of emotional twilight zone. The mind creating a shield against reality? A peculiar·form of denial? Abby could barely describe the phenomenon, let alone rationalize it. Then anger had burst upon her wholly unexpectedly, triggered when that ratty truck erupted from a side street. A pure, unadulterated rage which hit her so hard that she herself could have been the traffic victim. She had focused instead on the dog.

I just meant to keep him for a few days, she reminded herself, a resolve that had petered out quickly. Although perhaps her actions did make a crazy sort of sense. In a life rapidly careening out of control, here was one small thing she could accomplish. What she couldn't do for herself, she could do for the dog. She had resolved to shelter him from the winds of fate, to love him, to make him well and whole again.

"Is it all right with the professor who's renting to you?" Becky was asking.

The point of the pencil that Abby had been using for doodling snapped with the sudden pressure she applied. She knew full well that's not what her sister had intended to say. The long and short of it was that Becky doubted her sister's ability to handle one more complication in her life just now, only she didn't want to undermine Abby's self-confidence by saying so. *It's my kidneys, not my mind! I'm not a total invalid physically and certainly not mentally*, she silently protested. Then with chagrin she recalled her own self-doubts. Well, it was one thing to have them herself and quite another for someone to challenge her. But she tried to quell her irritation. Becky was only trying to help.

"I checked with Sorrell Lawrence and it's okay," she answered neutrally, playing along with the bogus scenario.

"At least the dog will be some sort of companion," Becky admitted reluctantly. "Maybe protection as well. I just hate to think of you being up there all alone."

Abby looked around at the comfortable book-lined room, the big fireplace which put out a faint odor of fires past, and the sunlight trickling in through the spruce in front of the house, creating a subtly shifting pattern of light and shadow. So far she had experienced the aloneness of solitude, not of isolation or abandonment. But who knew? Maybe these would come later.

"Missing Alfa Romeo aside, Flagstaff is hardly the crime capital of the world," she replied as she leaned down to pet the little animal curled up by her feet. Amazing how reassuring that soft, warm ball of fur could be.

"I still wish you'd chosen Prescott," Becky remarked wistfully. She and Charles had a second home in a summer community just west of Prescott called Iron Springs, and Abby knew that Becky had hoped to have her somewhere nearby.

"Becca, dear," Abby said, reverting to her sister's nickname, "you keep forgetting that my nephrologist has an office in Flagstaff, and I just don't have the energy to make the drive from Prescott to Phoenix or Prescott to Flagstaff to see him on a regular basis."

Fortunately Dr. Frankenthaller—the "kids' doctor" her ten-year-old nephew Sam had mistakenly dubbed him when his mother explained that a nephrologist was a *kid*ney doctor—had an office in Flagstaff as well as one in Phoenix. Frankenthaller had come highly recommended, both by the physician who had originally diagnosed her polycystic kidney disease and by the New York specialist Abby had then consulted. His Flagstaff office, together with Flagstaff's much vaunted summer climate, had made the city an obvious choice when Abby reluctantly concluded that a summer in the stifling heat of Phoenix would be intolerable.

There was, however, a bit more to it than that. Abby and Becky had always been close. This had been the case even before the death of their father from polycystic kidney disease and their mother shortly afterward from what had been diagnosed as heart failure, but the sisters had always thought was sheer exhaustion after the years of caring for her husband. A terrible time when the two sisters clung to each other, trying desperately to compensate for the lack of an older, more mature adult presence in their lives. A time that had brought them even closer together.

As her kidneys failed more noticeably, it was only natural for Abby to turn to her sister for support. When teaching ceased to be a viable option, Becky had done everything she could to smooth Abby's transition to Arizona. But in this scary business of learning to live with her disease, Abby had determined early on not to become too dependent. In Flagstaff she was only a few hours' drive from Becky whether Becky was in Phoenix or Prescott. Close but not too close. Certainly not living in her sister's pocket. To summer in

Prescott as well as wintering in Phoenix would definitely have been overdoing it. Deep inside herself Abby recognized that sooner or later she was going to have to stop running and work things out on her own. *And when would she have the courage to do that?* she wondered.

"But darling, it seems like you are *so far* away!" Becky tended to be a wee bit histrionic, Abby reminded herself. However, this was a trait she could easily overlook. She knew that her sister cared and cared deeply.

"I'm not that far, and the house is just fine," she said, deftly changing the subject. "Sorrell Lawrence really came through. Except that there are neighbors around, it's kind of like a little cabin in the big woods. Plank floors, braided throw rugs, sturdy blond oak furniture, and did I mention the stone fireplace? If you don't have a deep-seated aversion to red plaid—the Royal Stewart tartan, I do believe—this place couldn't be better. And from the back porch you can look across the yard into the forest. The dog and I love watching the squirrels."

She didn't add what a relief it was to have everything on one level. The leased townhouse in Phoenix with its two floors had increasingly become a challenge. She wasn't sure whether to laugh at herself or weep with frustration; the woman who had casually hiked precipitous mountain trails too fatigued to climb an ordinary set of stairs?

A few minutes later Abby hung up the phone with a sense of relief. Nothing today about the troubles besetting Charles, nothing more about the stolen Alfa Romeo, and nothing at all about the odious Foster Richmond. She knew that her sister was just trying to spare her, and for the time being she was grateful not to have to go over that particular ground again. Those topics were floating out there like an e-mail waiting to be retrieved from cyberspace, but endlessly rehashing them would prove nothing. Of course, however ineptly, at some point she needed to tackle the matter of the Alfa Romeo. She had told her sister she would. But even that could wait.

"Come on," she said to the little dog. "Let's take a walk."

* * *

"Is it all right if the girls pet your puppy?" asked a tall, slender lady swathed all in white—white turban, white tunic, and white leggings. In fact, the only thing about her pristine outfit that wasn't white was her leather sandals.

"They should be gentle," Abby cautioned, a warning that went unheeded as the two little girls who had come racing out of the house next door embraced the little animal with ecstatic, high-pitched squeals.

For the moment, Abby, the turbaned lady and her children provided the only action on the unassuming residential street lined with modest but well-maintained, mostly single-story houses. A street undoubtedly like countless others in the West, Abby thought as she looked around. Except, that was, for the dramatic backdrop of the San Francisco Peaks, the tallest of the three rising to almost 13,000 feet. Sacred peaks, home to the Hopi Kachinas and indicator of the southwest boundary of Navajo Land, she had read. Sheltering peaks, from the prehistoric Sinagua people to the present. Sentinels dominating the landscape of northern Arizona for hundreds of miles. And for her, friends that had soothed the last part of her drive up from Phoenix.

Mother or nanny, Abby wondered, turning back to the turbaned lady. But a closer look answered that question quickly enough. All three—woman and little girls—had the same delicate, pale skin and the same huge, almost colorless gray eyes.

As for the dog, a routine quickly developed. He put his head up through the arms of whichever little girl was hugging him and licked her face. She would squeal and back off; then it was the other one's turn to love and be loved.

"What happened to his leg?" the woman asked with concern.

"A truck hit him."

She gave a little gasp. "Oh, the driving in Arizona can be really terrible!"

"And he lost his tail," one of the girls piped up.

"Not really. Not from the truck anyway. Dogs like him are born without tails, or sometimes with very short stumps that are

27

docked—cut off, that is—immediately after they are born." While waiting to pick up the dog at the vet's Abby had leafed through a book on dog breeds. "He's a corgi and corgis are sheep and cattle dogs," she told the girls. "The idea was to make it easier for them to herd livestock through the underbrush."

"How does your dog feel about cats?" the woman inquired as a singularly large black and white long-haired cat with one well-chewed ear appeared from around the house.

"I really don't know," Abby admitted. But the dog didn't appear any more bothered by the cat than by the children. As for the cat—whose name was Sat, pronounced as if it were 'Sut,' the woman explained—he clearly considered himself to be a denizen of a far higher plane than one inhabited by a mere canine. In fact, Sat looked quite capable of taking on an entire sled team of huskies and positively relishing the experience. Definitely a cat with an attitude.

Sat selected a choice splash of sunlight on the doorstep, sat down, and proceeded to preen himself, carefully grooming whiskers, fur, and private parts. Task accomplished, he arose, stretched his long, supple body, then sauntered off haughtily, tail held high.

"By the way, my name is Abby Taylor," Abby put in when the regal Sat had disappeared around the house again.

"Oh, excuse me. I'm Sada Anand. That's Pooh and Bear," she nodded at the girls, still entranced with the dog, their shrieks of pleasure echoing down the quiet street. "Actually Susan and Sandra, only we never call them that."

"Are the children twins?" Abby guessed the girls to be around five.

"No, Bear's a year younger than Pooh, but they do look as if they could be twins, don't they? Bear is a bit big for her age," Sada Anand observed with pride.

"What's the puppy called?" one of the children asked.

"I'm not really sure. I've just adopted him." Abby smiled ruefully. She had to give the little animal a name. She thought for a moment. "I think I'll call him Francis after St. Francis, the saint who was so kind to animals," she answered on a whim.

"A saint?"

"A person who lives a really good life."

Not exactly a definitive description, but the girls seemed satisfied. Abby turned back to the mother.

"I've rented this house for the summer," she explained, nodding at the small, dark green block house distinguished from its neighbors by the stately spruce in front.

"Oh, the nice professor's house. Or, at least I assume he's nice. We've never met him except in passing. We just moved here in the spring ourselves. He was attending a conference, I heard, and then there was the end of semester rush. The next thing you know, he was off to spend a summer researching the impact of forest fires on national parks in the West. At least that's what a lady down the street told me."

Abby felt a twinge of disappointment at not learning more. As she settled in, the absent owner had begun to intrigue her. Living in another person's home had something peculiarly intimate about it. Clean note pads by the telephones, well-sharpened pencils, fresh dish towels, logs chopped and neatly stacked by the fireplace. The professor's doing or that of someone else? Conceivably Sorrell, through one of her minions, could have arranged all that. Another step toward perfection. But the meticulously organized kitchen, the choice of music, the books that lined the many shelves—all these spoke of the professor. Just what did they say?

"But where are my manners?" asked Sada Anand. "Please come in and have a glass of freshly made lemonade."

"That sounds delicious!"

"Do be careful with the puppy," Sada Anand warned when the children had settled down with the newly named Francis in the middle of the small, very white and utterly immaculate kitchen. "Remember, if he got hit by a truck he's probably still hurting."

Two pairs of translucent gray eyes looked up at their mother, then the little girls went back to the serious business of petting their newfound friend, who had stretched out on his stomach, his white paws with their black pads jutting straight out from behind, his long muzzle resting between and extending beyond white forepaws, and his big soft ears at the ready.

The few touches of color stood out against the pristine white of the kitchen like beacons—a pot of Swedish ivy hanging in the window, children's drawings tacked to a bulletin board on the wall behind the kitchen table, and a string of dried red chilies hung by the back door. A pot of mint flavored the air. Abby liked what she saw. Although her sister's Country French kitchen was all fine in its way, personally she preferred something more pared down, more basic.

She felt a sudden stab of envy. Would she ever again have a real place of her own, not leased, not rented, she wondered? She could certainly afford one, but would she ever have the will or energy to choose and then decorate a home? Or would the dialysis slowly, inexorably distance her from her surroundings as it had her father? Gradually he had drawn inward, always remaining gentle and kindly, yet somehow no longer really there, a shadow, a ghost.

"You're just here for the summer?" Sada Anand's question broke her train of thought.

"Escaping the heat of Phoenix," Abby answered, not lying, just telling a partial truth.

"Do you have a summer job?"

"No. I'm just . . . vacationing."

Sada Anand looked puzzled, as if she found the idea of "vacationing" over such an extended period of time entirely foreign. Abby felt compelled to elaborate further.

"Actually I'm a university professor."

Sada Anand's face cleared. "So you take the summer off to do research and prepare classes?" she asked as if she were familiar with the routine.

"That's right." Abby didn't feel up to explaining about the leave of absence, the illness that had robbed her of the job she loved so much and that even now, in spite of the invigorating tart-sweet taste of the lemonade, made her body feel sluggish and heavy.

"What do you teach?"

"English. Anglo-Saxon, that's Old English, the language, literature and culture. Beowulf and that sort of thing."

"Where do you teach? At Arizona State University?"

"No, at Vassar, a small liberal arts college in the East."

"Then you don't live in Phoenix on a regular basis. You must be on sabbatical."

Abby simply smiled and said, "You know a lot about college life."

Sada Anand shrugged slightly. "Flagstaff's a college town. Are you writing a book? It seems like the professors around here are always writing something. They say that they have to in order to move ahead in the system."

"I'm exploring some ideas," Abby answered noncommitally. How do you tell someone you've only just met that you're trying to find a life or maybe even invent one? Her stomach tightened at the thought.

Until recently she'd thought she'd been doing a pretty good job at this business of living. Professionally she'd been a success, rising steadily through the ranks at Vassar, where she'd earned her undergraduate degree before going off for an M.A. and Ph.D. at Yale. She was a full professor now, respected in her field and the possessor of a *curriculum vitae* listing an impressive number of honors and publications. But personally? She had numerous friends, and occasionally over the years there had been a man who was more than that. Yet, never since the accidental shooting death of her beloved Mark, had she met anyone she seriously considered marrying. Abby smiled sadly to herself. Her mother's generation deemed that only a gainfully employed husband and at least two children signified the good life. In that she had failed. However, judged by the standards of her own generation, she hadn't done so badly. Then the bolt from the blue. Polycystic kidney disease. Unstoppable. Incurable. Life prolonged, perhaps indefinitely, by dialysis.

Skillfully Abby turned the conversation away from herself and toward Sada Anand and her family. While they sipped their lemonade Abby learned that Sada Anand worked as a registered nurse at the hospital. Her husband, Soul Singh, was a cabinet maker. Sada Anand said that they were Sikhs, although Abby sincerely doubted that they had ever seen the Indian subcontinent. A family photograph she had noticed proudly displayed in the living room showed Soul Singh to be as Nordic as his wife and children. Evidently the Khalsas—Khalsa, Abby discovered, being the surname of all Sikhs—had become Sikhs as one might convert to any religion for its spiritual guidance and moral values.

"Isn't it awfully hectic to be working full-time while raising two small children?"

"Yes, but that's not unusual in Flagstaff. Although expenses are high and salaries are low, people want to live here anyway. A small-town atmosphere with all the advantages of the University. If you don't go in for music, opera, theater, and that sort of thing, there's hunting, fishing, hiking, and skiing in the winter. This place is growing by leaps and bounds and would be growing still faster if it weren't hemmed in by national forest."

"What do you do with the girls when you're working?" Abby glanced at Pooh and Bear, their squeals abated but still busy petting Francis.

"Come fall Pooh will be in kindergarten. For now a lady a few blocks over has a play group a couple of times a week. It's still a balancing act, but my brother Bob is visiting from Florida. He's been a great help."

"Oh?"

"He watches the girls when I need him to, does odd jobs around the house and, something I never would have expected of my brother . . . the ironing. But best of all he knows computers. Soul Singh invested in a computer and then couldn't do anything with it. Bob taught us both how to use it and even designed a software program specifically tailored to the needs of Soul Singh's carpentry business!" Sada Anand glowed with pride.

"How long will your brother be with you?"

There was a moment of hesitation, and the glow dimmed slightly like a rheostat being turned down. "I don't know exactly."

Abby gave her a quizzical glance. The man who came to dinner?

"He doesn't want to go back to Florida and he hasn't—" again a hesitation—"quite decided what next. He needs to finish his college degree . . . ."

Abby didn't point out the obvious: that right here in Flagstaff there was a fine university. Although she sensed she wasn't getting the whole story about the mysterious brother, she was reluctant to probe further. After all, it was really none of her business.

Later, much later, Abby would look back on this conversation with Sada Anand about her brother and wonder if she had experienced any intuition of how closely his fate would become entwined with her own. In retrospect she decided that she hadn't had an inkling.

* * *

"Your labs aren't too bad considering the circumstances. But the creatinine is gaining ground. And I don't like the look of the BUN. As I've told you before, I could put you on a very restrictive diet which would stave things off for a little while longer."

Abby thought of how strikingly this cubicle contrasted with Sorrell Lawrence's grand office. No windows, plain white walls, brownish linoleum. A large, functional steel desk across which Dr. Frankenthaller, garbed in chinos and a blue cotton short-sleeve shirt worn without a tie, peered at her through his tortoiseshell glasses. From time to time he turned his standard office swivel chair from side to side in a slight swaying motion. She herself sat on one of two chairs on the opposite side of the desk—chairs of simple wood, probably veneer, the seat and back cushioned in a nubby brown material that had the look and feel of something made to last. Personally she could not have lived long without windows, but otherwise the office wasn't as bleak as the decoration, or lack thereof, suggested. A large, worn Navajo rug—Two Gray Hills, she thought, remembering time spent wandering through the Heard Museum with its wealth of Indian art—covered much of the undistinguished linoleum, and the walls were almost entirely carpeted with pictures. Framed photograph after photograph of the Frankenthaller family crowded the requisite diplomas. A petite, dark-haired Mrs. Frankenthaller, two young girls and a boy water-skied, swam, and boated on Lake Powell. The family hiked Havasu canyon, the girls played tennis and appeared in school plays, the boy had evidently recently had his bar mitzvah.

Abby turned back from contemplating the Frankenthallers' active, happy family life to considering the grim realities of the picture painted by her nephrologist. She knew that the creatinine level together with that of the BUN—standing for blood, urea and nitrogen—were the standard means for measuring kidney function and that even the smallest change was significant. But no, Abby silently resolved, no restrictive diets. Of late she cared little enough about what she ate, and any sort of special shopping and preparation struck her as too exhausting to contemplate.

"It's up to you." Dr. Frankenthaller looked at her quizzically, head slightly cocked to one side in a way that reminded her of Francis. "But you're going to have to come to terms with the situation in the very near future. You can't put off dialysis indefinitely."

"Yes, I understand." She appreciated Dr. Frankenthaller because, unlike some members of the medical profession she had known, he didn't act as if he saw himself as God incarnate. He approached his patients as if they were rational human beings capable of considering alternatives and of participating in their own treatment. He never intimated that his way was the only way. Although he might cajole or even urge, he refrained from issuing commands and was never preemptive—not even now when, Abby thought, his frustration must be as great as hers.

"Once you get started with the dialysis, you will feel better and have more energy. Not so much nausea or any of the other symptoms. It will make quite a difference," he encouraged her.

Dialysis, the final indignity. She slumped back in her chair, unable to come to terms with the fact that she would spend her foreseeable future dependent on artificial means to stay alive. For her dialysis represented the ultimate loss of independence, and thus the ultimate loss of self. And there wasn't a damn thing she could do about it. Her body was hell bent on a destructive course, her fate not written in the stars but in her DNA.

All this was frightening and bewildering; it made a mockery of her beliefs. Their parents had taught Abby and Becky that what happened to them was the result of their own actions. Oh, not always of course; Mark's death had proved that. There was nothing anyone could have done to prevent a drug addict from buying a rifle and shooting up Yale. It was a tragic matter of being in the wrong place at the wrong time. But her basic lifestyle had evolved from the conviction that reason, discipline, and moderation produced a life that, even if the inevitable ups and downs couldn't be avoided, at least wouldn't slide out of control like so many others she had seen. All a bit stuffy sounding, she supposed, *"bor-ing!"* as her niece Sarah would say. But coming of age in the seventies she'd decided that she would rather be boring than blowing her mind out on any of the medley of drugs so readily available.

Yet, as the doctors had repeatedly told her, she could have done nothing to prevent the disease. Hereditary. If a parent had it, each child had a fifty-fifty chance of inheriting the disease. Strangely enough, no doctor had ever pinpointed the reason for her father's failed kidney function. But although polycystic kidney disease was by far the largest of all the hereditary life-threatening diseases, until the last ten or fifteen years little had been known about it. Once Abby had been diagnosed, Becky had immediately been tested. Negative, thank God! Ten-year-old Sam and his twelve-year-old sister, Sarah, would undoubtedly face their share of life's challenges, but these would not include polycystic kidney disease.

From beyond the door to Dr. Frankenthaller's office came the sounds of a busy medical practice. Phones rang. Nurses discussed patients and their care. The voice of the scheduler, raised as if trying to communicate with someone hard of hearing, attempted to explain that the doctor would be in Phoenix on the day the person at the other end of the line wanted to see him.

Perhaps it was just as well that she and Mark had never married, never started the family they had planned, Abby thought dispiritedly as she looked at young Frankenthallers romping through life. She would simply have to reconcile herself to the fact that some joys would never be hers.

Meanwhile, even had she known about the dreadful secret her body harbored, nothing she could have done would have prevented her disease's inexorable development. As the doctors had warned her, her kidney functioning was deteriorating with every passing day. And so every day brought her closer to the dreaded dialysis. She had tried to put it off as long as possible; perhaps in spite of what Dr. Frankenthaller was saying she could still do so a little longer.

"Procrastinating too long isn't at all a wise idea," he cautioned her gently, as if reading her mind. "We can't risk letting your health slide that way. You'd better make an appointment for the middle of the month. Get your blood work done a day or two in advance. I think that at that point we're going to have to map out a definite course of action."

* * *

After the appointment with her nephrologist Abby found herself too depressed to go home and read. Even a walk with Francis didn't have its usual appeal. She had already acquainted herself with the most significant sights of Flagstaff. Above all she looked forward to future visits to the Museum of Northern Arizona. But not today. Today she needed another project. Anything to keep her mind off dialysis. Almost automatically she turned the car toward the outskirts of town and the resort that had been the scene of the last, and disastrous, night of the Copper State 1000.

She was in luck. The first person she ran into was a slender young man, swarthy, with slicked-down dark hair and large, flashing eyes so dark she couldn't tell where the pupil began or ended. Wearing a forest green blazer with the resort's logo in gold on the pocket, he sat on the steps above the parking lot taking a cigarette break. His posture suggested that he was bored. This ought to be easy, she thought with satisfaction. Thanks to years of teaching, bored young people were a known and manageable commodity.

Abby sat down beside him. Yes, he did work for the resort, on the reception desk. Yes, he had been on duty the night—or actually the early morning hours—when the Alfa Romeo had been stolen. His dark eyes sparkled as he took a long, satisfied pull on his cigarette. Surely in his twenty-five some years the theft had been the most exciting thing that had ever happened to him. He was delighted to talk about it.

"You know, it was a setup from the start. Those guys that got mugged in New York—that wasn't any, what do they call it? Random act of violence. No way."

Abby agreed. Police and media commentators alike had considered it a bit too much of a coincidence that, just before the Copper State 1000, the mechanic and his assistant Foster Richmond normally used were mugged in New York City, their home town. One was badly shaken, and the other hospitalized. After a bit of scrambling, Foster had come up with two other mechanics capable of working on such a fine car as the Alfa Romeo, two well thought-of men with excellent reputations. The only problem was that the new mechanics had never met Foster personally until arriving in Phoenix, and over four hectic days of touring they didn't get to know their employer all that well, which was exactly what someone had counted on.

"I mean, those mechanics that Richmond fellow hired were good guys," the young man told Abby earnestly. "I talked to them some. Did you know that Alfa Romeo had an output of 85 horsepower at 4,500 rpm? Six cylinders. That baby could go up to 95 miles per hour, which is major for a car built that long ago. Those guys told me all about it. Like I said, they were really nice. But come on. They didn't know Richmond from the Easter bunny."

Abby nodded. She remembered one of the mechanics plaintively asking a TV commentator, "So what does a guy do when an owner appears at two in the morning and says he wants to take his car for a spin? The area where the machines were parked was lit okay. We could see this guy fine. He looked like Mr. Richmond, he talked like Mr. Richmond, he walked like Mr. Richmond. He'd maybe had a bit too much to drink, but he wasn't really drunk or anything. And after all it's *his* car."

"Besides, there were, like, a few distractions," the desk clerk added with a grin.

Abby agreed that the mechanic had done quite well to notice as much as he had. No other man up and around at that hour had been paying the slightest bit of attention to the fake Foster. All their attention had been riveted on the luscious blonde on his arm.

"Oh, Christ," the second mechanic had sighed in the TV interview. Then he had added, a slight Irish burr not disguising the longing in his voice, "Just looking at her was to be committing a mortal sin." The description that followed would have done justice to a lascivious poet. It certainly explained why the deception passed off so smoothly.

"Too bad no women were about," one of the investigating officers had later been quoted as saying. He knew there were plenty of women involved with the Copper State as co-drivers, wives or "friends" who joined their husbands or significant others for a pleasant, well-planned event involving beautiful scenery, a chance to tan and shop, and not too many hours each day on the road. However, in the wee hours of the morning they had all been catching up on their beauty rest, not checking up on the mechanics or the machines.

"No good," a colleague had been heard to reply. "The women would have been sizing up this blonde, too, and speculating on whether they were looking at the fifth, or maybe it's the sixth, Mrs. Richmond. That fellow Foster Richmond goes through wives the way some guys go through golf balls."

"Was the blonde as gorgeous as everyone says?" Abby asked the desk clerk curiously.

"Better." The dark eyes practically danced now. "Not just how she looked, but how she moved, too." He stopped for a moment, evidently hunting for the right words. "Sort of like oil oozing through clear water. Lucky there weren't too many people around at that hour of the morning. Otherwise, she might have started a riot."

Understandably no one had looked very hard at the pudgy, middle-aged man intent on taking a perfectly proportioned blonde on a moonlight ride. The mechanics, who, with no car to tinker with, had caught some much-needed rest, didn't realize that anything was amiss until the next morning when, the desk clerk related with relish, the real Foster Richmond, bleary-eyed and hung over, appeared demanding his Alfa Romeo. Then all hell broke loose.

"The word around here was that Richmond was shacked up with some gal, all right, but a redhead, not a blonde." The desk clerk took another long drag on his cigarette, then blew out a stream of sweet-tart smoke. "Some of the staff who saw him on his way to his room said he was too drunk to drive anyway. Red face, loud voice, weaving down the corridor. You gotta know, nobody here was too sorry about what happened A nasty, demanding sort of guy; never a nice word or a thank you. A real asshole if you ask me."

"The parking lot was well lit?" Abby asked for verification. When Becky and she had driven up to share the last night of the festivities with Charles she had had no reason to go out and check the parking accommodations. After all, she'd seen the cars at the send-off, and in April in the mountains the night air had a nip to it.

"Definitely. And they had a temporary chain link fence around it and guards. It would have been hard enough to sneak a wrench out of there. A car? No way."

"So what do you think happened to the Alfa Romeo?" Abby shifted uncomfortably on the concrete step. Tall, slender, she'd had excellent muscle tone until recently. Now that food had lost much of its appeal and she too often found herself throwing up what she had eaten, she didn't have enough padding to protect her butt from the step's hard, grainy surface.

"You know how these rich guys from the East and Europe get their machines out here? They FedEx them! Just drive them onto a cargo plane and out they come." The desk clerk shook his head as if such extravagance were beyond comprehension. "Only the Alfa Romeo didn't disappear that way. The cops checked and no cargo planes took off that night. But why not drive it down a forest road and onto one of those eighteen wheelers? Then off to California or maybe back East." The clerk indicated I-40, which was clearly visible from where they sat. They could hear the steady hum of the traffic, a muted background noise. "Course the Highway Patrol set up road blocks. But remember, they didn't know anything was wrong until morning."

Yes, Abby thought, how dead easy. Lots of unpaved forest roads little used, especially in the wee hours of the morning. Lots of forest, lots of trees. After all, Flagstaff had once been a logging capital, boasting the largest stand of ponderosa pines in the world. Although a lot of forest had been butchered like so much else in Arizona, there was still plenty of woods left in which to pack up and drive off a classic car without anybody the wiser. Risky, though, if someone had discovered the theft sooner.

"You think that environmental group that tried to use the theft for their own publicity had anything to do with it?" Abby asked, thinking back to the hawk man in the vet's office. The receptionist had said she thought he spent a lot of time hiking. If anybody would know the woods and its byways, it would be that sort of person.

"One Universe?" The young man shook his head, but looked pleased to have someone seek out his opinion. "At first I kind of thought so. But then they didn't do anything. I mean, if they had the car wouldn't they have done something to show people they had it and keep their attention?"

"And now?"

"That car's long gone," the young man replied philosophically. "Too bad, too. I looked at the machines before I went on duty that night, and it was a beauty. A real beauty."

* * *

Tracking down a few other members of the staff who had been on duty the night of the theft, Abby confirmed the desk clerk's story. But, although they were all happy enough to talk "the great car theft" almost ad nauseam, she learned nothing more from them. She returned home in a dark mood. Dialysis. The damned dialysis. Out there like a black hole just waiting to suck her in. In disgust she tossed her purse so hard that it skittered off the professor's dining table and plunked to the floor. Francis, hoping for a new game or perhaps a doggy treat, pounced. But he soon lost interest when he found that the purse offered no enticing food smells nor evidenced any inclination for further movement.

Dialysis ahead; the Alfa Romeo as elusive as ever. Abby flopped down on the couch. FedExing cars. What a life. She wondered idly what a 1929 Alfa Romeo 6C 1750 was worth. Nobody seemed to know exactly what Foster had paid for his. Such a bit of chance. Everyone had assumed that only a handful of these Alfa Romeo 6C's existed in the entire world, until a wealthy, very elderly woman—mid-nineties, perhaps—died on her Hudson River estate. When executors arrived to check things out, there it was, up on blocks in a heated garage.

According to the story her brother-in-law told Abby at the send-off for the Copper State in Phoenix, the woman's late husband had courted her in it all those years ago. She had always cherished it, especially after his death. From time to time she'd have it taken off the blocks for a spin on a fine day—but within the confines of her estate, so that she and her chauffeur were the only ones who realized that the car was still around. Then she'd died, no family remaining, and the executors had arrived to check things out.

"Out of the blue Foster appears and snaps up that car before anyone else realizes what's happening," Charles had said as they'd waited in the heat and crowd for the rally to begin. The tantalizing smell of coffee and Krispy Kreme donuts permeated the air. Over the PA system the Cowboy Junkies wailed about being miles from their home. Charles and Abby watched as a young man accompanied by a tall, attractive brunette wearing a poodle skirt in honor of the era they represented demonstrated the workings of a 1958 Ford Skyliner hardtop convertible. The hard top folded down into a large compartment in the trunk. The system didn't seem to leave much space for luggage, but it did work.

"How did he know it was available?" Abby asked.

"Insider knowledge," Charles said, then paused as he took a bite of a complimentary Krispy Kreme donut. "Probably through Mrs. Richmond, Foster's mother, quite an old dragon, or so I've heard. She's supposed to have met everyone worth knowing from Maryland to Maine. Foster's her precious only child and for him nothing is quite good enough. Not even a 1929 Alfa Romeo. In any case, nobody's sure what Foster forked up because the car *never* went on the market. But it would have been millions anyway."

"So Foster Richmond just up and buys this Alfa Romeo for millions, however many? One way or another that represents quite a lot of spare change," Abby remembered observing.

"Lots of money there," Charles had told her over the babble of conversation. A 1959 Mercedes 300SL was being much admired, while a 1968 Intermeccanica Italia Spider had attracted its own fans. On the PA system a group called the Dixie Chicks had replaced the Cowboy Junkies. "Family money plus his own, not always acquired all that ethically either, from what I hear. See that fellow over there?"

Charles had indicated a man of average height, probably like Foster Richmond in his mid-fifties. His face was obscured by mirrored, wraparound sunglasses and his nondescript brown hair, or at least what could be seen of it under a California Angels' baseball cap, like Foster's blond hair was streaked with gray. His skin seemed a size too large for his body. Abby surmised that he must recently have lost some weight, although he still had a bit to go, especially around the midriff. The man looked keyed up, nervous, definitely hyper. Probably on amphetamines, she guessed. She'd seen students that way. The man glanced around compulsively, but always back to the center of everyone's attention, the Alfa Romeo.

"Congressman Toby Barrett. Wealthy California family. Put his money into a blind trust when he ran for office. Foster Richmond churned the account and lost a bit more playing with the International Monetary Fund. Not that Barrett is exactly broke, but. . ." Her brother-in-law had shrugged.

"Isn't that illegal? What Foster did?" She shook her head. Shocking, but at least the gossip gave her something to take her mind off her discomfort. The April morning had been stunningly hot, a preview of the summer to come. Her clothes clung to her body and the sweat had felt like insects crawling over her scalp. Abby had wondered hopefully if she could duck into the air-conditioned Phoenix Art Museum, beside which the event was taking place.

"Certainly it's unethical. But what happens to a man like Foster Richmond? He gets slapped with a fine, which he can easily afford to pay."

"What did Barrett do about all this? A congressman does carry a certain amount of clout, you know."

"Barrett hasn't been in long enough to be deeply into the old boy network as yet," her brother-in-law had explained. "He hasn't built up enough seniority or gotten enough people obligated to him to bring down a man like Richmond. Richmond is very old money and has a lot—I do mean a lot—of very important connections."

"And these two are participating in the same event?"

"Barrett is the co-driver for his old friend Gene Turner, one of our MAC members from Scottsdale. I'm not sure whether or not Turner knew about Foster when he originally invited Toby Barrett. The entries had just started to come in. Once we began compiling the list and Foster Richmond's name was on it, Gene could hardly call up his old buddy and tell him to forget it. Or, maybe he did. Who knows? Barrett's said to love cars and may have wanted to come anyway."

Heat or no heat, the excitement grew as the cars had pulled out of the art museum's parking lot onto Alvarado Road, where a starter waved them off one at a time in measured intervals. A stirring sight, the meticulously maintained machines gleaming in the sun. A stately parade of excellence. Well worth watching, but Abby slunk away to find a cooler spot. The part of the memory that haunted her now was not her inability to withstand the rigors of the day—she could live with the idea of acting like a wimp from time to time, as long as it didn't happen too often—but the import of what Charles had told her, the realization that even a congressman had no effective defenses against a man like Foster Richmond. True, Barrett was only in his second term, as she had subsequently learned. And true, as her brother-in-law had said, he hadn't built up much seniority or gotten tightly locked into the old boy network as yet. But still, this man served in the United States Congress. If he were helpless against Foster Richmond, what chance had a relatively young trust officer like Charles?

CHAPTER 3

"You've got to wage war to make peace."

Pam Haines glanced around at the small group gathered on the screen porch of the Flagstaff house shared by two of the leaders of One Universe, Peter Rivers and Linda Wallace, and then around at the porch itself. One screen sagged and bowed out. The green trim that held the screens in place had begun to crack and peel. The floor, a once-painted concrete slab, had lost most of its original dark red. Pam and the others sat in wicker furniture that must have been bought new by someone's grandmother.

Pam smiled inwardly. The scene pleased her no end. It seemed that all of her life, or for as many of those nineteen years as she could remember, she had wanted to flee wholesome, boring, predictable Iowa, to fly over the rainbow to a land of excitement and adventure. But the details of her own Oz had remained elusive until one hot summer day when she was about twelve and had sought a cool refuge in her parents' basement, which contained, among other treasures, probably every *National Geographic* and *Life Magazine* ever printed. In an ancient, musty issue of *Life* she came across a lavishly illustrated article about Flower Children and the Summer of Love. Everything looked so colorful, everyone seemed so happy and free. Really letting it all hang out. That did it. She wanted to go back to the Sixties, to be a Flower Child.

Unfortunately there were no time-machines handy nor any helpful tornados like that which whisked Dorothy from Kansas to Oz. Moreover, Ottumwa, Iowa, didn't offer much in the way of props, either. Psychedelic definitely wasn't in. Various drugs were available, but Pam didn't feel she had to go *that* far. Sandals and flowered granny dresses were about the best she could do. Her mother would never have let her step a foot out of their own yard in bare feet.

And then she had come to Flagstaff, Arizona, to go to NAU. By chance she'd walked into Macy's Coffee House and Bakery and equally by chance found herself at a table with honest-to-goodness Sixties hippies. Aging, of course. But still the real thing and way cooler than anything in Iowa. Tall, cadaverous Peter with his long gray ponytail and short, plump Linda with her undisciplined long, brown hair now liberally streaked with gray. When asked, Peter and Linda even admitted participating in the Summer of Love. From that moment on she was theirs.

Pam discovered that now their focus was the environment; Peter Rivers and Linda Wallace led an environmental group known as One Universe. That suited her just fine. She'd never thought much about the environment in Iowa. Farms grew corn. Cities were just cities, some big, some small. But she'd been appalled flying into Phoenix for the first time. Hundreds of square miles of matchbox houses. Where was the open land, farm or otherwise? Driving up I-17 she'd been impressed and amazed by the huge many-armed cactus called saguaros (the "g" being pronounced like an "h," she'd been told) while at the same time being revolted at seeing land that presumably once grew these magnificent plants bulldozed flat for still more housing. She was an easy sell and soon became one of One Universe's most enthusiastic participants. And here she was almost two years later, right in the thick of things, accepted by the really important members of the movement. Well, maybe not exactly a movement. Pam mentally backpedaled a little. But she liked to see it that way, as something a little larger and more important than it was. A long way to go for a girl from Iowa.

"So how do we wage war?" someone challenged Peter.

"That's what we're here to decide," Peter countered.

"That car was the greatest," Pam sighed.

"Yeah," Peter agreed. "But we're unlikely to get that lucky again."

"Whatever we do, it's got to be something big. Something totally off the wall!" The voice was soft, almost musical. However, there was no mistaking the underlying firmness. Pam thought that Titus—last name never used and, at least by her, not even remembered—was the one member of the group who looked the part of a revolutionary, or in his case an eco-warrior, a knight errant out to save the world. He was a small, lean, wiry man with bushy hair and beard, gray and white strands interlaced with red the color of rust, who reminded her of some primordial woods spirit, a transplanted druid. She was sure that you could drop Titus in the Coconino National Forest which surrounded Flagstaff, or in any other forest in the world, and he would survive, becoming one with the land, its flora and fauna. In fact, Titus would undoubtedly be quite content in an environment not contaminated by the presence of other humans.

"You do anything too far out, you'll get arrested," Pam told Titus, and then blushed outrageously. She didn't know about Titus, but Peter took pride in a record of arrests as long as the number of volumes in her parents' set of leather-bound Encyclopedia Britannica, and Linda had her own tales about jail cells. The two had told her of participating in protests over segregation, protests over Vietnam, and now protests about destruction to the environment. These had resulted in confrontations with the police, clubbings and tear-gas, rides in paddy wagons and time in jail. And she was warning these people?

"So what the fucking hell? We're sure needing something to get our message across to those bastards that are mucking up the planet," Titus snarled, kicking a leg of the wicker armchair in which he sat with one of his combat boots, dislodging yet another flake of once-white paint.

"The result must balance the consequences. There is simply no sense in anyone going to jail unless we make our point clearly," Martha Van Dyke observed tartly. She reminded Pam of a feisty Scottish terrier that had belonged to her best friend growing up, not big but lots of spirit and bounce. Actually, in the canine line, Martha herself preferred dandy dinmots, and today as usual her faithful Terrence sat patiently beside her. Martha's white hair had been trimmed in a neat cap around her head. Her small, tidy figure was clothed in a starched, long-sleeve white cotton shirt and seersucker pants patterned in tiny black and white checks. With black espadrilles on her feet, Martha was about as informal as Martha ever got. A jacket to match the seersucker pants was neatly folded on the back of her chair, a back with which Martha with her rigid posture never made contact. Somehow seeing Martha always brought to mind Pam's high school's marching band all dressed up in spiffy white and gold uniforms, blaring out John Philip Sousa.

Martha was the oldest of the group, probably as ancient as Pam's grandmother, who still made yummy chocolate chip cookies whenever Pam came to visit. But in spite of her age, Martha's mind was sharp—she could have run rings around most of the kids in Pam's classes and probably the professors as well. Her body was admittedly still in darned good shape, and she had lots of important connections as well as lots of money. A truly awesome woman. Also one of the "Big Four," as Pam thought of them: Peter, Linda, Titus, and Martha. They were the people who made One Universe work, the ones behind all important decisions. Although she had attained a somewhat elevated status, the other members, mostly students at the University, were merely the rank and file.

"So far we've done quite well in making our presence known and alerting people to at least one of the more pressing problems facing our environment—species extinction. Of course it's part of the natural rhythm of things for species to disappear. But not at the present accelerated rate, which is the direct result of people's thoughtless actions." Martha pursed her lips and shook her head disapprovingly just the way Pam's fourth grade teacher had done when one of the boys had thrown a spit ball.

Again Pam looked around the screened porch with approval. She had always assumed that revolutionaries of whatever sort met in basements or attics, or perhaps in a loft in Haight-Ashbury. On the other hand, it was probably more fitting for eco-warriors, prepared as they were to do battle for the preservation of the environment, to meet in surroundings closer to nature. She watched as a squirrel balanced on his hind legs on the railing of a deck beyond the porch, fluffy gray tail lined with white rippling like a blanket getting a good spring shaking. He gorged himself at a bird feeder hung from a branch of a ponderosa pine. Above the feeder perched an acorn woodpecker, bright scarlet cap on his head and a mean look in his beady eyes, each eye looking as if a smooth black pebble had been tossed into a large round pool of white. The irate woodpecker screeched *ja-cob, ja-cob* in protest at the squirrel's inroads on the food supply. Did woodpeckers ever attack squirrels, she wondered? One thing you could say about nature, with or without eco-warriors, things weren't really so peaceful.

"As Pam pointed out, that Alfa Romeo was a godsend. Outstanding, nationwide publicity and no body count," Martha added with what Pam assumed was a trace of humor. Only Titus looked genuinely disappointed. "Well done, all of you."

"But where do we go from here?" asked Peter, a skeletal, seemingly colorless, washed-out figure with his gray ponytail, faded tan cotton shirt, chinos, and once-white tennis shoes turned gray with time. Colorless and washed out, that is, until a person noticed the intense, committed look in his pale blue eyes.

"What we need is something that will get more national media attention," Martha replied thoughtfully. "It's all well enough to try to get Arizonans to wake up and realize that in their greed they are destroying exactly the values they prized so much when they moved here—clean air, magnificent scenery, and a healthy lifestyle. But Arizona's not alone in this, and in making our point we need to go much further."

"Flagstaff doesn't normally attract national attention," Linda pointed out as she re-crossed her plumpish thighs, the outline of which could be seen under her loose, ankle-length denim dress. "We were just lucky about the Copper State 1000."

"What if a railroad car was to spill hazardous waste right in the middle of town?" There was a malevolent glint in Titus's green eyes. "That's the sort of thing that would make CNN and all the rest of those bastards come running. Give people a close look at the pollutants that are being spread around even if the powers that be won't admit it."

"Only it's too damned dangerous to fool with that stuff. Some kid might get hurt," Peter remonstrated from the deck beyond the screened porch, where he had gone to shoo off the persistent squirrel, which leaped to a branch a couple of yards above Peter's head and joined the woodpecker in protest. Pam knew Peter had done some pretty crazy things in his day, but she was glad to see he still had a conscience. Frankly she wasn't so sure about Titus.

"Let's concentrate for a minute on the message," Martha directed, absently patting Terrence, a shaggy gray and white creature with a silken topknot and large dark eyes, built low to the ground. "As I said, we have tried to awaken the public to the fact that species are going extinct at an unprecedented rate, and we have no one to blame but ourselves. Thanks to the mysterious disappearance of the Alfa Romeo, the centerpiece of the Copper State, we made some real headway. Our press release certainly got us excellent exposure. Perhaps some people have begun to ask themselves why they make such a fuss about a car when a whole species can disappear without a word of protest. But people in general don't think in large, abstract terms. They need specifics. If we could have shown the last of the passenger pigeons pining away in its zoo cage, the final specimen of an entire species wantonly slaughtered by man, the point might have been made. Sociable creatures, so easy to capture and kill, simply because they flocked around a tethered friend!" she observed sadly. "The origin, by the way, of our phrase 'stool pigeon'."

Pam thought that Martha Van Dyke must have made a first-class newspaper publisher, which is what she'd been following the death of her husband. As far as making an impact on people's opinions, Martha seemed to know exactly what she was talking about. The sight of the last poor passenger pigeon pining for its lost brethren would have wrung her own heart any day.

"We need an issue, right here in Arizona, preferably in Flagstaff. Something concrete that the ordinary person can relate to. And, if we handle things correctly, something that will also have wider appeal. Ideas?"

"Galloping urbanization?" Pam suggested timidly, remembering her own first sight of the urban sprawl known as "The Valley of the Sun."

"In Phoenix that would do well. But unfortunately it won't work in Flagstaff. Flagstaff's growing rapidly, and sometimes in a very ungainly fashion—yes. But it will never be like the Valley. There isn't enough private land. The city is too constricted by national forest."

"So what threatens the national forest?" asked Peter, who had returned from his squirrel-shooing mission and now paced back and forth to the extent the constricted space allowed. "Clear cutting, only even the loggers are beginning to see the economic problems with that. Grazing, but the cattlemen know the range isn't unlimited and the smart ones have gotten so environmentally conscious they're putting the Sierra Club to shame."

"And then," Linda said thoughtfully, running her fingers through long, unstyled hair, "there's the 1872 Mining Law.

"Do you realize that more than 5,000 acres of forest service land around the San Francisco Peaks have been claimed under the law?" she asked, her normally soft voice becoming as harsh and rasping as the irate woodpecker's. "That's 5,000 acres that can be mined with what Peter and I consider to be the most minimal environmental constraints. And speaking of mines, there's that damned Pycenium Mine right up next to the spotted owl habitat we've been trying so hard to protect."

"Despicable!" Martha snapped.

Mining Law? Claimed? Pam didn't have a clue as to what they were talking about, but she didn't want to admit her ignorance either. A trip to the library seemed to be in order. Not that she minded. Maybe she would run into that cute Bob Curtis. What a cool guy! And in the meantime, at least she knew about spotted owls. They were always good for some publicity.

* * *

Abby found to her relief that she really did feel measurably better in the high, cool, dry climate. The professor's house was comfortable, if a little too stridently plaid, Francis proved to be a reassuring presence, and her neighbors, the Khalsas, though never intrusive, were always ready to give her a helping hand. Even Bob Curtis, Sada Anand's at first elusive brother, turned out to be a good companion. A nice young man—bright, neat appearance, good manners. Yet under the clean, wholesome surface, Abby sensed something darker. She had noted an occasional brooding look, an extended silence, a quick, impatient gesture suggesting a barely restrained temper. But then he was young, mid-twenties she supposed, and maturing wasn't necessarily a smooth process even after the teenage years.

Bob and his two little nieces often joined Abby and her dog, who by now had only the barest trace of a limp, on their walks. The kindly Dr. Frankenthaller had suggested that his patients who kept moving did far better than those who became couch potatoes. For Abby the walks were valuable because they were something she *could* do, as well as something that gave focus to her days. Maybe they were really just another sort of running away, she had mused, an instinctive movement through space that precluded the necessity of meeting her problems straight on. Yet one way or another she was determined, no matter how fatigued, to keep them part of her agenda.

To Abby's delight, Bob Curtis seemed to know a great deal about the forest and could spot things she would have overlooked entirely. Every outing became a new adventure. Each day, though unremarkable in itself, was like a precious bead on a magic necklace. And always the inevitable question, how many more?

"A fawn, a baby deer," Bob quietly pointed out to Pooh and Bear. "Over there, with its mother."

"Oooooh," the girls sighed in unison.

"It's so tiny and delicate and vulnerable," Abby observed with wonderment. The legs looked too slender to support the barrel body, small though it was. The only things at all large about the animal were the tall gray ears which jutted out in a "V" from its long, skinny head.

"Very vulnerable," Bob agreed, the golden hair not covered by his hiking hat gleaming in the sunlight. A tall, well-conditioned young man, he undoubtedly could have stepped out at an impressive pace, Abby acknowledged. However, he patiently adapted his stride to hers and that of his nieces.

"Predators?" Abby asked.

"Sometimes, only there's not many of those left around. You

may think it's crazy to say, but that's too bad for the deer. They keep multiplying and there's just not enough food, especially in very dry years like this one. I think a quick death by mountain lion would be a whole lot better than slow starvation. The hunters thin them out a bit in the fall, but a lot of the deer are smarter than you'd think and seem to know exactly where they can't be hunted. It's pretty amazing to watch them flocking into the parks when hunting season begins."

Abby looked around and wondered what the poor things ate at the best of times. The long needles of the ponderosa pine? The lance-like leaves of the agave? The hard, shiny green leaves of the scrub live oak with their sharp, serrated edges? Or, the one viable candidate in sight, perhaps the fruits of the Gambel oak which, Bob had told her, produced edible acorns in season.

"Once in the parks they seem to know they're safe and people don't really frighten them. You should see them at El Tovar, the old hotel on the south rim of the Grand Canyon. In the winter when it gets dark and cold they lie down right next to the south side of the building because it's warm. The walls absorb heat during the day and release it at night."

Abby had quickly noticed that whenever Bob talked about anything in nature his voice resonated with enthusiasm and a passionate intensity.

"You're so keen on this sort of thing, have you ever thought of going into some sort of environmental studies?" she inquired, remembering Sada Anand's concern about her brother completing his degree.

Bob kicked a few of last year's brown pine needles with the toe of one of his Gore-Tex hiking boots. The little group came to a halt and he watched as the two girls carefully examined a choice selection of pine cones. Bob had given each of them a small sack and told them that they could only bring back as many pine cones as the sacks would hold so that the little girls would choose carefully. He had explained to Abby that he planned to take some thick, colorful Mexican yarn and staple it to the back end of the cones. Come December, the cones could be used as Christmas tree decorations.

His sister Sally—no, he had corrected himself—Sada Anand and Soul Singh didn't seem to mind having Christmas for the girls, even though it wasn't part of their new religion. The pine cones with their yarn would be bright and festive and remind the girls of their summer walks. Also they wouldn't stress the Khalsas' limited budget.

"There are all kinds of good programs, and Northern Arizona University strikes me as just the sort of place you might find one," Abby encouraged him, just the way she would have one of her Vassar students. Students who, time and distance having filtered out some of their more annoying characteristics like turning in papers late and saddling her with illegible exams, she remembered with great fondness.

Bob glanced away, looking unaccountably pained. "My father, well, he doesn't think anything counts except the law. He's a really big trial lawyer in Florida." He kicked aimlessly at a few more pine needles.

"You could be an environmental lawyer. There's an increasing demand for that sort of thing."

Bob didn't answer immediately and, the girls having made their selection, the small group moved on in silence. Abby gradually became aware of an acrid stench penetrating the clean, dry air.

"Oh, damn, look at that!" Bob stopped abruptly and pointed to a pile of black ashes where someone had lit a campfire.

Abby noted that whoever had been here had also strewn Red Dog beer cans about, left a half-empty sack of potato chips, and tossed a bottle of Union Jack Snakebite in the general direction of the bushes, where it had hit a rock and shattered into some nasty-looking shards. Francis sniffed around for a moment, then turned away in what could only be interpreted as canine disgust.

"The slobs can't pick up after themselves, and they're going to set the whole forest on fire if they don't get the idea that you can't build a safe fire under overhanging branches—shit, dead ones at that!" Bob's voice rang out harsh and tense with anger.

"And this isn't the first time this summer I've seen this sort of thing," he added, lowering his voice as if he had suddenly remembered the presence of the little girls. "I think it must be the same guys—unless everybody is going in for the same brands of beer and booze this year. They like this particular area. I've been thinking of hanging out here a few nights to see if I can catch them at it."

"What then?" Abby asked, not really sure she wanted to hear the answer.

"I'll think of something."

"Don't ask for trouble," Abby warned. Only one of Bob versus at least two party-going slobs who could quite well be doing drugs as well as liquor? Not good. Not good at all. She thought, as she had so often over the years, of Mark, his senseless death, the destructive rage that drugs could unleash, the dreadful consequences. The almost forgotten pain seared through her again. She had lost a lover that way. Now she didn't want to lose a friend as well.

"Me? Ask for trouble? No way." She could hardly miss the bitterness and sarcasm.

Bob strode on, then abruptly slowed his pace for Abby and the girls.

"About environmental law. . ."

"Naw, I don't want to be a lawyer. The law stinks!" he exploded. "Lawyers are bastards." He picked up a pebble and hurled it at a raven perched in a ponderosa pine. The raven gave a surprised screech and flew away, pumping his great black wings with a *zip, zip, zip* sound.

"Well, I guess the legal profession does have its share of detractors," Abby replied, more than a little taken aback at Bob's bitterness.

"Lawyers twist words! My dad thinks I'm stupid anyway, and then he makes me look like a fool. Even if I'm not brilliant like him, I'm not an idiot."

"Of course not!" Abby agreed, touched by his defensiveness and the sudden, dejected sag of his shoulder.

"I got into some real shit back in Florida." Bob's voice was low and tense. The girls lagged behind, seemingly oblivious. "Would the great lawyer help me out? No way. Made me get a court-appointed lawyer who totally fucked things up."

"Drugs?" Abby asked gently.

"Yeah," he admitted reluctantly, looking back at the two little girls, who were showing each other their pine cones. "The police in Florida know. My sister knows, and so does Soul Singh. I guess there's no reason why you shouldn't."

"Dealing?"

"Hell, no! Just an uninformed consumer. Some guys seem to be able to handle them. But not me."

"I doubt those guys manage in the long run. If so, I haven't seen it."

"Yeah, well, I really don't want to talk about it."

Abby, for her part, had no desire to push him. At least not now. And in the future? Maybe she shouldn't meddle, only it was almost impossible for someone with her teaching background to let a young person with brains and potential drift indefinitely. And after all, encouraging Bob to finish his education was a project for which she had a lot better preparation than finding out something about a missing Alfa Romeo.

* * *

Pam had never thought she'd love a library, but she did love the Flagstaff main public library, which she chose over the university library whenever she had a chance. The public library was awesome—truly the most beautiful building she'd ever seen. The view from the big windows made her feel like she was sitting in a park, only a park equipped with comfortable armchairs, desks, and even fireplaces. Not that the fireplaces actually burned wood. Even so they looked real enough in the winter when lit, making the library seem cozy and homelike as snow drifted down outside. Today she looked out on golden splashes of afternoon sunlight.

The library was also a great place to meet people like that awesome Bob Curtis. What a totally neat guy! Tall, blond, blue-eyed with a light tan and muscles from sailing, waterskiing, and whatever else they did down there in Florida. Could he ever get interested in a girl like her, she wondered? A girl still a little too well padded from a lifetime of solid Midwestern meals, with straight, dishwater blond hair that tended to be kind of on the limp side, sort of muddy brown eyes, and freckles. Oh, those awful freckles scattered right across the bridge of her nose where no one could miss them. Yuck! She rubbed at them as if that would make them go away. But Bob honestly seemed to like talking to her. At first he'd been kind of shy, but lately he'd begun to open up. The thought made her feel warm all over.

Pam found a librarian, a bouncy blonde who didn't look at all like the stern, grey-headed women with their conservative, tailored clothes and sensible shoes who ruled libraries in Iowa. "You know, the Mining Law's a real popular topic all of a sudden. Things go in waves like that. We do have some good material on the Mining Law, only someone's already requested it. See that fellow over there?" The librarian pointed discreetly. "Maybe he'd share."

Pam felt titillating ripples cross her stomach like a summer breeze riffling the surface of a pond. The fellow the librarian indicated was Bob Curtis.

"Hi," she said shyly as she sat down beside him.

"Pam!" He smiled and she thought his voice held pleasure.

She picked up one of the books in front of him, *The Mining Law: A Study in Perpetual Motion.* "Looks like you're reading up on the 1872 Mining Law. How come?"

"Well, I've kind of gotten interested in the forest, and there've been a series of articles in the newspaper on this Pycenium Mine. They say it's chewing up one of the flanks of the San Francisco Peaks and that has a lot of people very upset, especially the Native Americans. Hopis, Navajo, Apaches, Yavapais. You name it. The Sierra Club is talking about bringing a suit. The Forest Service doesn't seem to be very happy, either. But they say they can't do anything about it because of this Mining Law. I'd never heard of this law before and got curious. Do you know anything about it?"

"I've heard of the mine." Pam didn't want to admit that she didn't read the paper, only glanced at someone else's copy occasionally to check the movie schedule. "I'm a member of an environmental group called One Universe. They're as hot and bothered about it as the Sierra Club and the others. But tell me about the law." She gazed at him expectantly.

Bob paused a minute as if to gather his thoughts. "It's pretty curious," he admitted. "First off, this law gives anyone access to federal lands to look for minerals like gold, silver, and copper. You don't need any advance permission and don't have to inform anyone."

"You can just go anywhere?" she responded in amazement.

"Well, they've exempted Indian reservations and military installations, places like that."

"So you just take off with your mule and your pan and wear a big old hat." Pam stifled a giggle at the thought of Bob—clean shaven, hair neatly clipped, clothes ironed, smelling of soap—in a scroungy, wrinkled miner's outfit like they wore in the old, old movies and a battered, sweat-stained, broad-brimmed hat.

"Sort of. Only I think the miner and mule thing was pretty much out of the picture when the law was passed. Today we're talking mining companies, a lot of times big international corporations, you know."

She nodded, sagely she hoped.

"You've got to find a valuable mineral, or all bets are off. Gold or something like that. Then you just claim the land and mine it."

"Claim it?" The same word Linda had used.

"Announce that you've found a mineral, where it is, and that you intend to mine it."

"Don't you have to pay the government?"

"I think today there's some sort of fee for paperwork. But, no, you don't have to pay them for the minerals you mine. There's no sort of royalty. From what I can tell not even if you're a foreign company, as long as you're incorporated in the U.S. And you can mine as long as you like," Bob said, dropping his voice as a very large woman in tight white pants and a garishly bright flowered shirt, who was studying what appeared to be a cookbook, gave him a black look. "You're just expected to do at least a hundred dollars of work a year on your claim. The time you do pay the government is when you buy the land, if that's what you decide to do. In government speak it's called patenting."

Pam looked at the inner flap of the dust jacket of the book she had picked up from Bob's reading table. It could have been written in Sanskrit and she'd probably never have noticed. She was thinking how nice it was to be so close to Bob, actually within touching distance. Again little ripples ran across her stomach. The bouncy blonde librarian passed by, giving them a friendly smile.

"You can buy the land? What if it's in, like, Coconino National Forest?" Pam gulped, trying to come off thoughtful and concerned. Actually she was wondering if Bob had really gotten this whole thing right. It sounded really weird. She could imagine herself standing someplace in the forest, announcing that she had found her pot of gold and intended to claim the land on which it rested. Well, she thought, it probably didn't work *quite* that way. In the old movies the guys were usually hunkered over a stream sloshing water and gravel around in a pan. And today there were probably a zillion forms to be filled out. But still. . . . Her own little piece of the forest.

"You can buy it even if it's in a national forest, or at least you can after you've put five hundred dollars worth of work into your claim. And get this," Bob added eagerly, "the price is the same as it was in 1872: five dollars an acre for a lode claim, when the mineral runs in veins, and two fifty an acre if it's a placer claim; that's when the mineral's in particles."

"They sure as heck don't sell land for that price in Iowa."

"Not any place else I know of, either."

"And this really happens?"

"Sure. From what I've read there are whole developments of summer homes here in Arizona built on patented mining claims."

Pam wanted to ask him just what this Pycenium Mine, which had the Indians and the Sierra Club and a lot of other people including Linda and Peter so hot and bothered, was mining, only she didn't get the chance. Bob glanced at his watch, then jumped up.

"Sorry, I've got to run. It's my shift for baby-sitting."

Pam sat there stunned. Baby-sitting? Was Bob married? He wasn't wearing a wedding band, but then some people didn't. Or maybe he was divorced. Her parents would *hate* that. They didn't approve of divorce *at all*. When her Aunt Effy had split from Uncle Howard the whole family had declared themselves absolutely scandalized.

Pam felt like breaking down in tears right there at the library desk. It just wasn't fair. Here she'd finally met a really nice guy, no earrings in his nose or lips—very unusual for Flagstaff where body-piercing seemed to be a community fetish, and no gross tattoos on his biceps. Now she finds out that he's married or maybe divorced, which was almost as bad. What ever could she do about it?

* * *

When Abby got home from the walk with Bob, Pooh, and Bear she plopped down in an armchair and put her feet up on an overstuffed red plaid footstool. She checked her ankles—nope, no swelling. Good sign. Even if the kidneys weren't draining all the liquid and waste they should have from her body, at least the fluids weren't backing up too badly yet.

Encouraging about the ankles, but otherwise she felt rotten—tired, frustrated, and discouraged by her inability to accomplish anything that mattered. The woods walks were all fine and dandy and undoubtedly good for her health, physical and mental. She had brought happiness to a once-forlorn little animal. Otherwise? A big zero. What was she doing that made any difference to anyone? To date her probing into the disappearance of the Alfa Romeo, her one real project, had netted her nothing. She had managed to talk to the Flagstaff police, the Coconino County Sheriff's office, and the Arizona Department of Public Safety. Everyone had been uniformly polite and communicative, but no one had anything new to add to what the press had already ferreted out and broadcast or published. So much for the bright idea of shaking loose some new ideas! Abby freely admitted that she wasn't about to offer Kinsey Millhone or Anna Pidgeon any competition.

Her stomach roiled with frustration. When Mark died she had escaped the pain through work. In the intervening years she had thrown herself completely into her career, even small successes bringing with them a sense of fulfillment, a vindication of her existence as a human being. She could never forget that by sheer chance Mark had died and she had lived. She *had* to prove herself worthy of the life that had been so arbitrarily granted her, and she had to prove it by *doing* something. But now she was doing nothing at all, not teaching, not researching, not publishing. She didn't know what gnawed at her more, her guilt for living when Mark had died or her feeling of utter uselessness. What a crock life could be!

The telephone rang.

"*Darling*! How are you?

It was Becky, whom their mother had dubbed "Little Miss Sarah Bernhardt." Ebullient today, but definitely not as ebullient as usual.

"I'm fine," Abby lied. "How are you and the family?"

This elicited a lengthy account of golf and tennis lessons, swim team, and other activities in which Sarah and Sam were engaged during the early summer—before Becky and they settled in Iron Springs after the Fourth of July with Charles visiting for weekends. As her sister chatted away, Abby settled deeper into the big armchair, slipped off her shoes and rotated her feet one way and then the other, loosening up her ankles. Her unswollen ankles. Appreciate small blessings, she counseled herself sternly.

"And Charles?" Abby asked cautiously when her sister's monologue began to run down.

"Well. . . " Becky drew the word out like young Sam stretching a wad of bubble gum from his mouth, the pink thread becoming ever more attenuated until it finally snapped.

"The bank?"

"The president's an okay guy. Really very fair, but. . ."

But sling enough money and influence around the way Foster Richmond could and even a basically fair person might not remain impartial indefinitely, Abby completed the thought in her head.

"No one I've talked to here has had a word of criticism for the arrangements Charles made for the cars and mechanics."

But even as she spoke, Abby knew how limp her words sounded. Logic just didn't play a part in the "I've lost my toy so I'll break yours" world of Foster Richmond. Foster was going to shaft

Charles as surely as he had shafted that California congressman, that Toby Barrett.

"Why doesn't Foster take a shot at Earl Olson?" Abby asked, referring to the MAC member who had been in overall charge the fateful night in Flagstaff.

"Earl Olson has lots of money, lots of connections, that's why." Abby could almost hear her sister saying "duh!" as she had when they were children. "By the way, have you run into the Olsons? They're at their Flagstaff home now."

"I think half of Phoenix must be up here, judging by the traffic. The summer traffic in Flagstaff is as bad as the winter traffic in the Valley. I try to stay out of the center of town except at offbeat hours, so I haven't run into anybody."

"I've got to call Alice Olson anyway about the plans for the Phoenix Art Museum League's fall fashion show. I'll mention that you're renting in Flagstaff for the summer. The Olsons give *great* parties. Maybe they'll invite you to one with some good-looking men."

Abby made a non-committal sound. Nice thought on her sister's part, but faced with dialysis, men, no matter how good looking, were the last thing on her mind. She wondered if people on dialysis could be intimate, or if they even wanted to. As for the first, there was probably nothing to prevent it. As for the second, well, let's face it, she told herself, good sex takes energy and a positive outlook. Right now she had precious little of either. If a really great guy accidentally entered her life, would she even know what to do with him?

When Abby hung up, little Francis, who had been sunning himself in a patch of sunlight, got up, crossed the room, and settled down beside the armchair. She ran a bare foot through his thick, soft fur. She returned to the thoughts the phone call had interrupted. She craved, craved as much as a hiker craves a drink of cool water in the heat of the desert, the satisfaction of doing something, *anything*, above all for its own sake but also to keep her mind from dwelling on the fast-approaching dialysis. So far nothing, not even the elusive Alfa Romeo, had done the job. *Damn, damn, damn and double damn.* She felt an invisible vice beginning to tighten around her head, boring in at the temples until she could barely think or breathe. "The Headache," as she had dubbed it. It seemed to be just one more unpleasant aspect of renal failure.

As for the Alfa Romeo, she could think of one, and only one, avenue that she hadn't really explored, the environmental group, that One Universe. Would that nice vet give out the hawk man's phone number? Alternately she could go to the library, read or reread some of the articles that had been published about the theft of the car and get the names of some of the local people involved in One Universe. Maybe One Universe had a web site. They seemed to be into publicity. Or, she had yet another idea—but there was nothing she could do about it now, not with The Headache closing in on her, shutting down all her senses, leaving her with no links to external reality, only the awful pain.

CHAPTER 4

"Will it hurt a lot?" Bob asked tentatively.

Another day, another walk, another bead on the necklace—all the beads so remarkably the same and thus profoundly reassuring, Abby thought. It had taken her two days to recuperate from The Headache and the lassitude that washed over her afterward. Letting Francis in and out, checking his water and feeding him had sapped what little energy she had. But today she felt better, so she was back on the trail again. They weren't going very far, and definitely not very fast, but even that took an act of will. However, she counseled herself, walking was good for the mind, good for the soul. Worth the effort in spite of the summer heat and the constant, nagging fatigue that never quite went away. Also she wanted to act on her last structured thought before The Headache had grounded her. Did Bob, with his evident concern for the forest and all that lived there, have any contacts with One Universe?

Pooh and Bear were pursuing a large yellow butterfly with elegant black markings like the tracings on a late-nineteenth-century stained-glass window. The lovely creature, its beauty enhanced by blue dots on the end of its tail together with a few traces of red, clearly had a passion for thistles. Lighting on a pinkish-orange center, it rapidly opened and shut its wings like the handles of tiny, fairy bellows while it sucked up the nectar, then took off to sample another thistle with Pooh and Bear just behind. Giggling, the girls followed the butterfly as it fluttered insouciantly along just out of harm's way.

Francis watched this performance as if he couldn't quite believe the amount of effort expended over a creature that didn't have a delicious aroma, like a skunk or squirrel or even a rabbit. Thoughtfully he lifted a leg and anointed a small pine.

"Is it painful?" Bob prompted her gently. "Dialysis?"

63

"No, I don't think so. Lida, my dialysis nurse, says not." *Pain? Why did people always think in terms of physical pain? It could be bad all right. But The Headache had once again proved that she could withstand large doses, while other types of pain—mental pain—corroded the spirit like acid on naked flesh. To live only by recourse to artificial means, to lose her sense of independence, to relinquish a sense of self? Frankly she'd take The Headache any day.*

"Anyway, I've got to get through the operation to put the tube in for dialysis first." Abby winced, though not at the thought of the operation itself. Lida had assured her that the operation would be neither long nor painful and, since they would use a local anaesthetic, would have no unpleasant aftereffects. No, it was not the operation. It was the irrevocable step the operation represented that terrified Abby, made her heart pound as fast as the pulsating wings of the voracious butterfly. Once done, she would stand irretrievably on the brink of dialysis.

"Do you have to be tied to one of those big machines?" Concern darkened Bob's blue eyes.

"That's hemodialysis." She remembered her father and shuddered involuntarily. "For that you go to a clinic, usually three times a week, where they run your blood through an artificial kidney to get rid of the excess fluids and cleanse it." As usual when discussing polycystic kidney disease, dialysis, or any of the other awfuls that haunted her like coal-black ravens waiting in a pine to swoop down on a bit of road kill, she kept her voice low, calm, as neutral as possible. A good technique, she had found, to prevent herself from edging toward hysteria.

"And you're not going to do that?"

"I'm going to be on peritoneal, which I can do at home. I'll drain a special fluid into the peritoneal cavity," she pointed to her abdomen under the worn khaki shorts she was wearing with an old Vassar tee shirt in a rather bilious shade of pink with gray lettering, "into the region most people think of as the stomach, only it's not really. The fluid absorbs the impurities the kidneys would normally remove from the system and also the excess liquid. Then I drain that fluid out and put in some more." Abby felt proud of herself. She had repeated almost verbatim what the nurse Lida had told her and with no more emotion in her voice than she would have had in announcing the date of the mid-term exam.

"How often do you have to do that?" Bob asked, stopping a minute to take a swig from his water bottle, turning away so she could no longer read his eyes.

"Four times a day is the norm, although any dialysis regime is tailored for the individual, according to Lida. She's been teaching me about dialysis, how it works, what I have to do, and that sort of thing." Abby used her hiking staff to nudge a loose stone off the trail.

"Four times a day?" Bob's voice betrayed his distress.

"Four times a day."

For a moment he simply stood there as if trying to absorb what Abby had told him. She thought she heard him again mutter, "four times a day." Then, followed by the little group, he set off once more. They were moving slowly up a path strewn with gray rocks over earth that was bone-dry and friable. Difficult footing to Abby's way of thinking. So very easy to slip. Moisture tended to compact the soil, but today the whole forest looked as dry as the crumbling earth beneath her feet. The vibrant greens of late May and early June had noticeably lost some of their radiance. The tiny flowers that earlier in the season provided surprise and delight had faded or withered away. Even the deep blue sky looked harder, somehow more metallic. She thought of the party boys and their camp fires. In this tinder box a *very* bad idea indeed.

"And the operation?"

"It's to put in the tubing for the fluid, the dialysate as it's called. There'll be a tube—actually it's a catheter with a long name I can never remember—with a cap on it coming out of my peritoneal cavity. The dialysate goes in and out that way." In and out, in and out, in and out day after day after day. Her mind beat out the words like the *basso continuo* of a dirge.

Bob looked dubious.

"It has its advantages. Although admittedly given the new

techniques in hemodialysis, they can clean out your system very effectively that way." Also, she added to herself, frequently in much more pleasant surroundings than those endured by her father. She would never forget her last year in high school, driving her father to the dingy clinic in the hospital basement where he was forced to sit in a lumpy, aging Naugahyde recliner for up to four hours—though she had heard they did these things somewhat faster now—while the blood was drained out of him, cleansed in an artificial kidney, then returned to his body. Just the memory made her queasy. That awful, depressing clinic with the green and black linoleum floor and the government green walls. Noisy, too, with a wide-screen television always blaring, whether anyone wanted to watch it or not. The thought of it not only made her queasy, it gave her the shivers in spite of the heat of the day. The remembrance of the horror of the treatments and then the ultimate loss echoed dully down the years. Not all the sun of Arizona could brighten that dark corner of her life.

"With the peritoneal I'll be in charge of my own treatment," she announced brightly, as much to reassure herself as to reassure Bob. A control freak? She'd never really pictured herself that way. But as her world degenerated into chaos, she craved some measure of control, a small role in determining her destiny, a tiny bit of influence over the confusing and threatening events crowding in on her. She desperately wanted to be able to do something on her own behalf and so perhaps feel a little less helpless.

"When do you have this operation?" Bob looked uncomfortable as he mopped his face with a cotton kerchief. His color was high and, when he took off his broad-brimmed hat for a moment to mop the upper part of his forehead, Abby could see that sweat had plastered his blond hair to his scalp. The day had become unpleasantly hot, hot enough to bring out a sweat on the coolest cucumber, but the heat didn't account for the fact that Bob kept looking anywhere but at her. She sensed that he found the conversation thoroughly upsetting and distasteful, yet persisted because he needed to know the worst if he were going to be any good to her. Such a nice young man, she thought with an internal sigh.   She did so hope that he would go back to college, meet an equally nice young woman, and have a Pooh and Bear of his own. That's the way it was supposed to happen, wasn't it?

"The doctor says early July."

"That soon? Oh, shit."   He stabbed his hiking stick viciously at the ground, and with an obvious effort finally managed to meet her eyes.

"You know I'll do anything I can to help you. And don't forget that Sally, I mean Sada Anand, is a nurse. She'd help you any way she could, too. You seem so darned self-sufficient," he rushed on as if she were going to reject what he had to say, but he had to say it anyway. "Only sometimes people have just *got* to accept help. They can't do everything."

Bob's comment unexpectedly hit home.   She flinched instinctively. Since the death of her parents and even more so since Mark's, she'd tried to be independent, strong. She'd asked virtually nothing of her colleagues and friends. She'd even been chary about receiving any backup from her sister. Instead, she'd relied primarily on herself, who, ironically enough, had proved to be the weakest link of all.

No more loss, no more pain—or so she'd thought. She'd kept others at bay, not sharing with Becky, her closest friends, or the few men who had entered her life on a more than platonic basis her deepest hopes and fears.   In fact, even before the diagnosis of polycystic kidney disease she'd been putting her emotions in such a deep freeze that she wasn't really sure she had them anymore.   So when was strength really strength and when was it weakness? Her very strength, or at least what she'd thought of as her strength, seemed to have left her an empty husk, fragile, vulnerable.   *Accept help? Depend on another? Did she even know how?*

"Thank you," Abby said at last, unable to express to Bob how deeply his words had penetrated.

"When it comes time for the operation, I may well need some help with Francis," she went on, glancing down at the little dog. "My niece Sarah has allergies, and no way do I want to board him at the vet's. He might think he was being abandoned again! As for your sister, she's a really wonderful person. I'll call on her if I ever have to. Only I hope I don't have to because she's already such a busy lady—working, keeping house, raising Pooh and Bear."

They both glanced back at the girls, who had turned their big, searching gray eyes on a squirrel which sat on the low branch of a small pine squawking loudly at them, or more probably at Francis, who had chased him up there to begin with.

Suddenly a loud, grating noise drowned out the squirrel's protest. Instinctively Abby leashed Francis in and then looked up to see a couple of motorbikes come roaring over a rise. Two almost identical young men, both with long, greasy dark hair and each with three earrings on one ear, crouched low over the handlebars. Their torn, sleeveless black tee shirts exposed well-muscled arms tattooed with enough colors and patterns to decorate a mining-town bordello. They both wore skin-tight jeans, and short scruffy black boots of cracked, fake leather. The wheels of their bikes bit deeply into the dry soil, spitting up rocks and sand.

Bob exploded in fury.

"No motorized vehicles here," he shouted, shaking his fist as the bikes wove up a hill through the trees, maneuvering back and forth to gain elevation, grinding their tires deeper still into the ground as they did so. "You're ripping off the ground cover, you bastards. Go ride your bikes on some Forest Service road."

"Fuck off, man!" shouted one of the boys in return, raising a greasy middle finger as the two reached the top of the rise. Then they both laughed and sped away.

"Assholes," Bob yelled after the retreating figures. "Stupid, fucking assholes." He reached down, grabbed a stone, and flung it at them, but the bikers were already well out of range. "Somebody ought to grind their empty little heads against a boulder."

"Bob!" Abby put a restraining hand on his arm while the two little girls stared wide-eyed at their normally gentle uncle, his face flushed and twisted with fury.

"You're forgetting your nieces." Oh, that temper again. For a moment she thought he might run after the bikers, not that he could hope to catch them. Then, fists clenched, neck muscles corded, he stalked on. In a low voice he growled, "Just you wait. I'll catch those bastards."

* * *

All the way home Bob railed, *sotto voce* in deference to the girls, against everyone who desecrated the forest, bikers and party boys alike, dreaming up terrible fates for them. His favorite scenario involved tossing the offenders down an abandoned mine shaft to die of dehydration, a dreadful death which, in this dry climate, would come long before starvation. He pictured them gazing longingly up at the sky while their tongues began to swell and they began to hallucinate. Of course it was all fantasy, but at least he'd had the decency to keep his voice down. The abrupt change in personality had already shocked Pooh and Bear enough. As for Abby, it had been something like glimpsing the dark side of the moon. Caring, compassionate Bob had a lot of rage simmering just under the surface.

Afterward she realized that in all the excitement she'd never managed to ask Bob the question she'd wanted to put to him, did he know anyone at One Universe? Concerned as he was about the forest and about the environment in general, he might well have made contact with the group, either deliberately or by happenstance. Flagstaff wasn't all that large. The chances of people with similar interests getting to know each other were high.

She would have phoned him then and there, but he had said that as soon as they got back from the walk he was off to do errands for his sister. Well, a little time researching One Universe in the library wouldn't hurt her.

Abby showered quickly, then slipped on tailored navy slacks that looked like linen but were actually some crease-resistant blend and a light knit, scoop-neck, long-sleeve pullover in navy and white designed to go with the slacks. Navy loafers to match. Some of her friends could throw all sorts of clothes together with splendid effect. Abby left such agonizing decisions to the manufacturer.

* * *

Once again her research into the disappearance of the Alfa Romeo seemed to be taking her nowhere. She slipped off her reading glasses and pushed back from the reading table at the main Flagstaff public library for a moment to rest her eyes. Damned disease made them tire quickly. At least she assumed it was the disease, although this was one side-effect Dr. Frankenthaller had never mentioned. Maybe it was just another manifestation of the persistent fatigue. Or age. Dreadful how a disease could age a person.

She had just reread an article from *People Magazine* that at least had the virtue of being light and amusing and, further, was illustrated with some excellent photos. One showed a small group of people in animated conversation, the magnificent San Francisco Peaks looming above. *"No one cares about a species of bird or squirrel going extinct," says Martha Van Dyke, 75, former newspaper publisher and one of the leaders of the environmental group One Universe, "but lose a vintage Alfa Romeo and you'd think we were faced with a national tragedy,"* the caption read.

The story reconfirmed Abby's original impression that One Universe had milked the car's disappearance for all the publicity they could generate. Yet they had never demonstrated any tangible proof either that they'd orchestrated the theft or that they knew the fate of the Alfa Romeo. However, even though it was probably another dead end, Abby didn't want to drop One Universe altogether. At least they had a reason to steal the car, which is more than anyone else seemed to have.

After all, you couldn't sell a vintage Alfa Romeo without raising obvious questions, especially when there were only a few in the whole world, she reasoned. And it wasn't like a famous masterpiece "commissioned" by a fabulously wealthy collector who would then enjoy the work in the privacy of his own home. To be enjoyed a car had to be driven, but where could a person go? One of the great draws of the Copper State 1000 was a chance for classic car buffs to show off their machines; no one was likely to show off a "hot" car. Another draw was the chance, provided by the Department of Public Safety working in combination with some of the local Indian tribes, for the drivers to let their machines run full out on some of the scenic but less well-traveled roads of rural Arizona. Well, not much chance of running wild and free in a stolen Alfa Romeo.

Reinstating her glasses, Abby studied the photograph more carefully. The real subject seemed to be the Peaks, their dark green forested bases fading up into mauve and gray above the tree line, all three crowned at the summit with a pristine white cap of snow. Of course that had been April. As June approached, the snow had melted until now they were bare. But the Peaks remained perennially impressive, always dominating the landscape of north central Arizona. They were visible from the mountains west of Prescott to the Hopi mesas northeast of Flagstaff, and as far north as some sites on the North Rim of the Grand Canyon. For the Navajos, the Peaks marked the western boundary of Navajo land and were tacked to the earth by a sunbeam. This Abby had learned by studying the Harrison Begay paintings of the four cardinal points of the Navajo world in the Museum of Northern Arizona. The Hopis called the Peaks "the high place of the snows." In the olden days they had believed they were so high that when the sun shone on one side, the moon shone on the other.

In any case, the human figures in the *People* photo looked puny by comparison: Peter Rivers and Linda Wallace—names that meant nothing to Abby. With them were Martha Van Dyke, the former newspaper publisher who had been quoted, and, Abby suddenly realized, the hawk man, identified only as Titus. The fellow she'd seen in the veterinarian's office. She made a note of the names. All of them, but especially this Titus person, who presumably knew the forest quite well, would certainly bear looking into.

* * *

It must have been the conversation with Bob about dialysis, but that night Abby dreamed of blood. Blood draining out a vein in an arm through a catheter, flowing through transparent tubes. Blood that was supposed to be cleansed by an artificial kidney and then returned to the body, but in the dream was flowing, flowing off to nowhere. Blood she couldn't staunch.

Blood was life; blood was also death. Sacrifice and redemption.

Blood. Rivers of blood. Mark's blood, his chest red and

sticky and then that funny little rattle. No more Mark, and he had been so very young. And for her no chance to say goodby, no closure.

Her father dying. All the clean blood in the world couldn't cleanse the infection in one of the cysts that clogged his kidneys. Burning, not bleeding, to death, burning with fever.

And finally her mother. No blood there. Just fading away as if all her vitality had been drained by the blood that had, three times a week, been drawn out of her husband and run through the artificial kidney.

Abby awakened, her face wet with tears. Francis was on the bed beside her, licking a clenched fist with a rough, moist tongue. He had never jumped up on any piece of furniture before; the little animal somehow must have sensed her distress.

She lay for a moment, trying to regulate her ragged breathing and ease the arrhythmic pounding in her chest.

God, what an incredible nightmare! And yet like so many nightmares, the awful images, though dreadfully distorted, were based on reality. What her father had suffered in that dismal clinic; what her mother had suffered with him! The sisters had helped out through high school and when they came home from college—at least as far into their college years as their father had lasted. Still, the burden, physical and psychological, fell heaviest on their mother. No wonder she had outlived her husband by less than a year.

But dialysis worked, she had to grant the medical profession that. And gradually it was improving. They had come quite a long way from the early days when dialysis took much, much longer— twelve hours if she remembered correctly—and the availability of machines was severely limited. Someone had told her that a minister, a priest, and a rabbi had to choose who would have access to those machines, and in so doing, literally decided who would live and who would die. Not only die, but die a prolonged and miserable death. What a dreadful burden to bear! To know that you had condemned another human being to suffering—and, as she knew only too well, there could be a tremendous amount of suffering associated with end stage renal disease—and inevitably to death because only a few could be spared.

Which would have been worse? To be the judge or the condemned?

Abby turned on the light and took a sip of water from the glass on the bedside table. Gradually she got a grip on herself as she held tight to Francis's warm, soft body and sunk her fingers into his silky fur. Cushioning her head on him she could hear the steady beat of his heart, so reassuringly regular, unlike her own.

"I'm going to have to go to Phoenix soon now, little friend. To have a tube put in my stomach. That means I'm going to start dialysis. And then?"

She felt as if someone had pulled a thick, black curtain across her life, making it impossible for her to reach beyond the utter darkness toward the future. There was "now," the present, filled with the familiar sights and sounds, the tastes, smells, and other sensations to which she had long become accustomed. And there was a fast-approaching "then," the operation, dialysis, a time that, because she couldn't even begin to imagine it, loomed as a deep, intangible void, a great vortex sucking her into nothingness, a place as unfathomable as death itself.

Her chest constricted and her heart pounded still more wildly. "What. . . Just what am I going to do, Francis?"

Again the caressing tongue.

"I hope you're not going to have to find another owner," she whispered to the dog. But it wasn't death that terrified her. It was the idea of living.

* * *

Besides amenities like the big windows and the fireplaces she liked so much, the main Flagstaff public library had books, Pam sternly reminded herself. And if she didn't study those books and keep up her grade point average, her parents would have her back in Ottumwa so fast she wouldn't even be able to click her heels and say Oz. They hadn't been particularly keen about her going to college in Arizona to begin with, but she had wheedled and pleaded and promised to study very, very hard. Summer school had been a really hard sell, but her parents had to admit that so far she'd done better than anticipated.

Dutifully Pam tried to focus her attention on the book before her. The presidential election of 1800—wow, and people thought politics were dirty today. This early American history was actually pretty interesting stuff. Only it happened so long ago! She wanted to live right now, or better still in the Sixties with the Flower Children. Specifically, 1967, the Summer of Love; bell-bottoms, tie-dyed shirts and love beads. Linda and Peter were as close as she would ever get, but how lucky to have met them and been accepted by the "in" people at One Universe. Now if she could only get Bob involved. The idea, actually by no means a new one, popped into her mind involuntarily. But no, she quickly shoved it away. She had no intention of doing anything at all about Bob Curtis until she found out about this baby-sitting business.

* * *

The day burned bright and clear. Pines gave the thin, dry air a distinctive, spicy odor. Sunlight turned the tips of the branches of the Englemann spruce to a soft, fuzzy green. The elaborately twisted stems of old manzanita bushes with their intertwined stripes of gray and mahogany red looked like gnarled, slightly discolored barber's poles. From these sprouted red branches bearing bright green, almost oval leaves which stood out clearly against a delicate lace of lifeless gray twigs that the plants seemed reluctant to shed. A cocky Steller's jay, his blue body crowned by a distinctive black crest, called out a harsh *shaaak shaaak shaaak* as he zipped by. Above it all the San Francisco Peaks reared up against the intensely blue sky, almost purple at this altitude, like three majestic stallions frozen in time. Except for the noisy jay the silence was almost, but not quite, absolute.

Abby could see why Cecil B. DeMille had originally envisioned Flagstaff as the perfect place to make outdoor movies and had determined to turn it into the motion picture capital of the world. She had read that DeMille had taken one look at the setting from his westbound train, decided he had found just the spot for which he had been searching, and disembarked with the intention of staying. Fortunately she thought for Flagstaff, the next day a storm had blown down off the San Francisco Peaks bringing with it snow alternating with an icy drizzle. DeMille had packed up again, continued his westward journey, and ended up in Hollywood—the rest, as they say, being history.

Today, Abby saw, Bob was a man with a mission. U.S.G.S. map in hand, he strode forth in his khaki cargo shorts, short-sleeve mesh knit polo shirt in the color the Lands' End catalogue dubbed dark flagstone, his worn Wallaby—the Australian solution to the problem of a masculine sunhat—and Gore-Tex hiking boots. Since the trails they took were generally not difficult, Abby preferred her Asics, but Bob said he liked to keep his boots limber with regular use. However, they both agreed about carrying a staff. The loose soil could too easily become perilously slippery.

The two girls were surprisingly stout walkers and Abby, determinedly pushing herself as usual, was slow but game. It was obvious that Francis highly approved of any jaunt. His attitude was clear enough: so many trees to favor with his special attention; so many tantalizing smells to analyze with his long, sensitive nose; so many (uncatchable) squirrels to pursue. The walks usually worked out well for all concerned. However, today's walk had a different character. Abby had to call constantly to Bob to get him to slow down. He seemed jumpy, impatient, and not nearly as considerate of the needs of the others as he usually was.

"It's hot!" she complained. "Where are we going in such an all-fired hurry?" She stopped and very deliberately took a long, refreshing drink from her water bottle.

"You'll see. There's something I want to investigate. Something I've been reading about in the newspaper and talked about with a girl in the library."

"Oh?"

Bob blushed under his tan.

"Pam. She's a student at NAU. Really interested in the forest like I am. A member of an environmental group called One Universe."

"One Universe?" Abby's voice rose. That answered one question. "I'd like to meet some of those people."

"I'll check with Pam, if and when I see her. I had to run off pretty quickly the last time I talked to her. Maybe that wasn't such a good idea." He looked more embarrassed than ever. "She usually hangs out at the library, but lately she hasn't been around. I just hope she's not mad. I wish I'd gotten her number."

"Probably just busy with her studies."

"Yeah, maybe. She thinks she's going to change her major. She started out to be an elementary school teacher, but now she's thinking about something to do with the environment."

"Which is what you ought to consider," Abby said quickly, seizing this golden opportunity to proselytize. "You obviously know a lot about the forest, about how to get around it, the creatures who live here, what grows. Have you ever thought about talking with the professor whose house I'm renting? That is, when he gets back at the end of the summer. Professor Neale. He's a member of NAU's College of Forestry. Your problems in Florida may have barred a lot of avenues, but certainly not all. He might have some good ideas."

"Have you met him?" Bob asked skeptically.

"No, but living in his house I've formed a picture of him. Purely imaginary," she added. "I see him as a large, grandfatherly type, with maybe a pot belly. Just think about the size of his armchairs! I would assume he'd have a beard. Too much trouble to be clean shaven if you're going to be doing a lot of camping, which is how he's spending the summer. A white beard, white hair, and twinkling blue eyes."

"Blue eyes?" Bob asked curiously.

"No reason for the color, but I'm sure they twinkle because he must have a sense of humor. He's got some really off-the-wall books, like Edward Abbey's *The Monkey Wrench Gang* and John Nichols's *The Milagro Beanfield War*."

"Sounds like you've got this guy all worked out," Bob commented dryly, his brows furrowed as if still not convinced.

"Chinos, hiking boots, short-sleeve shirts—red plaid, but of course—which don't quite cover his girth. I'd say a pipe, only I haven't seen any signs of smoking. I think he'd be a great person to talk to."

"Yeah, sure."

Abby sighed. Bob certainly wasn't making this easy.

A slow, low-flying plane droned overhead, interrupting their conversation.

"Checking for any signs of smoke," Bob explained when he could make himself heard again. "With sixty-six fires burning out of control in the West, everybody's nervous. They've banned open fires in the forest. If I could catch the guys whose mess we saw the other day, they'd pay big time." His voice oozed satisfaction.

But Abby was no longer paying strict attention. She heard something rumbling faintly, ominously. Not the plane. It had passed on. The bikers again? No, this was a different sound, a low growl that grew louder and louder as they moved toward it. Soon it crescendoed into a menacing roar, a roar punctuated by sharp, staccato notes, high and piercing, the aural equivalent of carnivore incisors ripping into soft, defenseless flesh.

"What *is* it?" Abby shouted over the rising din.

"Earth-moving machinery."

"In the forest?"

"That's right. You'll see."

In a minute they came out of the trees onto a scene of purposeful activity and appalling devastation. The forest had simply been obliterated for acres—*one hundred? One hundred and fifty? Two hundred?* Unable to judge, Abby recoiled at the sight. She thought she might get physically ill, and this time not from anything that had to do with kidneys. Before her were no pines or spruce; no butterflies, deer, or jays; no thistles or manzanita bushes. The raccoon, gray squirrel, fox and rabbit in Harrison Begay's painting of the mythological San Francisco Peaks could never live here. Not a tree, not a bush, not a weed remained standing. The vast expanse of earth before them had been completely pulverized into pale, lifeless gray dust.

She realized that they'd been hearing the rumble of big engines, the *beep, beep, beep* of backing signals, and the crunch of steel jaws biting into earth. Bulldozers industriously gnawed away at what looked like a huge gravel pit, a hundred or more feet deep she guessed. Again it was difficult to tell. There was nothing left by which to calculate the size of the yawning gray maw.

A front-end loader filled with something that resembled sand and gravel took off toward an area with what looked like large screens, presumably used for some sort of separating process. The air was thick with dust, and the noise made Abby's head throb.

They all stared in awe, the girls' large, translucent gray eyes growing bigger than ever. Abby excavated her day pack to find a cotton kerchief with which to cover her nose, while Bob swivelled his head around trying to take in the whole scene. Francis dropped down on his haunches, cocked his head questioningly and coughed.

"What the hell is going on?" Abby demanded angrily.

"Mining," Bob answered shortly, his eyes glued to the scene that confronted them.

"In the middle of a national forest? How can they?"

"Something called the 1872 Mining Law."

"What are they mining?" she yelled.

"The newspaper said pumice, but we can make sure. Here comes someone now."

A red jeep circled the edge of the pit and headed toward them. It pulled up in a swirl of still more gray dust and a tall, athletically built man, almost movie-star handsome and unquestionably aware of it, leaped out. His dress could only be described as macho western: reptile skin cowboy boots with lots of tooling, snug Levis, a belt with an enormous silver buckle inlaid with turquoise, and a partly open red-and-blue plaid western shirt with pearl snaps. Above it all a big black Stetson crowned blond hair going gray at the temples. The man reached back into the jeep and said something into the car phone. In a minute or so the ruckus began to subside to the extent that they could carry on a conversation without shouting.

Meanwhile a smaller man got out from the passenger side. Boots, Levis, belt, western shirt, Stetson—all the same ingredients as the big, handsome man but none of it fancied up, all well-worn. His face and body were hard, lean, the face scored and abraded by the elements. Both men wore dark reflective glasses.

"What the hell are you doing here?" the big man demanded. "This is private property."

Bob started to say something when Abby stepped forward and addressed the man in her best schoolmarm fashion. "We are in a national forest, 'national' as in belonging to all the people of the country. So how can we also be on private property? It's an oxymoron."

"The hell it is," the shorter man snarled. "We've got the right to mine here, and that's just what we're doing." He stepped forward aggressively. A low, ominous rumbling came from Francis. The dog wasn't all that big, but there was nothing small about his growl or his full-sized teeth. Prudently the man stepped back out of what Francis seemed to consider the critical range.

Taking a good look at Francis and then at Abby, the taller man appeared to reassess the situation. Abby realized that she was hardly dressed for the part of confronting Mr. Hollywood, even though today she sported a glorious sea-green tee shirt from the California wine country with vines and grapes splashed with flecks of gold. But the tee shirt was hidden under a blue, long-sleeve Solumbra explorer shirt designed to protect her skin from the fierce, high-altitude sun. An elderly cotton duck sunhat, no longer in any way pristine, protected her face from its rays. Neither her khaki shorts nor her walking shoes were anything to excite a fashion frenzy. And yet through years of teaching she had cultivated a dignity and command of a situation which signaled that she was unlikely to be intimidated. Erect posture and five feet eight inches plus didn't hurt, either.

The replacement of his dark scowl by a more benign expression signaled that the big man had quickly concluded confrontation might not the best way to deal with these particular interlopers and that some diplomacy might be called for.

"Pardon me, but you startled us appearing from the woods like that," he said in a more conciliatory voice. "This is a hard-hat area and we don't encourage visitors. It's dangerous with the machinery in operation. We wouldn't want anything to happen to those two cute little girls you've got there." Well-spoken, no discernable accent, Abby noted. Moreover, he gave an impression of self-confidence and of being used to dealing with people. Probably the boss, she surmised.

Abby nodded slightly in acknowledgment of the explanation for his initial antagonism. "What are you mining?" She gestured at the enormous pit before them.

"Pumice," the big man said.

"What?" While the name was familiar, Abby couldn't recall any specifics.

"Pumice. It's a porous, volcanic glass."

"What in heaven's name do people do with it?"

"Ours goes for stonewashing. As in stonewashed jeans."

"All this for stonewashed jeans?" Abby's eyes widened as they traveled over the no-man's-land in front of her. The thought of the devastation of the almost magical forest through which they had been walking brought on another wave of nausea.

"It's a good business." The man smiled a toothpaste advertising smile. "By the way, I'm Jim Wilson and this is Shorty Dean." He indicated his companion.

"Abigail Taylor and Robert Lee Curtis," Abby supplied.

"Well, Ms. Taylor, Mr. Curtis, since you're here," he hesitated a minute, as if trying to reconcile himself to the idea but still not finding himself particularly happy about it, "can I answer any questions?"

"So how do you mine pumice?" Bob, who had been silent until now, asked abruptly, his frown suggesting that he was as horrified by the scene as Abby. She wondered if his question was a ploy to keep them from being sent packing immediately, or if he really was interested.

"It's basically a simple process." Mr. Hollywood shrugged slightly. "We have to take off the overburden—trees, boulders, soil—basically whatever is covering the pumice. The stuff can lie as much as 70 feet below grade. Then we sort the pumice by grades or sizes." He glanced around as if making sure he hadn't missed anything critical. "Oh, yes, and we try to keep it dry. Not much of a problem in this climate."

"Then you sell it, I suppose?" Abby rubbed her eyes, which itched from all the dust.

"Like I said, pumice—the sort of pumice used for stonewashing jeans—is a good business, a *very* good business," he explained with evident satisfaction. "This mine, the Pycenium, has made its investors some very happy campers."

For that she'd just have to take his word, Abby conceded. More to the point, there was no way an operation of this magnitude could be carried on in secret. If it were illegal, surely the authorities would have done something. But she couldn't wait to have Bob explain how a private venture could set up in the middle of a national forest.

"They're doing this legally?" she demanded of Bob, who was holding tight to the little girls' hands, when they were out of earshot. "Right in the middle of a national forest?" And she had thought clear-cutting was bad. At least a few shrubs were left. At the pumice mine there was nothing.

"Yes. It's legal." His voice was tight and tense.

"How in the world. . . ."

"As I said before, something called the 1872 Mining Law. There's been a lot about this mine in the paper, so I decided to do some checking. It seems that anybody can explore federal land for minerals and, if they find something worthwhile, file a claim and start mining it. While they're mining, and they mine as long as they want to as long as they do at least a hundred dollars worth of work a year, they can treat the land just like private property. Cut trees. Build an office. Build someplace to stay. Fence it in if they want to."

"They pay the government?"

"Nope. Oh, there's paperwork and some fees for that, but they don't pay for the minerals. The law's a sweet deal. It was dreamed up as a way to get people to come west when this was wide-open territory. Heck, after they've done five hundred dollars worth of work on their claims, those guys back there at the Pycenium could even patent that land. That's just a fancy way to say buy it. In their case for two dollars and fifty cents an acre. Same price as in 1872."

Abby's stomach did a final lurch and then started settling down as they proceeded further into the forest. Her jangled nerves began to untangle as they moved further away from the racket, which had churned up to full volume again as they left the Pycenium. The chirp of a finch, the chatter of a squirrel, an especially large and imposing ponderosa gave her reassuring evidence of the forest's vitality.

"Why would they bother to buy it? It seems like they're getting everything they want anyway." Abby's voice was tired, cross, and crabby. It expressed exactly how she felt. Maybe she should stop trying to push her reluctant body as hard as she had been. Maybe take more time off. Maybe. . . but all that would be cravenly giving in to the disease.

"The mining companies say that it's easier to go to the bank for a loan. Less government interference, not that there seems to be a whole lot now. Less hassle from the environmentalists. And perhaps, after the pumice's all gone, put up some cabins. There're a lot of old summer cabins built on played-out mining claims around Arizona."

Impatient, the two girls broke loose from their uncle and romped ahead. Francis, evidently wanting to join in the fun, strained at his leash.

"You said that your friend Pam is a member of One Universe? They're supposed to be concerned with protecting the environment. Do they plan to do something about this situation?"

"I don't know for sure." Abby noticed that, at the mention of Pam's name, Bob's face again flushed. "I'll ask her when I run into her."

CHAPTER 5

Pam's stomach flip-flopped as if she was riding on a really fast elevator. It seemed to her that she had spent all of her non-class time the last three days wandering back and forth between the main Flagstaff public library and Macy's Coffee House and Bakery hoping to run into Bob. And now there he was, at one of the outside tables at Macy's with two of the cutest little girls she had ever seen. Precious little girls. And she did see a family resemblance, only Bob's eyes were blue, not gray, and his hair was a much brighter blond than their pale, wheat-colored locks. Her heart sank precipitously, as if the elevator had come loose from its cable. So he *was* married!

"Oh shit," she said to herself—a gauge of her distress since her mother had pounded it into her since childhood that it was truly uncouth for a woman to use four-letter words. She would have slunk off quietly if Bob hadn't spotted her and called out.

"Yo, Pam! Come sit with us."

"Well. . . ." She looked dubiously at the girls.

"My nieces." Bob smiled affectionately at his companions. "Pooh and Bear."

Pam's stomach took off on the elevator again, this time streaming upward as if it would explode through the roof. Then she realized that she was staring like some tongue-tied idiot at Bob and his nieces, who were finishing up the crumbs from what she guessed were outsized cookies. "Oh, that's great you've got family here." Did she sound as stupid as she thought she did?

"Hey, Pam, sit down. You want a cup of coffee or some iced tea?"

"I'll get it. Save me a seat. Would you like a breakfast roll or something?"

"No. Right now I'm staying with my sister and her family.

She feeds me well. Only no coffee, no caffeine. So I have to cheat a bit," he said with a smile so warm and sweet that Pam felt it radiating all the way down to the tips of her toes.

She left reluctantly to get her order and returned shortly with milk and a breakfast roll. The girls had gone down the sidewalk a bit to play some sort of jumping game so that she had Bob all to herself, but she couldn't think of one single thing to say. Fortunately Bob solved that problem.

"I visited that mine you and I were talking about the other day."

"The Pycenium? I've heard they don't like visitors."

"They don't exactly welcome them with open arms. But what're they going to do? Use physical force with two little kids in tow and a lady professor? Abby Taylor," he explained. "She likes to hike—well, it's really just walking—with the girls and me."

"Does she teach at NAU?" Pam didn't recognize the name, but then the university was a big place.

"Naw. Back east. She's on a leave of absence."

"So what's the mine like?"

"Picture a huge, and I do mean huge, hole in the ground. A no-man's-land. Just some earthmovers and eighteen-wheel haul trucks, which kind of look like insects crawling around in a hole that big. And lots and lots of dust."

Pam took a sip of her milk and tried to form a picture in her mind. She shook her head at the effort. "Pretty bad?"

"Pretty bad. Three-or-four-hundred-year-old ponderosas gone. Bushes and everything else stripped away. Not even any boulders. No birds. No animals. Like I said, a no-man's-land."

"Awesome." Pam curled a strand of hair around her right index finger and glanced at it—mousy-blond, what else could you say? Not long, not short, clean but no real style. She looked again at Bob's bright blond hair gleaming in the late morning sun. She'd kill for hair like that; any girl would. Why had a guy been lucky enough to get it? "So what are they mining?"

"Pumice. Just like the paper said." He rested his arms on the varnished wooden table. He had rolled the sleeves of his blue work

84

shirt up to the elbows, and she could see the strands of bright blond hair on his lower arms. She would have loved to brush her fingers over them.

"Pumice?" Pam wasn't too sure what that was, but it didn't sound very exciting. "You told me for that law, that Mining Law, to work there had to be something really valuable to mine, like gold or silver."

"Yeah, I know, pumice doesn't seem all that special, does it?" He stretched out his long legs and Pam noticed that his jeans, though faded and worn, were not only clean but ironed as carefully as his shirt, every crease in place. In her red and white horizontally striped cotton scoop-neck L.L. Bean tee shirt and denim shorts she felt adequately dressed for a hot summer day in Flagstaff, but she knew she could never quite duplicate Bob's starched, pressed look.

Pam took a tentative bite of her roll. Probably a zillion calories, but oh, so very good—the soft, sweet dough, the extra-sweet icing, and just the right touch of cinnamon.

"What must have been the boss man told us pumice mining is a great business and the investors are all real happy. They use the stuff for stonewashed jeans, and you know there are plenty of those around."

Pam momentarily gave herself over to the succulent pleasures of the sweet roll. Under the sweet taste of the dough she could detect a base of rich farm butter. Just like home.

"Remember I told you I'm a member of an environmental group called One Universe?" she inquired tentatively when another delicious bite had been washed down with a swallow of cold milk.

Bob nodded as he finished up his coffee. Both fell silent for a few minutes as a train rumbled slowly and noisily by on the Santa Fe tracks a couple of blocks away. Afterward the side street on which Macy's was located became relatively quiet again.

"I talked to Peter Rivers last night," Pam said when the train had gone its way. "He's, like, sort of the top guy. Peter is really excited because there's a congressman coming through Flagstaff just before the Fourth of July on his way home to California for some sort of Independence Day celebration. Toby Barrett?

Congressman Barrett?"

"Barrett? Nope, never heard of him," Bob said as he finished his coffee.

"Peter says he's a friend of Earl Olson, who's a big investor in the Pycenium. Olson asked him to give a speech to tell everyone how great the mine is, how it's wonderful for the local economy and all that sort of thing. One Universe is planning to stage a protest, something original and really terrific and altogether cool, Peter says." Pam's voice rose with enthusiasm, then she broke off to fiddle with her roll. "We can always use an extra protester," she added shyly.

"Sounds great, but I've got a problem." Bob glanced over at the girls, who were by now playing quietly with some napkins and rocks they had found. "I got into some real shit back in Florida and, well, I don't want to attract too much attention, especially not from the cops."

"Big trouble?" She gazed with concern at Bob's face, suddenly dark, brooding, as if a cloud had passed over the sun.

"Yeah. Sort of the fitting end to—what can I say?—an unfortunate childhood? For this I need more coffee. Do you want more milk?"

She shook her head.

"Just keep an eye on the girls for a minute."

Bob returned with his coffee and sat silently for a minute or two as if gathering his thoughts. Then in a rambling fashion he confessed to a childhood that to Pam's mind went far beyond being merely unfortunate.

Evidently Mom was a sun-leathered, sun-wizened woman whose life consisted of three, and only three, activities: golf, bridge, and drinking dry gin martinis with other women rich enough not to have to worry about mundane things like housework and cooking or, heaven forbid, jobs. Bob and his sister, Sally, seemed to have dropped into her life by accident. After Bob had come along his mom had made certain that such an occurrence never again disrupted her life. What two births had done to her golf handicap, though only temporarily, was not to be repeated, as she made quite clear to anyone willing to listen.

But Mom, a real neutral in the big scheme of things, was considerably better than Dad. "You either do things my dad's way or suffer the consequences," Bob told Pam ruefully. "You've got to be just the way he thinks you should be or forget it. When I was a kid it wasn't too awful because I was pretty good at sports and not too bad in school, at least in the subjects I liked. The trouble came later when I couldn't quite make varsity in any sport. Things really started to unravel when my GPA and SAT's weren't good enough to interest Tulane, Dad's alma mater."

Bob took a gulp of coffee and shifted uncomfortably in his chair. "Maybe if I'd done something outstanding like get elected president of my class or win a science award. . . Well, *maybe* things might have been different."

Pam's heart went out to him as he haltingly explained that while he was never a complete failure, in his dad's eyes he was never quite good enough either. His father's tongue became ever more blistering. Eventually there was nothing Bob could do right— not make good enough grades, not choose the right friends, not even wear the right clothes.

"So stupid me, I got into the drugs. Screwed up big time. There I was at Florida State College drinking with the guys and, well, sampling everything around. Of course I got caught. I wasn't half as smart as the rest of the crowd I ran with. The dumb one. The fall guy. And my hot-shot lawyer dad? No help, no help at all," he observed caustically, his face twisting with the pain of the memory.

"Wouldn't even represent me in court. Said I was eighteen and could damn well manage on my own. Made me get a court-appointed lawyer who fucked things up but totally," Bob confided bitterly. But Pam could tell that what really got to him was his dad's indifference. His only son had screwed up; that was the end of it. No encouragement. No forgiveness. No second chances. She didn't know quite what to say. Maybe nothing could ever make Bob feel better. She gave his hand a quick squeeze, then blushed and quickly removed hers.

"I can see why you don't want to get mixed up with the cops." Pam chewed thoughtfully on the last of her roll, which had lost much of its delight as she had listened to Bob's story.

"Not if I ever want to see the inside of a university again, which is what both my sister and Abby Taylor want me to do," he replied with a grimace.

"And you?"

"I guess I kind of do and kind of don't," he admitted reluctantly. "Last time turned out to be such a bust.   But no degree is like a dead-end. My sister's a saint. She's willing to keep me for as long as I want to stay, until I get my life back together.   But having a record really cuts down on the options.   I mean, I'd love to do something with the environment, something like Park Service, Forest Service—you know, that kind of thing.   Only they've got so many people applying they'd never take anybody like me, and anyway, they probably have some damned rule about hiring someone who's had a conviction."   Looking embarrassed and uncomfortable, he shifted his legs, then shifted them again to yet another position.

"So what can you do?"

"I'm pretty good with computers."   With shy pride Bob told her about some of the things he had done, including designing a software program for his brother-in-law's carpentry business.

"Well," Pam said with satisfaction, "so maybe there's something you can do with both computers and the environment." And, while you're at it, spend more time with me, she added to herself.

* * *

"Yeah, this guy is really into computers," Pam assured Peter Rivers when she dropped by Peter and Linda's home that evening to see if she could find a role for Bob in One Universe. The two were sitting on the screen porch sipping beer and watching the birds still attacking the feeder in the late summer light. To Pam's way of thinking a beer seemed awfully mundane for Flower Children, but she supposed that a cold beer did taste good at the end of a long, hot day.

"He designed a cool software program for his brother-in-law's business and he knows all about that stuff without being a nerd." Well, Pam reflected, at least she knew Bob wasn't a nerd and he sure seemed to understand a lot about computers, although it was kind of hard for her to judge since she'd never used one for anything except word processing.

"And he really, really cares about the forest." Here Pam felt on safer ground. "In his spare time he's always reading about it. Like researching that mining law. That's how I met him, in the library. And he's always trying to protect the forest. Like there're some bikers who've been chewing up trails. He's just watching for them. He said he'd love to get a hold of those guys and shake them 'til their teeth rattle! Then there are some other guys who've been trashing the forest and starting really dangerous fires. He's on the lookout for them, too." A real eco-warrior, she reflected with pride.

A tattered calico cat slipped out of the lengthening shadows. The birds at the feeder squawked loudly at the approach of danger, yet were clearly reluctant to abandon their dinner. On the other hand the cat's presence didn't seem to faze the hummingbirds still diving at a large, red plastic flower filled with sugar water a few yards away. Perhaps they were too fast to fear feline claws, but the slower birds had every reason for concern, she noted, as the cat suddenly leaped up to the railing beneath the feeder and swiped out with a wicked paw that narrowly missed its intended victim. Pam imagined that Bob would be just like that cat, carefully stalking his prey, then pouncing. Only Bob wouldn't do anything as drastic as the calico would to a bird, she assured herself. Just teach those guys a good lesson.

"He's willing to take chances?" Peter asked her.

"Up to a point, I guess," Pam answered honestly. "He got into some trouble back in Florida. I don't think he wants to tangle with the authorities again, so he wouldn't do anything totally illegal like monkey wrenching. But he sure does love the forest. And he hates people who destroy it."

"Do you think he could create a web site for One Universe?"

"Oh, definitely," she replied with relief. Nothing illegal about that.

"Also, Titus has come up with some interesting ideas." Peter started to go on, then hesitated. He continued slowly, as if he were revising what he'd first intended to say. "But he needs more information. . . computer-generated information."

"No problem." Pam bobbed her head in assent.

"About Bob Curtis, what do you think, Linda?" Peter asked his companion.

"It sounds as if we should give the young man a chance."

* * *

Abby wished she could dislike Becky's Phoenix friends, the Olsons, their house, and/or their friends, only it wasn't quite that simple. Earl and Alice Olson proved to be gracious almost to the extreme. They remembered her from the Copper State and professed themselves to be absolutely delighted Becky had called to say that her sister was in Flagstaff for the summer. What a nice surprise! And how happy they were that Abby could join them and some other friends for cocktails!

Abby feared her enthusiasm failed to match theirs and felt correspondingly guilty. Grateful to have the opportunity to get out and talk to new people, glad to have something to distract her from the ever-darkening specter of dialysis, she had accepted their invitation without hesitation. But she had not expected anything so totally. . . well, overwhelming. And she was not sure that at present she had sufficient energy to meet the challenge.

The Olsons' spacious home had a beautiful view out over a plush green golf course and boasted every comfort. Libations flowed freely. The other cocktail guests exuded enthusiasm as if they might get low marks in the art of being entertained if the air were not continually filled with expressions of amazement and delight, or if a fellow guest were even momentarily neglected. Maybe that explained why she felt so uncomfortable. Everything—hosts, house, and fellow guests—was a bit too much. Like a great big wad of cotton candy, fine up to a point and then, suddenly, too much of a good thing.

The house, for example. . . Abby looked around again. It was enormous: acres of double-glazing to keep the winter cold at bay, countless rugged-stone fireplaces all big enough to roast an ox, and great high-beamed ceilings that would have done quite nicely for the mead hall of an Anglo-Saxon king. The decorating scheme involved a great deal of the sort of fabric with geometric patterns in pale peachy pinks and soft turquoise that denoted the "Santa Fe" style, although until the last few years Abby had never seen anything like it in Santa Fe itself.

Whatever its origins, Abby liked the style well enough. However, one less swag above the endless windows, fewer decorative pillows on the huge four-poster beds (at least one for each of the five big bedrooms Alice had proudly shown her and a few of the other guests on an impromptu house tour), the removal of a flounce or two from the skirts of the upholstered chairs—what a difference it would make.

The Olsons struck her as being a lot like their house. So gracious, so outgoing, so, well, persistent, they seemed to absorb all the oxygen around her until she could barely breathe. Her fellow guests were equally exhausting. All of them talked in loud, boisterous voices and with great enthusiasm about people she had never met. Desperately, she tried to steer the conversation into more general areas, but national politics proved to be a bust (not an election year) and Arizona politics got her no further. No one except she seemed to have paid much attention to the Museum of Northern Arizona with its outstanding displays of natural history, archaeology, and Native American art. And even the renowned Grand Canyon music festival elicited only passing acknowledgment. Abby wished desperately that she could curl up among the too-numerous pillows on one of the big beds and sleep until it was late enough to excuse herself decently.

Under the circumstances she found it almost a relief to run into the Pycenium Mine's Jim Wilson. Even though their first meeting had not been entirely amicable, here at last was someone with whom she had a viable topic of conversation in common.

"Well, if it's not Miz Taylor. Where's that funny-looking dog of yours?" he asked with a friendly grin. Her first impression of movie-star handsome held true. She had to admit that the man was shockingly good-looking, just weathered enough to avoid being too handsome in a conventional way. If the pumice gave out, Jim Wilson could always seek a second career as a Marlboro man.

"I don't normally take Francis to cocktail parties, Mr. Wilson." She shook her head with mock sadness. "Not much of a party animal. He doesn't drink, and too many people shouting loudly at one another only makes him cross."

"And where's Robert Curtis?"

"At home like Francis," she answered, although as far as she knew he could be chasing pyromaniac slobs through the forest or lying in wait for erosion-causing bikers. "Bob isn't much of a party type either."

"That's not the story I've heard," Jim Wilson retorted with a knowing look.

"Oh? So what have you been told?"

"One of the men who works at the mine is from Florida and he recognized him. I hear that Bob's father is a power player down there, a real hot-shot lawyer. Golfs with the governor, hobnobs with the legislators, manipulates the old-boy network for all it's worth. So it made quite a splash when his son got himself into trouble. DUI and then drugs. The media loved it: 'Scion of old Florida family accused of possession of an illegal substance,' 'Trial lawyer refuses to represent son'—that sort of thing. But I assume you're aware of all this."

"As a matter of fact I am, but things have changed," Abby replied defensively, stepping back to put some space between herself and the large man before her. "Bob's getting his act together. No more alcohol, no more drugs. I think he may even return to college—out here, of course. As you can well imagine, he has no interest in returning to Florida."

At that moment one of the catering staff passed by with a large plate of finger food. Abby chose a tiny spinach quiche, delicious but extremely rich. Jim Wilson sampled a couple of Swedish meatballs, some stuffed mushrooms, and also a quiche.

"What does he plan on doing? *If* he gets another chance, that is," Wilson asked when the server passed on.

Abby narrowed her eyes but chose to ignore Wilson's insinuation. "His real interest is the environment. I'm beginning to get the impression that the situation in Florida was badly mishandled. If it could be declared a mistrial, then Bob's slate might be cleared. A lot of opportunities would be open to him."

"So, an environmentalist?" Wilson made it sound as if Bob had an infectious disease, Ebola or maybe rickettsial fever. "Sierra Club? Earth First? God help us, not One Universe? How far left has he gone?"

"As far as I know, he's not 'gone' any place," she shot back. A statement that was less than the whole truth, but Wilson already seemed so sure that he had Bob pegged she didn't want to give him the satisfaction of confirming his suspicions. Besides, as far as she could tell, at least to date, Bob hadn't done anything more radical than making a friend who was a member of One Universe.

"I never heard of One Universe until the theft of the Alfa Romeo. It's local, isn't it?" she asked, subtly shifting the direction of the conversation.

"It's based here in Flagstaff and is fairly new," Wilson answered as he hooked another quiche from a passing tray. "So far it doesn't have much impact outside of northern Arizona. However, they have their aspirations. All these groups do," he added with disdain.

"Oh?"

"They all have a message and want to shout it as loudly as possible. One Universe is all hot and bothered about species extinction."

"What have they done about that so far—besides using the publicity generated by the Alfa Romeo to their advantage?"

"The usual sorts of things. They've written endless letters to the newspaper and put up posters about saving forest habitat. Early this spring a bunch of them lay down in front of bulldozers preparing the terrain for a new golf course. Some 'non-compliants,' as they're called, were arrested and then released soon after. The Flagstaff police are savvy enough to keep things low key."

"But no monkey wrenching? Nothing like pouring sugar in the bulldozers' gas tanks?"

"No, thank God, although the potential's there. Peter Rivers, their leader, was in Vietnam and I think a fellow named Titus was, too. A tough school. They came home and demonstrated for peace. Both racked up a string of arrests, as did Linda, another member of the group. Can't think of her last name now. That's according to what the newspaper dug up when they were investigating the golf course episode. Evidently those three scored still more arrests as members of other protest groups."

God, Abby thought with an inward groan. What if Bob got involved with these people? What might he be getting himself into?

"You seem to know a lot about it."

"I keep my eye on all these tree huggers." He gazed at her intensely so she couldn't possibly miss the point. "Hell, we're running a business. A very profitable one, may I add. I've got investors to satisfy, big shots like our host, Earl Olson. I don't want those environmental bastards messing with my equipment! God help them if they try anything destructive at the Pycenium!"

Wilson took a large swallow from his highball, ice cubes clinking. "As I said, I watch the environmentalists damn closely. I must say the Rivers fellow seems to have learned some discretion and restraint over time. But not that Titus. He'd do almost anything and worry about the consequences later. Maybe never worry at all."

"And the women involved?" Abby took a sip of her Chardonnay.

"Linda—oh, yes, it's Wallace—has been with Rivers forever. A bright lady, I've heard. But the group's real ace in the hole is Martha Van Dyke. Her late husband was owner and publisher of one of the largest newspapers in the state and she took over after his death. She's retired now, but that woman still has enormous clout and a lot of money and isn't shy about using any of it. Phenomenal media contacts. Very savvy." Wilson took another swallow of his drink and plucked yet another quiche off a passing tray.

"Retired? None of these people sounds very young."

"They're trying to get in some new blood. They've recruited a university student named Pam something-or-other for their inner council, and at least twenty to twenty-five students are closely connected to the group, plus a lot more who get involved from time to time. But don't let age fool you. Martha Van Dyke's the oldest member by far, and I'd never make the mistake of underestimating her. She's one powerful, determined woman."

Interestingly enough, Wilson sounded more impressed than intimidated by the idea of an intelligent, focused, determined woman. Evidently strong women didn't faze him, and for that Abby had to give him credit. A lot of credit. Also he ate quiche. Although she seriously doubted that a man's eating habits were quite the clue to his personality that current pop psychology would claim, Wilson seemed to have more facets to him than their initial encounter had suggested.

"Speaking about environmentalists, I apologize for being so abrupt the other day, but *somebody* has been spying on us," he said as if he really were sorry about his original hostility. "The men have caught a glimpse of a figure from time to time through the trees."

Wilson watched her closely, as if waiting for some sort of reaction. Without his dark glasses on, she could see his eyes—very dark marine blue. They reminded her of the ocean off Kauai. She remembered drifting lazily along in the clear water, admiring the brightly colored fish that darted about below the surface, when suddenly she had felt the lethal embrace of the undertow—a vast unseen, unexpected force drawing her inexorably away from shore. Even for a strong swimmer the experience had been terrifying.

Abby turned away from those disturbing eyes and gazed out one of the large windows at an extended vista of thick, green fairway bordered by tall pines. "What you're doing is legal, so why should that bother you?"

"The monkey wrenching!"

"Hire guards."

"We've got a couple, and soon we're going to go to the expense of fencing the whole area we're mining. But still. . . . A guy dodging around in the woods? Who knows what he might be up to."

"Well, if you're thinking of Bob, forget it. He'd never been to the mine before he happened on it with me and his two nieces. Those precious little girls aren't mine, you know," she explained, turning back to him.

"Yes, Alice Olson mentioned that you were single, never married," he said with a twinkle in his eyes. And what else had Alice said, Abby wondered?

"How do you like Flagstaff? Or are you from here originally?" Abby asked, trying to find a less personal direction for the conversation. She had to admit to herself that Jim Wilson definitely had his attractions, and she could hardly blame him for the mine, could she? A person had to earn a living. But still... In any case, for her there was the dialysis, always the dialysis. A damaged woman. No time to be contemplating any sort of involvement.

"Southern California. The Flagstaff summers are fine, but winter here is cold as hell." He gazed out the double-glazed window as if seeing the now green fairway covered by deep, white drifts of snow, the sprinkling of deciduous trees among the pines stripped bare of leaves, icicles extending like sharp glass swords from the eaves.

"Do you plan to go back to California eventually?" She wondered how long a pumice mine was good for. At what point did it play out, or could Wilson and his pal Shorty Dean go on almost indefinitely?

"Probably. I sure wouldn't spend another winter in Flagstaff if I didn't have to."

But, she thought to herself, there are warm places like Phoenix not so far away.

A boisterous wave of laughter broke out from a group of guests standing on a deck overlooking the golf course.

"This part of Flagstaff is certainly lovely," Abby remarked as she in turn gazed out the window. "It seems like there's not a lot of private property around here for development, not with the national forest and all. But I gather that this development where the Olsons live is extensive, an eighteen-hole golf course, the works."

"Thirty-six holes, plus an eighteen-hole putting course. Spa, two clubhouses, tennis, volleyball, basketball, playgrounds for the kids."

"Good lord! How did the developers get the land?"

"Funny you should ask, since in a way it goes back to dogs like yours."

"What?" she asked, checking to make sure he wasn't joking—but if so, he showed no sign of it.

"The land belonged to a doctor who never married, just took care of his patients and raised corgis. Things weren't so crowded then, and he bought up a lot of land over the years. When the doctor died he willed a generous amount of money to the two women who had taken care of him—no family, you see—and left the land to a foundation he'd established, mostly for scholarships. Eventually the land was sold and got developed. More than a thousand acres of absolutely prime real estate in an area that, as you pointed out, doesn't have much private land."

Having seen the Phoenix metropolitan sprawl, Abby thought that Flagstaff was actually very fortunate in that regard. But before she could get the opportunity to express her concerns about the development of Flagstaff, the conversation was interrupted by a loud, cheerful voice.

"My dear, you are absolutely *monopolizing* the handsomest man here." Alice Olson swooped down upon them and thrust her arm through Jim's. A large, heavily built woman wearing dressy western boots, a full denim skirt and a ruffled blouse of the same peachy pink featured so prominently in the house's decoration, she looked as if she were all ready to take off line dancing.

"I'm going to have to steal him from you because there is someone else simply dying to meet him."

"Oh, no you're not, Alice. I'm going to reclaim him." Sorrell Lawrence, the Realtor, looking absolutely spectacular in a short black and gold leopard-print silk dress with spaghetti straps, which showed off her broad shoulders while doing nothing whatsoever to make them look the slightest bit masculine, moved smoothly to Wilson's side. A sleek predator on the prowl. The skimpy dress revealed long, firm arms—not a trace of flab on their upper undersides—

ending in perfectly manicured hands.   Strappy, high-heeled gold sandals emphasized elegant legs, also long and firm.   Sorrell radiated a health and vigor that made her seem more alive than anyone else around.   Abby felt a wave of jealousy engulf her.   Not that she herself didn't look quite striking in her off-white St. John knit slacks suit, matching low heels, and silk neck scarf in an abstract pattern based on a design of Frank Lloyd Wright.   But Sorrell. . .   Thank heaven she had decided that her life held no room for entanglement at present,   Abby thought as Sorrell rested her hand lightly on Wilson's shoulder, a not-so-subtle sign of possession.

"Still liking the house?" Sorrell asked Abby.

"Yes, of course," was all that Abby could think of to say.

"So glad.   We do try to please," Sorrell said with her self-satisfied look and a toss of her thick, silvery mane.   "Now, if you don't mind."   She gave Alice and Abby each a large, though not especially warm smile as she whisked Jim Wilson away.

And that was the last Abby saw of Wilson, at least at close range.   He did, however, provide Abby with a most satisfactory topic of conversation.   Predictably none of the Olsons' guests had any interest in pumice mining per se, but they were generally quite interested in Wilson as a person.   No one that big and good-looking could go unnoticed or unremarked upon.

"A nice guy, but watch out for that Sorrell Lawrence," one woman warned.   "A Realtor from California," she added, the words sounding as if Sorrell were being accused of having some very questionable personal habits.

"Should have stayed on the coast," a man grumbled.   "Too aggressive.   Dreadful the sort of people who get broker's licenses in Arizona today."

"Grabs whatever she wants," another woman said, her eyes lingering longingly on Jim Wilson.

"Oh, she can be entertaining," the first woman observed, "but a bit overbearing, don't you think?   One wonders about her background.   Certainly not top quality."

Jim Wilson fared better as far as the gossip went.   From the women Abby learned that Wilson, as he had indicated, was from

California ("Los Angeles, probably, anyway definitely not San Francisco"), had been divorced several years before, and was the father of two teenage sons ("perfectly dreadful children, completely out of control, but they live with their mother").

From the men she discovered that Wilson had been in real-estate development in California, had suffered reverses in a downturn of the market ("like plenty of other people, you know"), had done a bit of this and that, then gotten into pumice ("good stuff with the present fad for stonewashed jeans; the business seems to be thriving").

"Though it won't last forever, of course," said one corpulent, balding man. "These fads never do. But his investment can't have been too great—just his own time, really. The expense of leasing equipment and hiring somebody to run it would have been covered by his investors. He would have had to prove that his operation complied with environmental regulations, a tedious process and not inexpensive, but those California boys are weaned on that sort of thing. The environmental types are screaming about mining on the Peaks, of course, but they're always grousing about something. Legally there's not a damned thing they can do. Have you ever seen them stage a rally? Interesting how many of *them* wear those stonewashed jeans."

"Oh, some of you men! You make it sound like the environmentalists are responsible for *everything*," complained a skinny, stridently blond woman whose original hair coloring was shrouded in the mists of time. "You'd think they invented the spotted owl just to make you miserable."

"Wouldn't put it past them," the corpulent man rejoined jovially. "They bring those owls up at every turn. Their weapon of choice, so to speak."

"How about that Alfa Romeo that got stolen?" commented another of the men. "That car got the bunch from One Universe a lot further than the owls, at least for awhile."

"Just talk, talk, talk," the heavy, balding man cut in. "If they'd really had the car they would have found some more concrete way to use it for the publicity."

"Such as threatening to dismember it piece by piece if we didn't meet some incredible demands—like going back to the horse and buggy era so we don't pollute the atmosphere with lead and carbon monoxide or whatever it's supposed to be.   Only I can't think that all those horse droppings around town would be too wonderful, either."   The blonde turned up her nose in disgust.

Abby thought the blonde's idea of dismembering the car wasn't so far-fetched.   Send back one purposely damaged part at a time, the way kidnappers send back a severed finger or toe.   That would have riveted people's attention.   But not a trace of the car had turned up.   Just talk, talk, talk, as the fat man said.

* * *

"You're not going to do anything foolish, are you?"   Abby asked Bob as they turned off the pavement and drove up a well-maintained gravel road toward the Pycenium Mine.   Her last hours of freedom, she thought, since Dr. Frankenthaller, finally having convinced her that the dialysis could no longer be put off without a severe risk to her health, had scheduled her surgery for right after the Fourth of July.   And in her final few days of unencumbered freedom she had agreed to go hear some dull congressman praise the virtues of a pug-ugly mine and watch some retro demonstrators? Instead she felt like climbing Mt. Humphrey, at 12,611 feet the highest of the San Francisco Peaks, and railing at the gods, or running naked through the forest screaming like a maenad—in other words, doing *something, anything* to give the finger to fate.   But here she was, driving *sedately* along.   *Disgusting*.   Her only excuse was that at last she'd get to see One Universe in action.

"Naw.   Besides, I'm beginning to think there may be better ways of stopping the mine than demonstrating, anyway."

"Such as?"

"Too early to say."

Abby didn't have a chance to pursue the matter, for at that moment they came upon the mine and a guard who directed her toward an area cleared for parking.   Another guard directed them toward where the congressman would speak.   A tent had been erected to provide shade for the folding chairs that had been set up.

A platform had been hung with the United States and Arizona flags and red, white, and blue bunting. Off to the side waited a refreshment table, as yet without refreshments. Beyond it two catering trucks stood beside a double-wide trailer, the mine's headquarters. Other than a couple of metal storage sheds, the Pycenium boasted no other buildings. Just the huge hole and acres and acres of gray dust which had purposely been camouflaged by positioning the tent so that the forest beyond the mine's perimeter served as a backdrop.

A young woman, surely Bob's friend Pam, waved at Bob and Abby. Abby recognized other members of One Universe from the photograph in *People Magazine*. They were mixed in with curious Flagstaffians, university students, and anyone else who was ready to trade a dull political speech for what might, with luck, be very good eats. At the far side of the tent Titus, the hawk man from the veterinarian's waiting room, talked with Peter Rivers—Ichabod Crane with a long, limp gray ponytail—while Linda Wallace, with graying brown hair and somewhat on the dumpy side, listened intently to their conversation. Martha Van Dyke—neatly attired in a white pants suit, black silk blouse and black and white low-heeled spectator shoes—chatted amiably with what the constant presence of press and cameras signaled to be the key players: Earl Olson, Jim Wilson and today's speaker, whom Abby recognized immediately as the twitchy Toby Barrett from the Copper State 1000.

Then it was "I'll rub your back, you rub mine" time. Someone from the Arizona State Legislature introduced Jim Wilson, who introduced Earl Olson, who introduced the speaker, while complimentary adjectives flowed so fast and thick it occurred to Abby that, if they had they been edible, everyone present would have had at least a month's worth of empty calories. When it finally came his turn, Congressman Barrett, who was evidently on the subcommittee on Forestry and Public Land Management, which gave him some rationale for being in Flagstaff, praised the Pycenium Mine profusely for its stimulus to the local economy. Abby yawned. Jobs, jobs, jobs. Barrett was obsessed with the idea, but from what Abby had seen pumice mining was about as un-labor intensive as you could get. The congressman was full of it.

Looking around for some source of diversion, Abby watched the caterers quietly bringing out refreshments from the mine's office and from the catering trucks parked next to it. Then a collective gasp from the crowd brought her attention back to the podium. In front of it eight extremely well-endowed young ladies had leapt up and were pulling off their shirts and forming a chorus line. Although the tee shirts they had worn under their other shirts were dry, any one of the girls could easily have won a wet-shirt contest any time. Every shirt had on it an image of some animal that lived in the forest. Two local television cameramen looked as if they might pass out in the arms of Miss Bobcat, who would have required a triple-D cup if wearing a bra had fit her agenda. Even Congressman Barrett, his lips a tight, straight line, maneuvered to get a better look at Miss Chipmunk. The Rockette wannabes bobbed up and down in a ragged chorus line as they chanted something about saving the forest creatures.

"Brilliant, absolutely brilliant," shouted the woman next to Abby over the ensuing hullabaloo. "Better than placards any day!"

The girls bobbed and bounced over to Peter Rivers, who extracted something from Linda Wallace's capacious handbag. Then they worked him into a position just beyond the tent, right in front of the hole. Peter unfurled a pair of stonewashed jeans and holding them aloft shouted, "Is a pair of jeans really worth this destruction of *our* forest?"

Abby turned to agree with the assessment of the woman next to her and caught sight of Titus slinking out from the double-wide with some papers in his hand. No one else seemed to notice, for even the security men had become totally engrossed with the delectable sight of bouncing boobs. Just what is the hawk man up to now, she wondered?

CHAPTER 6

Later Abby could not have said whether it was her fatigue and profound depression or whether she really did experience a premonition of disaster when approaching her rented house.

Lida, her dialysis nurse, had thoughtfully arranged her monthly visit to her mother in Phoenix so that she could bring Abby back from her sister's, where she had been recuperating from the operation to insert the catheter. Most of the way up I-17 Abby had dozed, rallying only within the city limits of Flagstaff to give Lida a few pointers about the best route to take to the professor's house.

Instinctively she patted her stomach. Beneath her clothes the catheter emerged from her peritoneal cavity, coiled around like a serpent, and was secured by a strip of adhesive tape. Although it didn't hurt, it seemed a strange, alien thing. Worse, it represented dependency, utter dependency. It was an irrefutable sign that her body could no longer function on its own. She felt tears of fatigue and frustration pool in her eyes and blinked rapidly to hold them back. She just wanted to get home, to take Francis in her arms and tell those trusting brown eyes how her life had gone to hell. Despite Becky's and her family's kindness all Abby had been able to think about over the past few days, besides the hated catheter, was getting back to Francis. Friends and family constantly offered well-meaning suggestions; a dog knew when to remain silent. Dogs didn't criticize, they didn't advise. They just loved unconditionally.

In contrast to her own unsettled state, the neighborhood looked tranquil enough. It was early evening, a time of long, golden light. The setting sun brushed the tips of the San Francisco Peaks with gold leaf. Above them hovered a couple of puffy cumulus clouds like dollops of whipped cream sprayed out of a can. After the heat of the day, her street was coming alive again. Children played tag. A neighbor mowed his grass while another washed her car. An older couple in shorts and tee shirts briskly paced each other. But when Lida drew up to the professor's house it had a desolate feel; not a sign of life, not a friendly bark. Perhaps Francis was at the Khalsas' with Bob, who had been caring for him, Abby thought.

Sada Anand, who must have been keeping a lookout for her, rushed out as soon as Abby stepped out of the car.

"Oh, Abby, they're gone. Gone! Bob and Francis," she said in a choked voice. "They've been gone for two days."

Abby felt her body freeze as if a witch had hexed her. Turned to salt, Lot's wife could not have been more thoroughly paralyzed. For an endlessly attenuated moment everything around her stopped like a halted frame on a VCR. Try as hard as she might, she couldn't seem to get enough oxygen into her lungs. She sucked in air but couldn't get it past the constriction in her throat.

Grasping her arm, Lida broke the spell and hustled the two women inside.

Abby, who immediately collapsed in her favorite armchair, noted that Sada Anand, who had seated herself on the very edge of the couch, looked almost as pale as the immaculate white she always wore. Her lips, as usual free of any lipstick or gloss, were twisted together and clamped tight. Furrows traced across her high, normally smooth forehead. Even her thin, straight nose looked pinched. Fatigue rimmed her translucent gray eyes with dark shadows.

"No note or anything?" Abby, swallowing to ease her throat, managed to ask.

"Nothing."

"Gone since when?"

"Wednesday."

By now it was Friday evening. Yes, gone two days! Sada Anand had every reason to panic. And where, dear God, was Francis?

"Wednesday was the play group for Pooh and Bear," Sada Anand explained in a tense, uncharacteristically high voice. "I was working at the hospital. Bob promised to do some things for me around the house, which he did. I don't have any idea when they— Bob and Francis, that is—left, only that they weren't home at the end of the day. I looked around and found that Bob had taken his day pack, some food and water bottles. At first I wasn't worried. I thought maybe he wanted to watch the forest animals at sunset, when they're feeding and the night creatures are coming out. He's been really interested in the spotted owls. . . ."

Sada Anand looked carefully at Abby to make sure she was taking all this in.

"Yes?" Abby was taking it all in, at least on the surface level. On a deeper level she simply could not comprehend what she was hearing. Gone? Two days? Impossible. Bob had showed himself to be responsible in the way he helped his sister out and cared for Pooh and Bear. People like that didn't just disappear.

"Bob loves the forest. You know that." Sada Anand dropped her eyes as if there were too much pain in direct contact and stared at her slender fingers as they picked nervously at the hem of her white tunic. "But to be gone so long without a word. . . .   I know it can't be deliberate! Bob would *never* make me worry like this. He's always so sensitive, so very considerate."

"Have you called the police?" asked Lida, who had positioned herself between the living room and the front entryway as if to protect the other two women from who-knew-what.

"Yes. And I stayed home from work yesterday so the girls and I could explore the areas where they usually walk with Bob. Soul Singh searched too, but there wasn't a sign. That's when I called."

"What did the police say?" Abby pushed herself further back into the armchair, as if she could find comfort in its embrace.

"I got the impression that the police hate to touch the disappearance of an adult. As far as they're concerned, any adult who wanders off probably left on purpose. The city police wouldn't do anything, nothing at all. So I waited another night. Still nothing." Her voice broke and she took a moment to compose herself before continuing.

"This morning I tried again and finally convinced the Sheriff's office that there must have been an accident. Bob just never would have gone off. . .on. . . on some permanent basis without telling me. And he certainly wouldn't leave with your dog." Sada Anand's voice faltered again momentarily.

"The Sheriff agreed with that," she continued. "They're much readier to search for someone if they think there's been a climbing or hiking accident. You know, with the mountains and forests and all, they get a lot of that sort of thing around here."

"Do you think that's what's happened?" What Sada Anand was saying was simply too dreadful to take in. Abby felt that she was observing the scene from a long way off. It was as if she had distanced herself physically, although she was, in fact, still sitting in the living room in the Royal Stewart-plaid chair. But the living room didn't have its usual cozy feel. It seemed suddenly very cold and impersonal, like a set for a scene in a play when the actors themselves have left the stage.

"I, I don't know!" Sada Anand cried out, then lowered her voice to a more normal level. "Even if Bob twisted an ankle or something like that, he has basic medical supplies in his pack. I know he has an ace bandage and pain pills. He joked with me about those pills. He said he'd tried everything when he was into drugs, but now he wouldn't touch anything except a vitamin C unless it was a total emergency. He only carried the pills to keep from going into shock if. . . if he had a bad fall. But he wasn't climbing. So how would he do that?"

Abby considered the terrain as she knew it. "Clambering over some boulders? Sliding into a ravine hidden by brush when he was going across country? With the heat and dryness, even the regular paths have become awfully slippery." She remembered the loose, crumbly soil. "He could have fallen going down a very steep part of the trail. Badly wrenched a knee and been unable to move."

And then there were the uncovered mine shafts, she thought with a shudder. The mineral-rich slopes of the San Francisco Peaks were peppered with them. Too many to begin to cap them all. So easy to tumble into, often impossible to get out of, as Bob himself had recognized when he designed fanciful fates for anyone who desecrated the forest. Abby remembered that a poor homeless man had lost his life that way only a few weeks earlier. Definitely not a good subject to bring up with Bob's sister, who was already so distraught.

"He has good boots, very good boots," Sada Anand was saying. "And Bob's got a wonderful sense of balance. He's a natural athlete, you know. Never quite A-team in any of the popular, attention-getting sports, and never good enough to satisfy our father. But still, he's in great shape and very coordinated. Hiking is a natural for someone like him." Her eyes filled with tears.

"Still, anyone can fall."

"Yes, but Bob would have made it back, or at least to a spot where we could find him. He knows the forest, how to deal with it, how to survive there."

The two women sat in thoughtful silence while Lida went out to collect Abby's things from the car. Then she rummaged around the kitchen, producing three mugs and a pot of hot tea. With the coming of darkness the air had suddenly grown chill, or so it seemed to Abby, who started to shiver. She wondered idly if the shivering was caused by the aftereffects of the operation, the shock of what she was hearing, or the actual temperature. Whatever the cause, hot tea was a welcome antidote.

As the three women sipped the tea they considered the possibilities. Yet nothing that had not already been said occurred to any of them. Surely there must have been an accident, but of what sort? And why hadn't Bob been found yet by the Sheriff's rescue team? Yes, the forest was enormous. However, the members of the rescue team were surely knowledgeable, with plenty of training and experience. Bob and Francis had gone on foot. How far could they go? Although Bob with those long legs of his might cover a fair distance, certainly not Francis.

Francis, she thought, grasping the mug more tightly. How long had it been since the little dog had eaten? Far more important, how long had he gone without water? She always carried water on their walks together with a little tin measuring cup for Francis to drink from. Bob would have done the same. But if Bob was disabled, or even unconscious, what then? Cool pine forests aside, and frankly they hadn't been so cool of late, this was still the arid southwest where surface water was not easy to come by. No rain in months, so there wasn't even a puddle.

Abby shuddered slightly. In spite of the tea she felt cold, so very cold. Perhaps she should ask one of the other two women to light the fire she had laid weeks earlier in what had proved to be the overly optimistic hope of enjoying it on a rainy night. However, talking required an almost insupportable effort. Gradually they had all fallen silent, waiting for no one knew what.

The sound of the doorbell drew them back to the moment. Sada Anand jumped up and hurried to open it. The door frame was filled with two very large uniformed men.

"Mrs. Khalsa?" one of them, who identified himself as Lieutenant Henderson, inquired.

"Yes."

"Harry here is going to take you back to your home. I'm afraid our news isn't good, and I think you should be with your husband when you hear it. You go with Harry now," he gently urged Sada Anand, who stood motionless, as if she'd been turned into a pillar of white marble. "I'll be over in just a minute."

"Ms. Taylor?" Lieutenant Henderson turned to the two remaining women as Sada Anand, coming slowly out of her rigid posture, slipped silently out like a wraith.

"Yes," Abby answered in a very faint voice.

"Fortunately, we have some good news as well as the bad. Your dog is fine." Abby's heart jolted. Just for a moment the unexpected, glorious relief that surged through her canceled out even the terrible knowledge that something awful had happened to Bob.

"A little dehydrated, but basically okay. He's being checked out by a vet, just by chance the one who's seen him before. She says he'll be perfectly fine in a day or two. One of my men will be bringing him home as soon as she's finished with him."

"Oh. . . oh, thank God," Abby breathed. "But Bob, Robert that is, Robert Curtis? What. . . ." She couldn't bring herself to finish the question.

"Dead, I'm afraid, Ms. Taylor."

The joy that had flooded her on hearing of Francis turned to bile. No, no, no, it *couldn't* be true!

"You're sure?" she asked, and realized immediately that this was a very stupid thing to say. Lieutenant Henderson wouldn't have made the statement had he not been certain. But the situation seemed so utterly unbelievable. How could the same young man who was so very much alive when she took the shuttle to Phoenix on Sunday be dead now? Oh God, her worst nightmare. Mark all over again.

"Yes, we're sure," the big man told her.

"But. . . but what happened?"

"Drugs. It looks like he OD'd. Overdosed, you know."

* * *

No, Abby repeated to herself when the officer had gone, Bob couldn't have died of an overdose! It was hard enough to take in the fact that he was dead, but completely impossible to believe that his death had been caused by his doing drugs. She didn't care how many needle tracks they'd found or how much drug paraphernalia. Although maybe, given time, she could accept the fact of Bob's death, she could never accept that way of dying.

She rubbed her temples in an attempt to stimulate the blood flow to her brain, but her jumbled thoughts failed to clear. She remembered her much earlier protestations that mentally she was okay. Well, she had lied to herself. She might be doing better mentally than physically, but she was still no great shakes. No getting away from it; of late, her mind had not worked in anything like a normal manner. It was like a car with a sluggish engine, one badly in need of a tuneup. Although she eventually got where she was going, worked through the problem at hand, it was as if she were proceeding on half or even quarter power. Perhaps her mental processes would speed up when the dialysis cleaned out her system. Well, she'd find out soon enough.

As for Bob, what had really happened? And when? Bob had shown not the least sign of taking anything before she left for Phoenix on Sunday. He'd disappeared on Wednesday. If something had gone wrong in the short space between Sunday and Wednesday, if Bob showed any sign of being back on drugs, Sada Anand would have known. Wouldn't she? She was a nurse after all.

Abby began to tremble violently. Lida found a heavy sweater

and slipped it around her shoulders. But Abby continued to shake—with cold, with grief, with a sense of events beyond her control overpowering her.

Quietly Lida asked if she could light the fire in the fireplace. Abby nodded and felt tears she had not even known were there slide down her face. Lida got the fire going. Abby stared into it, watching the flames cavort hypnotically. Just looking, not thinking. Suspended in time.

The doorbell rang again. When Lida answered the door, there was another uniformed man, this one with Francis. The dog gave a joyous yelp, then the man dropped the leash and Francis made a bee line toward Abby, flinging himself into her waiting arms. The officer, a very young man with nut-brown skin and dancing dark eyes, grinned broadly. "I got the right place, don't I?"

"Oh, yes. Quite definitely. Thank you so very, very much, Officer," Abby managed to croak, her voice sounding hoarse and far away.

Francis curled up in Abby's lap, and she stroked his soft pelt gently. The dog almost vibrated with contentment. He had come home, he knew it, and home he intended to stay.

"Would you like to sit down? Have some tea or a soft drink?" Abby asked, belatedly remembering her manners.

"No, ma'am. I've got to get going. But Lieutenant Henderson, he told me I had to get this dog home safely. You know, your dog never left that man who died." The young man gave Francis a look of respect.

"Stayed right there beside him. I don't know if we ever would of found him if the dog hadn't been along."

Abby gazed down at Francis and silently thanked him with her whole heart. He couldn't save Bob, but he'd tried.

"The forest is a real hard spot to find people. Ridges, washes, trees, snags. And all the old mine shafts and drifts, you know. You've seen the drifts? Like shafts only they don't go straight down but down on a easy angle."

She nodded. Bob had pointed some out to her. Drifts, though not quite as hazardous as shafts, still had their problems. The wooden beams used to shore up the ceilings might easily be a century old. An injudicious move and the whole tunnel could collapse. A scene, Abby recalled, that was much beloved by the producers of grade B Westerns.

"As it was, the body was down in a drainage—where the water runs. . . that is, when there's any water," the officer added for Abby's benefit.

"Lots of overgrowth. We'd probably of ended up using the hounds, so maybe we would of come across the guy sooner or later. Only it's awful hard for them in a place like that with so many scents one on top of the other. Anyway, a couple of our men were looking in that general area and the dog came out and got their attention. Sure enough. There was the body."

That was something Abby didn't care to dwell on.

"How did my dog get along without water?"

"Well, ma'am, he was lucky. If there's a guardian angel for dogs, he's got one. There was this old cattle tank nearby. Of course it was too high for a dog like yours to get to the water, but there was some seepage. Just enough to make a puddle. Your dog used that. Only he was still a bit dehydrated the vet said. Nice the vet already knew him. We just took him there just because the vet is good friends with Lieutenant Henderson."

"And she says that other than the dehydration my dog is all right?" Abby craved reassurance.

"Yes, ma'am, although he's been without food, too. She says only feed him a little at a time, real small meals but pretty often. Otherwise he'll just get sick. She wrote you out instructions."

The young man gave Abby a neatly written list.

"Thank you again."

"That's a brave little mutt you've got yourself there," he said admiringly.

"He's not a mutt," Abby corrected him with pride in her voice. "He's a Pembroke Welsh corgi."

* * *

Sada Anand didn't break down until after the officers had left and she had spoken with her parents. Only when she had hung up

111

the phone did she start to sob. Soul Singh put his arms around her protectively and held her as gently as he would have one of their little girls.

"They don't care. They don't care at all," she choked out. "Mom and Dad said they'd send the money to cover funeral expenses, but they weren't going to come out here and *please* not to send the body back to Florida. Dad has a big court case, and Mom has too many social commitments to think of canceling them all. Their son is *dead* and all they can think about is business, golf, and bridge."

She broke down again. Soul Singh slipped off her turban and stroked the pale hair that drifted down around the strained white face.

"If something happened to Pooh or Bear I'd feel as if someone were cutting out my heart without benefit of anaesthetic! They just sounded miffed at being awakened in the middle of the night but were too polite to say so."

She rested her head against his shoulder and cried bitterly, without restraint.

"You can't change them, you know," he reminded her gently. "We discussed this long ago. Remember you have your own home now, your own family. We have peace and love and above all each other."

"But Bob. . . ." she gasped.

"Your brother's death is a terrible thing. But somehow we've got to come to terms with it, and above all help the girls. It's going to be an awful blow," he sighed. "You were right in telling the police that Bob would never have done this to himself. He loved Pooh and Bear and wouldn't have hurt them for the world. He wouldn't have touched drugs because of the awful example it would have set. I don't know what happened, but I'm as sure as you that it wasn't how it looks. Something's very wrong there."

"He was doing so well and he had such potential. He was talking about finishing college." Sada Anand caught her lower lip between her teeth and bit it until it turned as red as if she'd been wearing a lip gloss. "He had so much to live for. Why, oh, why did he have to die?"

Pam Haines would have paced the floor, but in the cramped quarters she shared with two other girls there just wasn't room enough to go much of anyplace.

Why didn't Bob call? She hadn't seen him since the demonstration. Yes, she and her roommates had joined a group of friends water-skiing over the Fourth up at Lake Powell, where her class-cutting roommates still hung out. But she'd been back for several days. Not that she expected him to call every day, but after all, it was by now late Friday. She didn't want to phone him. When they'd exchanged telephone numbers Bob had explained how hard his sister and brother-in-law worked. Their precious time at home with their two little girls didn't need to be interrupted. Besides, it was probably too late now to call anyone who got up at the crack of dawn, which seemed to be the regime in the Khalsa household.

As Pam stood in the middle of the apartment's tiny living room, pretty well picked up but pathetically shabby, she found herself filled with self-doubts. Had Bob tired of her so quickly? Maybe he had found someone else? Abby Taylor? Pam felt faintly nauseated. Bob had said that Dr. Taylor was darned attractive for an older woman and, if she were the woman with Bob at the demonstration, Pam had to agree. Tall, slender, a bit of chestnut hair visible under a straw sunhat. Although dark glasses made it impossible to see her eyes, they didn't prevent Pam from admiring her regular, oval face. But "old" was the operative word. She'd bet there was some gray in the chestnut unless the professor colored her hair, and that the skin which looked so smooth from a distance showed fine lines closer up. That woman had to be nearly old enough to be Bob's mother.

Pam sighed and took a swig of Diet Coke. She had thought things were going really well. She just couldn't believe that Bob was avoiding her.

She had a couple of good reasons to talk to him. Above all she wanted to relive with him One Universe's awesome triumph at the Pycenium.

Pam picked up the videotape she had made from the news

reports, toyed with it, then set it down again on the television which, together with a few lamps, a lumpy couch, two unmatched garage-sale chairs and a small, unsteady table accounted for all the furnishings. Even so, the small room seemed crowded.

She fingered the tape for a moment, then turned away. Better to wait to watch the tape again until she could watch it with Bob. It represented a triumph to be shared and savored.

Obviously, the visit of a junior congressman—especially one from California, a state that most Arizonans seemed to view with great suspicion—wasn't exactly a major event. But except for the wild fires that were flaring up throughout the state as a result of the unusually hot, dry summer, not much else was going on. Consequently the news media had been well represented at the Pycenium. Admittedly their plan had been hokey and sexist, as Martha Van Dyke had stated straight out. But it had worked. The coverage had been sensational.

The tape she was saving for Bob showed it all. The cameramen, and even the one woman among them, had focused on the bouncing boobs and then on Peter Rivers. He had positioned himself squarely in front of what had once been a green, sheltering ponderosa forest, home to deer, mountain lion, bobcat, and all sorts of other critters. Now it was chewed into a great hole, just acres and acres of acres of gray powder. Home to nothing. The mine reminded Pam of an aerial photograph she'd once seen of an avalanche. Only this wasn't cool, clean snow that would melt and nourish the land. This was all that remained when the porous, froth-like volcanic glass they called pumice had been gouged from the earth.

Enormous havoc and destruction, and for what? As Peter Rivers had informed the media and the others who had gathered to hear the congressman, it wasn't exactly as if the world couldn't get along without pumice. Especially this sort of pumice. Pumice to produce more stonewashed jeans?

Flapping a pair of stonewashed jeans, pointing to the desolation behind him, Peter had shouted, "Is it worth it?" The media had caught every word, every gesture, every detail.

Pam had tried to talk to Bob at the end of the demonstration. However, in all the confusion she'd not managed to catch up with him and the woman who was presumably the professor. Now, beyond relishing the Pycenium success, she wanted to ask Bob what was going on with Titus. Those two were up to something for sure, she thought as she dumped a bunch of books and papers off one of the garage-sale chairs, so pathetic it looked like the poor thing was molting, and plopped down.

The idea of getting Bob involved in One Universe had been for him to spend more time with *her*. Only all that time seemed to be going to Titus, Pam thought with disgust as she gripped her Coke can more tightly. They'd become as thick as. . .well, the proverbial thieves. Just what were they up to?

* * *

Later, when both the officer returning Francis and Lida had gone, Abby continued to sit in the chair, stroking Francis. Occasionally he turned his head to give her hand a reassuring lick with his long, pink tongue.

Abby had found it hard to convince Lida that it was all right to leave her, but, after all, Lida had her own husband and children to care for, and, in any case, for the present there was little more she could do. All Abby's things had been brought in, properly stored and the dialysis equipment rechecked. A sensible precaution, although she wouldn't actually begin the dialysis until sometime next week, since first the catheter needed time to settle in. Lida had made some more tea and reluctantly departed.

Only then, with the house quiet except for the crackle of the burning wood, could Abby concentrate on all that had happened.

Bob had been preoccupied lately, but there was no indication his preoccupation had anything to do with drugs. Or was there? The more she thought about it, the more convinced she became that he'd been up to something. Something he didn't want to share with her because it lay on the fringe of the law? Because he thought she would have disapproved for some reason? Once she thought she'd glimpsed him talking with the hawk man at Macy's. But Macy's was a casual place where people talked quite naturally with strangers. It could have been coincidence. Or maybe they were discussing some issue that concerned the forest. Both had a common interest there.

With his track record would Bob risk involvement in anything illegal? He had seemed truly happy with the turn his life was taking. The love and support of his sister and her family appeared to be gradually repairing his shattered self-confidence. The unquestioning adoration of his two little nieces, who clearly viewed him as some sort of superior being, had played its part. And then there was that girl from One Universe, Pam—Pam Haines. The way that Bob kept bringing her name into conversations had convinced Abby that he had more than a passing interest in the young woman. Meanwhile, although he hadn't made any definite commitment about returning to college, he wasn't fighting the idea as hard as he once had either.

One of the fire logs shifted, sending up a shower of sparks.

Bob had demonstrated that, given the right circumstances, he had a hair-trigger temper. Could he have run into someone doing something destructive to the forest? Someone doing drugs? If he'd interfered they might have beaten him up, sure. But why waste drugs on him? Or maybe he'd been hanging around the mine, and someone like Shorty Dean decided to make it look like Bob had gotten back into the drug scene so his sister would send him back to Florida. A strategy gone awry? On the other hand, why him? From what she'd seen at the demonstration, the Pycenium management should have been worrying about that sneaky Titus, not Bob.

Abby stared into the fire. She didn't know the answers to her questions, and she couldn't bear to think about Bob any longer. She was too tired, too depressed to make sense of anything. She could only grieve—for Bob, for herself, perhaps for the whole messed-up world which let people like Bob and Mark die so young, and for no reason.

She felt shaky, shaky from the inside, and cold, so very cold in spite of the tea and the fire. A physical reaction in the aftermath of the operation? Becky had probably been right. Perhaps she shouldn't have come back to Flagstaff so soon. But she hadn't experienced any real postoperative pain, discomfort at most, and Dr. Frankenthaller said the incision was healing nicely.

Cold, shaky, tired and depressed. She pulled Francis closer. More depressed than when she'd been diagnosed with the disease; more depressed than she'd been in the weeks leading up to the operation when she'd tried so futilely to penetrate the black, fathomless future. Worst of all, illogical though it may have been, she felt oppressive guilt. Again someone she cared for had died while she had lived. Why should she be spared?

Abby felt as if she stood on a cliff before a gulf, a gulf as great as the Grand Canyon and as dark as that enormous cavity on a starless, moonless night. Desperately she wanted to slip over the edge, to disappear forever into the darkness and silence, to glide off into the seemingly endless space like some huge night bird. The image came to her so strongly that Abby could almost smell the pungent scent of the piñon and juniper that grew along the canyon's rim. She could practically hear the slight movement of wind riffling the edges of the canyon's stillness. She could nearly touch the black velvet void drawing her inexorably into its depths.

How long she poised there on the edge of oblivion she couldn't have said, but suddenly her reverie was shattered by the sound of the doorbell.

Abby glanced down at her watch. A little after ten. Not nearly as late as she'd thought, but later than she was accustomed to staying up. Probably the police again. Lieutenant Henderson had mentioned something about more questions, only she'd thought he'd meant to come back tomorrow.

She carefully lowered Francis to the floor and went to answer the door. The man standing there was someone she had never seen before and was not in uniform. He wore a royal purple tee shirt silk-screened with a picture of three snow-flaked wolves howling at a huge, luminous full moon, old Levis, and scuffed jogging shoes which Francis sniffed with evident interest.

"Excuse me," he said. "I wouldn't have bothered you except that the lights were still on. I'm David Neale and I. . . ."

"You can't be David Neale!" Abby protested, incredulous at the sight of this man claiming to be her absent landlord. The man before her was definitely not a large, round, grandfatherly sort of person. He was about her age, not a great deal taller than she, and certainly not in the least bit rotund. His thick dark hair showed strands of gray, but no white. And where was the beard she'd envisioned? Although this man could certainly use a shave, that was it. The only thing she'd been right about were the eyes, as blue as the Flagstaff sky and sparkling with humor and vitality.

"Why ever can't I be? I'll show you some identification if you'd like." He seemed amused at her greeting and not the least bit offended.

"No, no, I guess I believe you," she replied, hearing the skepticism still in her voice. "What can I do for you?"

"I was just coming down from Wyoming and decided to drive by and see if anyone was home. I finished my field work early and wanted to pick up a disk I left here so I could start running some of my data through the mainframe at the university first thing tomorrow. Look, I'm really sorry. I shouldn't have presumed to come by at this hour. Clearly it's not a good time. I'll come back tomorrow."

"No, I'm sorry to be so rude. I do apologize. Please come in and get your disk." She was too tired to care if he really was who he said he was. In any case, she had nothing worth stealing, and one good scream would bring the Khalsas running. She doubted that they would be sleeping much tonight.

Still feeling shaky and uncertain of her legs, Abby settled down again in the chair by the fire. Professor Neale didn't need her help to find his disk. She picked up Francis and held him close. As soon as the professor had gotten what he wanted, she intended to go to bed, to shut out reality, to forget everything until tomorrow.

The professor started toward the bedroom used as a study, and then paused. "A fire? Not that I mind, but isn't it a bit unusual to have one in the middle of the summer? At least when there's not been a storm to cool things down. Of course, it is cheering," he added dubiously.

"Yes, it is cheering." Abby's voice trembled slightly. "And

it's been a. . . a thoroughly miserable day."

Then it hit her all at once, the operation she'd just had, the dialysis she faced, Bob's death, how close she had come to losing Francis. To her horror she completely lost control and, right in front of this man she'd never even met before, she began to sob.

CHAPTER 7

Saturday dawned fresh and clear, but already with a hint of the heat to come. No classes, Pam Haines noted with pleasure as she tried hard not to think about Bob. She looked longingly at the news tape she hoped to share with him. Most of the footage, the really great stuff, was on the demonstration, but there were a few shots of that stupid congressman, that Toby Barrett, who thought it was really cool that acres and acres of forest had been destroyed for a few jobs. How did such an idiot ever get elected to Congress?

Pam pulled on her jogging shoes and double knotted them. She started a few preparatory stretches. Better to jog now before the heat built up. And if she didn't jog regularly she would probably turn into pudding.

Remembering the congressman made her think of the Pycenium, and the Pycenium made her think of the forest again. Pam wondered if the continued drought would force the Forest Service to close Coconino National Forest. They had been talking about it since before the Fourth of July. Not, of course, that the authorities could forcibly deny access to such a large area, but there would be a stiff fine to pay for anyone caught ignoring the injunction.

When she had come out from Iowa she had assumed that Arizona was hot and dry, only this summer it was unusually so. Even Flagstaff, along with the White Mountains and the North Rim of the Grand Canyon, among the coolest spots in Arizona, had begun to feel the effects of the abnormally harsh summer, with temperatures now rising well above normal. A summer like this meant fire and already several wildfires burned around the state, for once not the result of human carelessness but rather of lightning strikes. Dry lightning. Lightning without rain. The media was full of dire warnings about the problems that lay ahead if the monsoons failed to materialize.

She turned on the television and continued her stretches. Local news. Nothing about closing the forest, but another reminder that the Forest Service had prohibited fires there until further notice. An update on a wildfire burning off I-17 and news of a pile-up on I-40. All the usual stuff.

Turning her mind to other things, she had lost the thread of the narrative when suddenly the commentator's saccharine voice penetrated her consciousness. She had been touching her toes, trying to loosen those tight, grouchy hamstrings. Now she stood up and stared at the female newscaster, who tried to look so very serious while still being upbeat.

"Bob Curtis, found dead?" Pam didn't know whether she spoke aloud or simply deep within herself. No, it couldn't be. It just couldn't be. Time seemed to be suspended, as if someone had flipped a universal circuit breaker. Everything came to an abrupt halt. Even the dust motes sliding down a beam of sunlight were for a moment frozen in place. People her age didn't die. Except maybe for some awful accident like a car crash, it just didn't happen. Her stomach lurched as if she had just hit a hillock skiing too fast down the slopes at the Snow Bowl. She thought she would throw up the jellied donut she'd scarfed down for breakfast.

After the first wave of shock had passed, she tried to recall the newscaster's exact words. "Last night the body of a young man identified as Robert Lee Curtis was found in Coconino National Forest. The Sheriff's office is investigating." Then the newscaster had gone right on chirpily to other subjects—the effect of the hot, dry summer on tourism, a proposed new gated community stirring up controversy, and the question of a possible raise in teachers' salaries. Pam could take none of it in. She was too shaken even to cry. When at last her stomach had come to terms with the donut she picked up the phone and dialed Peter Rivers. Somehow Peter, and therefore One Universe, always had the latest news about what was happening.

"Drugs?" Pam asked in amazement when Peter, who evidently had a source in the Sheriff's office, had filled her in on the continuing investigation. "No way!"

"They say that's what it looks like. An overdose. Too bad, he was a nice kid."

"But Peter, he wasn't into that stuff," Pam protested. She had turned the sound down on the television but pictures kept floating by. She tuned them out, only peripherally aware of color and movement.

"Come on, Pam, you can't be sure. You weren't living with him, were you?"

"No." As a matter of fact, their relationship hadn't even become what you'd call intimate. Bob wasn't the sort to try to force himself on her like some guys. Maybe in time. . . but now there never would be time. She choked back a sob.

"So how much do you really know about this guy anyway? Bob Curtis was someone you met in the library. You liked him. You trusted him. He cared about the environment. You were right about that. And he wasn't quite as intimidated about the authorities as you thought he might be."

"Oh?" Pam heard a whistle hoot, the sound of a train rolling slowly down the Santa Fe tracks, and the low, hollow cry of the engine's whistle. The images on the television continued to drift silently past. Someone in the building was cooking bacon for breakfast—the sharp, pungent odor unmistakable. Everything so ordinary yet now so irreversibly different.

"I liked him too, and he was impressive with a computer." Peter sighed audibly. "Hate to lose him just when. . . ." His voice trailed off, and he failed to complete his thought. "Anyway, now we've got to go on from here."

"Yeah. I guess. That's the kind of stuff my mom says. But I still don't believe the bit about the drugs." Pam fought to keep the tears out of her voice. "Bob had been there before and never wanted to have any part of that sort of thing again," she added defiantly.

"Look, Pam, you've been around enough to realize that sometimes people do things they had no intention of doing. Who knows what happened with Bob? But whatever went wrong, there's nothing we can do about it now. He's dead. A good kid, but dead. Shit happens," he reminded her philosophically.

* * *

Abby awakened in a room half-lit with sun filtering around the edges of the shades. For a moment she couldn't figure out where she was. Flagstaff, it came to her, she was in Flagstaff, Arizona. And, oh God, she thought as she instinctively touched her abdomen, the tube, the catheter, wasn't just a nightmare. It really was there. Coiled, serpentine, a symbol of her body's bondage.

She closed her eyes again in an attempt to shut out the light, and to shut out reality. She definitely didn't want to think about facing the day. The catheter wasn't the only thing wrong, she remembered with a rush. Bob was gone. Bob was dead. Her gentle, kindly friend. And Francis? No furry body curled up beside her. No pink tongue reached out to caress her arm. Where was Francis?

"Francis?" Her voice was shrill, panicky, as she sat up abruptly, then stood on legs still wobbly and headed for the bedroom door, which she threw open so hard it slammed against the wall.

Francis, looking none the worse for wear, trotted up to her, his long, pointed ears at the ready and his hindquarters vibrating with the motion she had come to think of as the tailless tail-wag.

And behind Francis came her landlord, David Neale, freshly shaven this morning, thick dark hair with its strands of gray parted on one side, undoubtedly the same old Levis but a fresh tee shirt, this one sporting a coyote, head thrown back to howl, atop a gold and purple mesa. Last night—the tears, the hysteria, it all came back to her. God, but she'd made an ass of herself! This man must think he'd turned over his house to an utter idiot.

Abby dropped to her knees and hid her face against the little dog's soft fur. "Are you all right, Francis?" she asked him gently. She thought she heard her landlord mumble something about the dog looking a good deal more "all right" than his mistress, which, whether he'd actually said it or not, was undoubtedly true.

"Your little dog scratched, very gently I might add, on your bedroom door a while ago. His intent was quite clear. I let him out into the backyard, then fed him some breakfast. No," David Neale added before she could speak. "Not too much. I saw the vet's instructions. By the way, from the look of things the dog's the only one who eats around here."

"Thanks for the help with Francis." Abby felt awkward, confused, as if she couldn't quite get a grip on the situation. If this were the aftereffect of a sleeping pill, why did anyone ever take them? Standing up again, it suddenly occurred to her that she was still in her nightgown. In front of a strange man. "I think I need to get some clothes on," she said with all the dignity she could muster, and hastily retreated back into the bedroom.

"Don't worry," he laughed after her. "You should see some of the things my female students turn up in for summer school! Fortunately the Flagstaff weather constrains them in winter."

Abby put on sandals and a soft, loose-fitting dress in old rose. Normally she would have chosen slacks and a shirt, but Lida had warned her to add some casual dresses that didn't bind to her wardrobe. Slacks or shorts would tend to chafe the catheter until it had settled in. The dress with its Empire waist was perfect under the circumstances.

Suitably attired to leave the bedroom, she slipped through the hall to the bath. Peering into the mirror, she thought that David Neale must have a strong stomach not to have run screaming at the sight. Her skin was an unnatural shade of gray. The shadows under her eyes were so pronounced that they made her look like a first cousin to a raccoon. Only the shape of her long neck and oval face looked familiar.

As for her hair, what a disaster! Most of her adult life she had worn her hair long, usually in a chignon at the back of her neck—so very professorial, she had thought. But as her health had ebbed she had found it more and more tiring to care for it. In despair, she had gone to her sister's hairdresser and had her hair cut short. A good cut, only right now the hair stuck out at all sorts of odd angles like the snakes of Medusa. Her poor hair. Whatever had happened to the lustrous chestnut brown with the pronounced red highlights? Though it had enjoyed the benefit of enriching shampoo and the best conditioners on the market, her hair still appeared lackluster. Abby admitted to herself that she would simply never qualify as one of those Romantic nineteenth-century heroines who faded gently away, heartbreakingly fragile and delicately beautiful to the very end.

As she gazed at the image in the mirror a wave of nausea washed over her. She fought to keep from vomiting. *Damn*, she cursed silently. Neither an unusual occurrence nor a singular reaction to the image before her. Just one more symptom of her disease. She reflected that if this was what morning sickness entailed, her sister must have been a brave woman to opt for a second child.

Fighting down the nausea, she washed her hands and face and generously applied lotion. Her hands were dreadfully dry and flaky, evidently not uncommon for someone with failing kidneys. Abby applied some makeup, which only slightly improved matters.

"You're still here," Abby said to David Neale as she entered the small, precisely ordered kitchen. White walls and floor but vintage green tiles on the countertops. A large refrigerator. Gas stove, dishwasher, all the necessary appliances. Abby marveled again at the peg board wall with its colorful array of cooking utensils and other objects, presumably also used for cooking. Abby, in spite of having examined them carefully, could still not manage to identify all of them. Unless there was a significant other someplace around, and she had seen no sign of that, this man was seriously into cooking.

"I mean, did you go away last night and come back? Or did you stay?"

"I stayed," he answered matter-of-factly. "Between the catheter operation and losing your friend Bob, you'd had all a person could take. It didn't seem to be a good idea to leave you alone. After you and Francis had retired, I was too tired to go anyplace anyway."

"Thank you." And she supposed that she should also thank him for convincing her to take one of the sleeping pills Dr. Frankenthaller had prescribed for her. After all, she'd desperately needed the rest. On the other hand, the pill had left her feeling groggy and with a light headache, which didn't make her feel so grateful. But at least her stomach was calming down.

"Do I smell coffee?" she asked hopefully.

"You do. After checking the kitchen out I put in an emergency call to an old graduate student of mine. Does anyone eat around here but the dog? In any case, my graduate student provided, and provided well I might add."

The kitchen being too small for a table and chairs, David placed a mug on the dining room table and filled it from a thermos. Without consulting Abby, he added a generous measure of cream and sugar. Abby accepted the doctored coffee without protest.

"Would you like a breakfast roll?"

"Please. It's from Macy's!" she noted with pleasure.

"Oh, yes," David confirmed dryly. "From the look of things around here you don't believe in food, but I do. And nothing but the best."

"I was in Phoenix this week," she defended herself. But as a matter of fact she had discovered that when the kidneys fail they take the appetite with them.

"How about some huevos rancheros?"

"Sounds delicious," Abby agreed, suddenly remembering that she'd eaten nothing since a light lunch the previous day.

She soon found she had made a wise decision. He must have had all the ingredients ready, because it didn't take him more than a few minutes to prepare the eggs. He lightly scrambled them with salsa, chives, a touch of chili powder and abundant sharp cheddar. Then he served them with extra salsa, thick and juicy, a fresh flour tortilla, and sliced cantaloup on a bed of lettuce on the side. Definitely gourmet.

Not only was the meal delicious, David Neale had used his imagination to make the setting special. Plain white Noritake china, straw mats, forest green and white checked napkins of some fabric that didn't require ironing, and quality stainless steel tableware— all this had become quite familiar to her. But David had gone beyond the basics by placing a few pine sprigs and several cones in a piece of Indian pottery to create a simple but attractive centerpiece, something she had never thought of doing.

"Did you drive all the way down from Wyoming yesterday?" Abby asked after she had put away half of the eggs.

"Night before last I camped out near Flaming Gorge Reservoir.

Then yesterday I came down through Utah." He described driving through Vernal, a nice enough farming community, through Moab, a once charming town set amid brilliant vermillion cliffs before it had the misfortune of becoming what he theorized must be the ATV capital of the world. Then on down through Monticello, Blanding, Bluff, and into Arizona. He told her that from there he had headed through Monument Valley, across the Big Reservation, past the trading post at Cameron and into Flagstaff. A very long drive, a very long day.

Abby was delighted by the tale of his trip through places she had never seen, some she had never even heard of before. His account was light and descriptive, and somehow made towns like Moab and Vernal come alive. She listened intently, asking a question here and there. Anything to get her mind off Bob, the catheter, and even that damn Alfa Romeo, although she had to admit that the missing car had taken up very little of her mental time of late. Nor had it been mentioned while she was in Phoenix. But she couldn't ignore the strain the missing car was putting on Becky and Charles. Charles's normally jovial face had showed lines of tension that had not been there before and, throughout her stay, Becky had bounced around nervously like a demented June bug.

"There are some calls for you on the answering machine," David informed Abby as they finished off the last morsels of the eggs. "Didn't want to answer it myself and have to answer a bunch of questions about who I am and what I'm doing here. I don't expect any of my friends to call since for all they know I'm still in Wyoming."

"Nothing pressing, I hope?" she asked as she polished off the last of the sweet roll.

"A 'Becca' called twice."

"My sister, Becky."

"You should call her later this morning at Iron Springs, wherever that might be. She said that 'they' hoped to arrive around noon."

Abby nodded.

"And Lida."

"The nurse who brought me back from Phoenix."

The last slice of cantaloup, the last shred of lettuce disappeared from her plate.

"So what are your plans now that you've finished your research?" Abby inquired, thinking with part of her mind that she really ought to do something about the breakfast dishes, but she didn't feel as if she had the energy to move. "You don't. . . ."

"No, your lease is good for the summer," he chuckled. "No sense ousting a good tenant who pays the rent on time and hasn't complained about anything so far as I've heard. I'm just going to put my notes on the computer at the university—it'll take a few days, perhaps the better part of the week, but don't worry. I've got plenty of friends I can bunk with. Then I'll head off for some serious backpacking in Colorado," David told her as he gathered up their plates and utensils and took them out to the kitchen. Abby didn't discourage him. It wouldn't be hard to get used to this sort of service.

The phone rang and she got up reluctantly to answer it.

"Lida, the nurse," Abby explained when she had hung up and sat back down at the table to sip her coffee. "She's such a dear person. A husband, three young boys, and she can still take time to phone on a Saturday when you know they are all frantically busy going six directions at once. The older two boys are on two different Little League teams, while the youngest one is in some sort of swimming program. And her husband likes to take the whole family fishing on the weekend."

"Does she like to fish?" David, who had returned to the dining nook with the thermos and refreshed their coffee mugs, asked curiously. "Or is she one of those women who just goes dutifully along?"

"Loves it. Probably the only time she gets to sit calmly and just think about life."

"Hmmm, well, with three young boys you're probably right. You say she's a nurse?"

"My dialysis nurse. She's been teaching me about the equipment—that sort of thing. We've gotten to be friends in the process. She even planned her monthly visit to her mother in Phoenix at a time she could bring me back up here. Otherwise, my sister would have insisted on rearranging her whole schedule, and she's already such a busy person."

"You mentioned the dialysis last night. When do you start?"

"Next week. You can't start immediately because the catheter has to have a chance to settle in. But then you can't wait too long either because it might clog up if it's not used," she replied, keeping her voice as level as possible.

"Are you diabetic? Is that why your kidneys failed? Oh, my God, and all that sugar!" He looked in horror at the mug in which he'd served her well-sweetened coffee. "The sweet rolls, too."

"No," she answered to his evident relief. "No diabetes and no problem with sugar, although I try to take it easy with the protein. That stresses the kidneys." She thought about the eggs and cheese, for once feeling no twinge of regret. "And most people with failing kidneys have to be very careful with potassium. Fortunately I haven't had a problem yet in that regard, so you don't need to worry about the melon. My doctor thinks I sweat it off while walking." Just one more incentive to keep walking, she reflected. Even though, faced with the constant fatigue, it was often a matter of sheer willpower. Now without Bob—God, she couldn't think of that.

"But why did you think to ask? About the diabetes? So many people aren't aware of the connection."

Absently David reached down to pat Francis, who had positioned himself between their chairs in hopeful anticipation of a dropped morsel. "My wife. . . my late wife, that is." Abby heard a distinct catch in his voice. "She was Navajo. Diabetes is like a plague on the Big Reservation. I've been told that a third of the Navajos and Hopis are diabetic now. I don't know if that figure's exactly right, but I can guarantee that diabetes is a major problem."

"There are good new drugs, I've heard. And, depending on the circumstances, to a certain extent diabetes can be controlled through diet," Abby offered.

"I know, I know." He stopped petting Francis, who immediately put his head on David's knee to ask for more. "But

129

there's not enough early training on the Rez, and so many of them persist in doing everything wrong. Like my wife's uncle who drank regular Coke with his donuts on the theory that the Coke washed out the sugar!"

Abby shook her head in amazement. "Good lord! And of course the diabetes must be playing havoc with their kidneys."

"It's so bad that they have a dialysis clinic, no two now, I believe, in Tuba City and even one in Peach Springs."

"Peach Springs?"

"Peach Springs. About fifty miles northeast of Kingman on old Highway 66. Not exactly a world class metropolis, although they do have a couple of motels and a gas station."

"And a dialysis clinic?"

"And a dialysis clinic."

"Is that what happened to your wife?" Abby asked gently. "Diabetes?"

"No, a drunk driver. The other great plague of the reservation," he replied bitterly. "Nina had gone up to visit a sick aunt. Broad daylight and the bastard was too drunk to navigate. Came right over the center line and hit her head on." His normally twinkling eyes turned steely and from the veins that stood out on his hand she could see that he was gripping the coffee mug with great force.

"Oh, David," she said, using his name aloud for the first time. "I'm so sorry. I know that sounds dreadfully inadequate, but I am so very sorry." She dropped her eyes to stare at her own coffee mug, unable to bear the look of pain that pinched his face.

"Nina, the drunk driver, and at least one of the other people with him in his truck were killed instantly. But our son survived." Francis gave a slight cough to establish his presence and David absently stroked his head a few times, then forgot about the dog. Francis, having satisfied his immediate craving for affection, settled down under the table.

"Was he badly injured?"

"Surprisingly not." David's tight voice relaxed a little. "Nina always made sure he wore his safety belt. They think that saved him."

"Where is he now?"

"This summer he's fighting fires up on the Arizona Strip," David told her with pride.

She looked at him quizzically.

"The area between the Colorado River and Utah."

"So he's grown?"

"He's nineteen. An independent kid with an apartment of his own. Nina died almost ten years ago."

But Abby could tell that even a decade was not enough to dull the pain completely. She often thought about Mark, and sometimes she still remembered him with searing vividness. At those moments she could even hear the timbre of his voice. But he had long since ceased to be a constant presence in her life. After all, as she often reminded herself, she didn't even know if it would have worked out between them in the long run. They had been young, only graduate students. Would they have married as they assumed they would? Would the marriage have lasted as so many didn't today? In recent years the unanswered questions had begun to plague her not less but more. An important part of her life had been left unresolved, uncompleted.

"What's your son's name?" she asked. At least David Neale had something tangible left of the woman he'd loved, although his life as a single parent could not have been an easy one.

"Andrew."

"Andrew. And Andrew. . ." But for the present Abby was not to learn more of Andrew. The doorbell rang and when she opened it there was the large form of Lieutenant Henderson. The subject of Bob could not be dodged any longer, she thought with a sigh. But what could she really tell the lieutenant?

* * *

The Honorable Toby Barrett superimposed the image of long, sun-dappled fairways lined with pines over the dark waters of the Potomac which ran below his condominium. He pictured the clear blue skies of Flagstaff in place of the lowering clouds that hung ominously over the nation's capital. Washington presented a depressing scene. No golf today. Those clouds suggested no golf tomorrow, either. Another hot, wet weekend. Ah, well, he consoled himself, summer recess would soon be here.

The days since he had returned from California had been particularly tedious. As usual the ritualistic visits of leading constituents, so-called supporters who made constant forays to Washington either for self-indulgence at corporate expense or to prove to themselves that they were as important on the Hill as in California, had eaten voraciously into his time. There had been a bill of particular interest to some of his monied backers which had stalled on the floor. And as always, here, there, everywhere, the media stood ready to puff the most trivial remark into a grand statement of policy, usually to his disadvantage.

Speaking of which, he sure in hell appreciated the fact that Earl Olson wasn't blaming him for that goddamned screw-up in Arizona. Of course, it hadn't been *his* fault. Jesus, all he'd wanted was to shine a positive light on the Pycenium Pumice Mine, which was under constant attack from the goddamned environmentalists, especially those bastards from One Universe. It was the least he could do for Earl, his generous host, good golfing buddy, and political backer. After all, Earl had business interests in California as well as Arizona. A boost for Earl as a major investor in the mine and a boost, too, for Jim Wilson. Even if Jim wasn't at present a real player in the California scene, he still had important connections on the coast. One more pipeline to his constituents.

The idea had been to counteract the allegations of those damned interfering environmentalists, and Barrett had thought he knew just how to do it.

"More jobs!" "Stimulate the economy!" Arizonans, he had found, loved the sound of those words. Christ, but they usually responded like Pavlov's dog to these rallying cries. Those environmentalist s.o.b.s could rage all they wanted, and nobody was about to believe that the extinction of the spotted owl spelled the end of western civilization.

Better still, nobody really cared. Run a contest between the owl and the creation of even a half-a-dozen short-term jobs, and the jobs would win any day. People in Arizona wanted money, quick money, not environment. Develop a copper mine with all the leachate that implied, including arsenic and beryllium, in a riverbed upstream from the Phoenix water supply? No problem. Salt River Project could tackle the cleanup when the inevitable contamination occurred. Create trashy concrete sewers à la Los Angeles from perfectly good natural drainages? Of course! It was undoubtedly good for the concrete business. Flatten out another stretch of desert for yet another housing development? Why not? Desert was expendable but tax dollars weren't. So why the big fuss about a small section of the Coconino National Forest just because it was on the slope of one of the San Francisco Peaks? Hell, by the time Wilson's company reforested, it would be better than ever. Anyway, that's what the Environmental Impact Statement claimed.

And so everything had been just fine until those damned tree huggers demonstrated, he thought, hurtling the section of the *Washington Post* he had just finished to the floor. Earl had told him that one of the bastards had even slipped into the mine office while everybody else was staring at the chesty dancers. It was open for the catering staff, and they didn't know that the guy had no right to be there. Stole some financial data and some government reports. "Now why in the hell would anyone want that?" Toby Barrett demanded aloud.

But one thing he could say in favor of the environmentalists. They'd inadvertently given him some valuable tips in dealing with that fat ass Foster Richmond and his Alfa Romeo.

* * *

"So you noticed no sign of drugs?"

"No, Lieutenant, and believe me, after years of teaching I'm sensitive to that sort of thing."

They were sitting around enjoying the comforts of the red-plaid living room and more coffee. It seemed that David's graduate student had brought a bag of beans along with the already brewed coffee and the other goodies they had enjoyed for breakfast. In her forays into the kitchen to prepare her simple meals, Abby had paid no attention to the grinder David now pulled out of a cabinet. The percolator, a bit harder to overlook, had held no interest because she made do with instant. But David knew his kitchen and appeared intent on making sure that they didn't run short of the fresh-perked stuff. Actually he looked far more at home in the kitchen than in the well-appointed red-plaid palace, as Abby had come to think of the living room. While Lieutenant Henderson appeared perfectly at ease in one of the oversized armchairs, they were really a bit large for a David Neale. What was David, five ten or eleven? A fit, wiry body. He wasn't small but he wasn't built on the scale of the furniture, either.

"Is it 'Doctor' or 'Professor'? You are a professor, aren't you? Do you prefer to use your title?" Lieutenant Henderson asked Abby.

"'Yes' to the first, although I'm on an indefinite leave of absence for health reasons. And 'no' to the second. At Vassar we don't use our academic titles as a rule. I only bring mine out and dust it off when I'm feeling particularly huffy."

"Ms. Taylor then," he said with an encouraging smile.

"I suppose that's as good as anything."

"Tell me some more about Robert Curtis," the lieutenant suggested as he settled more comfortably into his chair. Yes, Abby refined her impression of last night, a big man. Six four at least, large boned but carrying no extra weight. Square face, protruding ears, thinning gray hair. "You first met him, in early May, I believe, not long after he'd come to live with his sister?"

"That's right."

"And what sort of person was he?"

"He struck me as someone who was really trying very hard to get a grip on his life." Abby paused a moment to order her thoughts. "The experience in Florida—being expelled, doing time—devastated him. He had real problems handling the indifference of his parents, particularly that of his father. He rarely said anything directly about all this, you understand, but if you listened carefully the message came through clearly enough."

"Yes, I imagine it would," the lieutenant agreed, and thoughtfully sipped his coffee. "Did he change at all during the period you knew him? Was anything different lately?"

"He seemed to be gradually coming to terms with himself. As they say, he was getting his act together. His sister and her family were a tremendous help. That and being so close to the forest. Bob loved the out-of-doors in every form, but especially this area. Very different from Florida! He'd pretty well decided to try again with college and, if he were accepted, work for his degree in forestry. We'd speculated that perhaps Professor Neale here might offer some assistance."

"Ah ha! A hidden agenda," David commented with a grin. "I was a marked man."

"It was just a thought. Remember, neither one of us had met you. You might have been the worst sort of old curmudgeon." Although how many old curmudgeons liked jolly red plaid, Abby asked herself?

"Nothing had happened lately to set Bob off? To make him want to get drunk or do drugs?" the lieutenant inquired.

"Not unless it happened after Sunday when I took the shuttle for Phoenix. In any case, I doubt it. As I said before, Bob really did seem be getting his act together. He even had a girlfriend."

"His sister mentioned a Pam Haines."

"That's right. A student at the University. She's also a member of One Universe and, so I gather, wanted to get Bob involved in the group. He was interested, but not in harassment and definitely not in monkey wrenching. That sort of thing would have gotten Bob right back into trouble with the law, which he knew full well, and mucked up any plans he might have been making for a university education. Besides, he didn't think that sort of action was the most effective way to attack environmental problems. I was surprised, but he even expressed doubts about the value of demonstrating."

"Was he out at the Pycenium Mine when the congressman spoke?"

"Yes, but with me, *not* demonstrating."

"Congressman? Which one?" David asked.

"Barrett of California," the lieutenant replied.

"I've heard of him," David volunteered. He slouched back into his chair, following the dialogue intently. "Barrett's on the sub-committee on Forestry and Public Land Management. So what's he doing visiting a pumice mine in Arizona?"

"Earl Olson, one of the investors in the mine, is a golfing buddy of his, also a political supporter from what I hear. The mine has been taking a real beating from the environmental community, particularly One Universe. Barrett was there to publicize the economic benefits of pumice mining, only it backfired, at least to some extent," Henderson explained.

"What happened?"

Henderson filled David in on the bouncing boobs and the stonewashed jeans.

"Sorry I wasn't there," David chuckled. "Nothing that interesting was happening up in Wyoming."

"So we know that Bob Curtis had made at least one friend, Pam Haines. How about enemies?" Lieutenant Henderson asked, turning back to Abby.

"He did much better on that score." Abby's voice was tinged with irony. She related their various run-ins with people Bob thought to be harming the forest. "Bob was basically a gentle person. Very kind and thoughtful. But he did have a quick temper. A very quick temper when anything to do with the forest was involved."

"Do you think that any of these people could have had anything to do with his death?"

"If he'd died as a result of a beating, I'd think it highly likely. But drugs? Not really." Abby shared her scattered thoughts of last night. "And it seems a bit too much to suppose that he was killed accidently by someone who didn't know dosages. A drug charge would be serious enough, but one involving a fatality? That would be an enormous risk to take even for someone a bit stoned at the time."

"Very risky," Henderson agreed, draining the last of his coffee. "Anything else that you can think of?"

"Just before I left for Phoenix, Bob was busy with some project, so I saw somewhat less of him than before. But there wasn't a sign of anything to do with drugs. He spent a lot of time with his, or rather Soul Singh's, computer and he'd been putting in a lot of hours in the library."

"Any idea what he was doing there? After all, he wasn't taking any classes."

"Besides 'accidentally' running into Pam Haines?" asked Abby, sure that this was at least part of the answer. "I have a good guess. I would bet that he was getting more background on forests, forestry and perhaps general environmental problems in this area."

"To snow me?" David asked, clearly amused to have been the focus of so much attention.

"I shouldn't be surprised."

"And what if I did turn out to be that worst sort of old curmudgeon? The Khalsas couldn't vouch for me. They're new neighbors, and when they moved in I was so busy with the usual demands of the semester and getting my research organized for the summer that I couldn't have exchanged more than a word or two with them before I took off for Wyoming."

"If you proved to be surly and unapproachable, the chances were that we could have found a more friendly member of the faculty," Abby answered him honestly. "However, and although not strictly relevant, you didn't mind having Francis. Such toleration speaks well of anyone," she added with the hint of a smile.

The lieutenant finished his questions. As David walked Henderson out to the car, the phone rang.

"Oh, *darling*, I've been so worried about you!"

Had her sister heard about Bob already, Abby wondered? She'd intended to drop that one on Becca very gently and hopefully not in the immediate future.

"No call last night! No answer this morning!"

"I'm sorry." Abby sat down in the chair next to the phone, relieved that she didn't have to explain Bob's death just yet. "That was really inconsiderate of me. Yesterday was a. . . a long, tough day and this morning I slept late. I unplugged the phone in the bedroom."

"A pretty miserable day here, too. The bank's president casually mentioned to Charles how he might be needing someone with just his talents at the branch in Yuma or maybe

Lake Havasu City."

"Oh, Becky!"

"Yes, major demotion." Becky's voice trailed off. Abby felt
a stab of guilt. Between Bob and the catheter she'd thought so
little about the Alfa Romeo.

"I'm sorry, Becca. What can I do? As I told you before, I
have been asking around. Only so far nothing."

"I'm sure you've done your best."

Abby wasn't so confident of that. She hadn't, after all, yet
established communication with One Universe.

"There's one angle left to try." She offered the small sop, hoping
it might raise Becky's spirits.

"Don't worry," her sister sighed. "After all, you've got to
concentrate now on the dialysis."

Not a thought on which Abby cared to dwell. "I guess I just
don't have well-honed skills as a sleuth," she said, averting the
subject. Too bad, too, because, as it was slowly dawning on Abby,
if Bob himself hadn't been fooling with drugs and someone hadn't
accidently given him an overdose, he'd been murdered. But why?
Why Bob Curtis? And as his friend and frequent companion, was
she herself in any danger?

CHAPTER 8

Normally Abby wouldn't have wasted time and energy on going to a beauty shop, but after the image she had seen in the mirror that morning she decided she had no choice in the matter. Even if she'd thought she could rehabilitate her hair herself, she didn't have the energy to try. Such a small gesture as lifting her hands above her head long enough to wash her hair had become immensely tiring.

Where could she find a good hairdresser in Flagstaff, she wondered? She certainly didn't want to go into any place from which she would emerge as a tightly curled poodle or, perhaps, a windblown rag. Should she call Lida? No, she thought not. Although Abby liked Lida's short, blunt cut and would be happy to have something like it, Lida would undoubtedly be off by now with her husband and sons. Even had she considered contacting Sada Anand in her grief for anything less than a very compelling reason, Sada Anand's hair never emerged from her turban and undoubtedly had not been subject to a hair stylist since she was called Sally.

Abby felt at a loss. She knew so few women in Flagstaff. Lida, Sada Anand, Sorrell Lawrence—as if she would seek advice from her on anything personal—and. . . yes, Alice Olson. If anyone would know what could be done to hair in Flagstaff, it was her sister's friend Alice.

A telephone call established that Alice would be delighted to introduce Abby to her own salon, where she was going that very afternoon. Not to worry that it was Saturday, a very popular day to be coifed. Alice would make all the arrangements and pick Abby up at two.

True to her word, Alice arrived on the dot of two in a car as big as the QE2. Cadillac or Lincoln? Something of the sort, Abby presumed. She hadn't realized that even Detroit made cars that big any longer.

Alice's beauty salon was also something out of another era. None of this unisex bit, Abby noted, not a man in sight. Everything was pink, from the walls to the floors and doors, from the patrons' adjustable chairs to the decorative molding around the mirrors, from the carts stuffed with mousse, hair spray, combs, and hair pins to the uniforms of the stylists. The manicurist had her own pink rolling table with a pink, heated cup in which to soak nails and a small pink fan for drying them. Her table also featured a display of emery boards, cuticle sticks, nail polish remover, clear base, and every conceivable color of polish, each type of equipment in its own neat pink plastic container. *People Magazine* had replaced the movie magazines of yore, but otherwise Abby could have been a little kid tagging along to a beauty parlor with her mother.

"Mrs. Olson," the pink-clad receptionist greeted them with a broad smile. "Glad that you brought your friend."

"*So good* of you to work her in on a Saturday afternoon. How are Jack and the kids?"

When it had been established that a chiropractor had realigned the receptionist's husband's ailing back and that her kids were doing no worse than might be expected of normal teenagers, Alice and Abby were ushered into the pink bowels of the salon and seated side by side in front of the pink-framed mirrors. Abby's stylist critically examined what was surely her challenge of the week if not the year.

"Ms. Taylor, would you like a little highlighting?" she asked, viewing Abby from all sides. Although it wasn't the sort of thing Abby would usually go in for, she felt that she looked so grim that anything that brought a little life to the gray skin and dull hair was worth trying. "You'll be happy with it," her stylist assured her. "And maybe a trim?"

Abby agreed. Might as well do the whole thing while she was at it, she reasoned.

The *snip, snip, snip* of the stylist's scissors made Abby nervous. Reflexively she stiffened. But she wanted to give the woman a chance to do her thing, and hair would grow back. Or maybe it wouldn't. The strange goo the stylist was now applying might

140

make it all fall out.

"You've had the operation?" Alice asked while they waited for the goo to settle and for whatever had been put on Alice's hair to settle or ripen or do whatever these mysterious potions did.

"Yes," Abby confirmed. Evidently Becky had told Alice about her illness and concomitant problems. "At the beginning of the week."

"And how are you feeling, my dear?"

After last night? Like death warmed over, and I look it, too. "Tired, shaky, some minor discomfort but no real pain."

"I take it you must have stayed with Becky and Charles while recuperating?"

"Yes. I just got back to Flagstaff late yesterday. And, oh, it was such a miserable homecoming." Abby discovered that Alice was a remarkably easy person to talk to now that she wasn't surrounded by a hoard of happy guests. As the two women were led off to adjoining pink basins, Abby found herself telling Alice all about Bob's tragedy. It came as a relief to talk about it, in part counteracting the sense of dislocation arising from doing something as mundane as having her hair done when there was so much sorrow in her heart. And not only hers. So many people suffering—Sada Anand, her husband, the little girls, and surely Pam Haines, too.

"It wasn't that I had known him all that long," she concluded, trying desperately to quash the slight tremor that insisted on creeping into her voice. "Just a couple months. But some people you instinctively like and form a bond with right from the start."

"*How difficult* to accept the death of such a young person, especially one you've described as having so much potential," Alice observed sympathetically as their heads were lathered up with a peach-scented shampoo.

Strong fingers massaged her scalp. Abby waited for the sound of rinsing water to subside before responding. "Once I adjust to the initial shock, I'm sure I'll be okay." Lord knew, she'd had enough practice with that sort of thing. "Although I can hardly say the same of his sister and her family. But I don't believe I'll ever accept the idea that out of the blue he got back into drugs and died as a result."

"From what you've told me it does seem unlikely that he would fall off the wagon, or whatever it's called with drugs, so suddenly and apparently without cause," Alice observed as the women were treated to a second peach-scented sudsing followed by another spray of water, an application of conditioner, and a final rinse.

"What do the police think?" Alice asked once they had returned to their outpost before the mirrors.

Abby repeated the morning's conversation with Lieutenant Henderson. "Unless the lieutenant's holding something important back, I don't think they know much of anything," she concluded.

"So your Bob was there at the demonstration at the Pycenium? I couldn't be there myself, but I watched a rebroadcast of the highlights on the news. My husband has rather a good deal of money invested in the Pycenium. He's the one who worked it out for Congressman Barrett to give his little talk there. Toby Barrett is a long-time personal friend of ours."

"At the time I wondered why a U.S. congressman from California happened to be giving a press conference in Flagstaff, Arizona."

"Toby was just trying to help Earl. As well as get in a few holes of golf," Alice confided. "Earl's originally from southern California, you see. His parents moved out there from Minnesota in the Thirties. The families—the Olsons and the Barretts—knew each other well. Toby is *much* younger than Earl. But they've always gotten along quite well. Earl enjoys having Toby over here to play golf, whether we're in Phoenix or Flagstaff. And Toby *loves* to get away from the rat race. Poor Toby. It's a shame he ever ran for Congress. It's not his sort of thing at all. Although I must say he's been helpful to Earl with a few matters in California, where we still have business interests."

"Poor Toby?" Abby asked curiously as the stylist gently pulled her hair around puffy pink curlers.

"Oh, Toby was divorced and at loose ends and thought it would be such a *thrill* to be a congressman. Only it hasn't happened that way. He put his money into a blind trust which was badly abused by that dreadful Foster Richmond, the owner, you know, of the stolen Alfa Romeo. Bad enough in its own way, but Toby also found life as a congressman wasn't all that it's cracked up to be. Too much work, too much kowtowing to his backers, and much too much time away from the fairways and greens. Toby is a nice enough young man. He's bright and clever, really *very* imaginative. But not one to buckle down willingly to the day-to-day grind."

"So Barrett was helping your husband?" Abby had a hard time thinking of someone in his mid-fifties with a pot on him as "young," but then Alice was seeing Toby Barrett from a different perspective.

"As I said, Earl has invested in the Pycenium Mine rather heavily. And there's been *so much* flack about the mine from the environmentalists! Particularly One Universe. Toby was only trying to tell the other side of the story."

"What could the environmentalists actually do? Besides protest, that is. Could they jeopardize your husband's investment?"

"Yes and no, my dear," Alice said as her stylist pinned another fat pink roller into place. "I don't think they could do anything about mining on claims that have already been staked, about two hundred some acres in our case. Those are secure now that the EIS—the Environmental Impact Statement, that is—has been accepted, the necessary permits granted, and they're actually mining. But there is some possibility that they could prevent more claims from being staked, or prevent the claims we have now from being patented."

Abby nodded. She had begun to get a fairly clear picture of the workings of the 1872 Mining Law from her conversations with Bob. "At which point you would own the land you've claimed outright."

"Yes, indeed. Once claims are patented you own the land just like we own the land on which our house is built. Of course then you have to pay taxes, but it makes it easier to go to the bank for loans. And, *most importantly*, the whole question is entirely out of the hands of the environmentalists, because now you're dealing with private property. Of course the land's treated just like private property once it's claimed, but after the patenting there's no doubt whatsoever. I know those environmentalists mean well. I even count one or two, like Martha Van Dyke, as friends. But in general they can be *such* a thorn in the side." She shook her head, which the stylist firmly steadied again in order to secure the last of the rollers.

"Well, I guess Congressman Barrett won't soon forget Miss Chipmunk."

"I should say not!" Alice responded with a hearty laugh.

"I hope that at least he got in his golf."

"Oh, yes. Poor boy had been so disappointed not to get in a round when he came out for the Copper State."

"Speaking of the Copper State, what do you think about the theft of the Alfa Romeo?" Abby asked as her stylist spritzed something light and refreshing with a hint of lemon about it on her hair, now tidily contained by curlers.

"A slick maneuver. Very, very slick," Alice pronounced with a touch of awe in her voice.

"You know the situation a lot better than I. After all, your husband was in overall charge of the stop in Flagstaff. Do you have any theories?"

"I'd suspect my own husband—you should have seen him drooling over that car—but Earl would *never* do anything illegal. Actually every man there felt the same way about the Alfa Romeo. Why, Toby himself would have loved to have gotten his hands on that car." Alice's second chin wobbled with the force of the laughter. "But I don't see any way he could have been responsible for the setup. He's imaginative, as I said, but no good at all with organization and details. And he could hardly assign the theft to his administrative assistant, now could he? The people involved must have been professionals to have passed off the deception so smoothly. That mugging in New York that left Foster's two usual mechanics out of commission? Definitely professional. Besides, what would Toby or Earl or anybody else have done with the car once he'd gotten it?"

"My thoughts exactly," Abby agreed with Alice, who turned

to look as someone made an entrance.

"Oh, my," she continued in a lower voice. "You do remember Sorrell Lawrence?"

Abby nodded.

"Well, she *just* walked in."

As a matter of fact, Abby could have figured that out without looking. Whereas Alice's voice was loud and warm, Sorrell's was penetrating and demanding. Though not actually raised, it carried, filled with the confidence that Sorrell would have her own way and have it without delay.

"I'm so sorry I'm a bit late. I had a very important call about a house I've got listed down in the Valley. But Cindy, could you please," the "please" being like a knife through butter, "start on me as soon as possible?"

Fortunately, this was quite possible because Cindy, Abby's stylist, was all ready to pop Abby under the drier. The three women exchanged greetings. Then Cindy settled Abby under a drier and provided her with a recent copy of *People*. Alice's coif took a bit longer, but soon she, too, was settled in to dry.

The heat of the drier together with its steady purr made Abby drowsy. She'd nearly fallen asleep by the time Cindy retrieved her. Once the pins and curlers and other paraphernalia had been removed, the effect was indeed astonishing. Cindy had been as good as her word. Abby's natural red highlights had reappeared, and traces of some new highlights gave still more life to her hair and hence to her face. No attempt had been made to disguise the narrow line of gray that swept up the from the left side of her forehead. Although the curlers had given Abby cause for concern, Cindy had refrained from turning her into a poodle, opting instead for a soft, layered look. Abby thought that at last she really did look human! Almost a new woman. Too bad Cindy couldn't work her magic internally as well as externally, wash away the pain of Bob's death and the despair engendered by the catheter.

Alice, on the other hand, finished looking the same as always—white curls massed about a round, smiling face with full, pink cheeks that reminded Abby of Mrs. Santa Claus.

"Tell me more about Sorrell," Abby asked Alice when they were back in the car. "I gather she has claims on Jim Wilson?"

"Not *serious* ones, my dear," Alice assured her as she maneuvered the enormous vehicle out of the confines of the parking lot. "Although they do go back together a fairly long ways. Jim and Sorrell were both in real estate on the coast. Jim was a developer, and I get the impression that Sorrell was more than a tad jealous of him since she wanted to be the head honcho, planner/developer for her own project. Only somehow she never got the chance. Well, anyway, she didn't drop any big money when land values slumped. Things were pretty stale in California for a while so she came here, got an Arizona broker's license, and at some point looked up her old friend Jim, who had come to Arizona and taken up mining. All business, you see." Alice reached over and gave Abby's hand a little pat. "I'm sure Jim has given her some good entrees."

Remembering the predatory gleam in Sorrell's eyes at the Olsons', Abby didn't buy the "all business" reading of the relationship. Undoubtedly it was just as well that between failing kidneys and dialysis she herself had no designs on the man. Abby recalled the leopard-print party dress Sorrell had worn. Like a big cat, the woman struck her as being potentially dangerous. She was certainly determined to have her own way and didn't seem the type to give any quarter.

"And how has business been for Sorrell?"

"Booming," Alice confirmed what Abby had already surmised. "She works primarily in the Valley—Phoenix, Scottsdale, Paradise Valley. But enough of her clients from down there come up here in the summer to make it profitable for her to work this market, too. As you know, there are some *very nice* developments in this area."

"Like the one your place is in."

"Well, thank you, my dear. Yes, like that, and since the homes are rather pricey, Sorrell does quite well while getting out of the heat."

"I wouldn't think the heat would bother her."

Alice laughed broadly at that, although Abby hadn't meant her comment quite the way Alice interpreted it. "She's a cold one, isn't she? Do anything, absolutely *anything* for a sale. But I've never thought it was the money so much as a sense of control. That woman wants to dominate. Which is, of course, why she and Jim could *never* have a lasting relationship. He's tolerant enough of strong women, actually seems to enjoy them, but he's not the sort ever to become 'Mr. Sorrell Lawrence.' So don't look at him as taken."

As if, Abby thought, she really wanted him or anyone else right now. Give her the slightest clue to what happened to the Alfa Romeo or to her friend Bob, and she would be well satisfied.

* * *

"I gather that you don't think Bob's death was natural."

Abby shook her head. Not that any drug-induced death could properly be categorized as "natural," but she knew David Neale was really asking if Bob had deliberately been doing drugs, and she was as sure as she was of anything that he hadn't. She'd thought that ground had already been covered, but evidently David was double-checking.

They sat in the fading evening light on the back porch in large, dark green old Lloyd Loom lawn chairs with their elegant wicker look. The chairs were provided with patterned green and white Sumbrella pillows, which could resist the water should the rain ever blow in. Bats, tiny winged forms against the pearl gray sky, darted precipitously after insects. Lights began to go on in the neighborhood. After his nightly tour of inspection around the yard, Francis stretched out on his stomach at Abby's feet, his long nose extending beyond his front paws, his ears standing up at the ready so that, Abby presumed, even in his somnolent state he would miss nothing. At the rear his little white paws with their bottom pads up like tiny black cushions continued on a direct line with his elongated body.

"Henderson may well agree with you. Only if something doesn't turn up to prove otherwise, I'm sure he'll have to let the matter drop."

"Yes, I don't suppose he'll have a choice."

That evening Abby hadn't mentioned the "m" word, saying

nothing more of murder by accidental overdose and certainly not raising the possibility of murder with premeditation. After some deliberation she'd assured herself that Henderson was a competent police officer. If there were anything to investigate along those lines he'd look into it. As for being in any danger herself, on further reflection she seriously doubted it. Why had such an absurd idea popped into her mind? She'd never heard that paranoia was a symptom of her disease, but at this point she wasn't all that confident in her mental abilities. She didn't want to make an absolute fool of herself by suggesting that Bob's death might have any implications for her own safety.

"It's a shame for someone to die so young. And, based on your impressions, someone with so much promise."

"Yes," Abby murmured. "Such a dreadful waste of potential." She wasn't sure she was up to discussing Bob any more, or anything else for that matter. She felt detached, like a balloon wafting gently on a light breeze, occasionally touching ground and lightly bouncing up again, but mostly just floating along. As she could hardly attribute such a sensation to a half a glass of Sauvignon Blanc, she assumed it was some sort of reaction, both physical and mental, to a moment of calm after the recent stress and the overload on her sensory system.

Perhaps the sleeping pill last night had also played its part. Heaven knew that since then she had done a remarkable amount of sleeping. When Lieutenant Henderson departed around noon, she had chatted with Becky and talked to Alice. Then Francis, who never passed up the opportunity for a snooze, and she had returned to bed for a short nap before Alice arrived to take her to the beauty parlor. Later she had almost fallen asleep again under the drier.

Arriving home once more she had been determined to avoid yet another nap, and so took Francis on a short walk. As they meandered through the pines, the thought of Bob and his death never strayed far from her mind. She recalled *The Wanderer*, one of her favorite Anglo-Saxon poems, and the Wanderer's heartfelt lament that "No man is living/no comrade left." The poor man. With his lord gone, his kinsmen and comrades as well, the very structure of his world had ceased to exist. All had been conquered by war and fate. Through the stanzas of the poem, the crashing seas and the cry of the sea bird echoed the Wanderer's wail of woe and created a chorus for his grief. Nature itself gave tongue to his thoughts. The result was an heroic dirge, a great drama in spite of its short length, a wonderful poem that, even in translation, spoke eloquently over the centuries.

Here, she had reflected, it could not be more different. No drama, no tumult, no reverberations of grief troubled the Coconino National Forest; no driving storm, no snow, no hail, no tossing sea. The forest remained mute. Only the nearly inaudible hum of insects, the chirp of a somnolent bird, and the occasional rustle of some unseen creature passing through last year's dried pine needles suggested sensate life beyond her own and that of the faithful Francis. It was as if Bob had simply disappeared as did the insects with the frost. This seemed very wrong indeed. Someone should make more of his life. Someone should loudly protest his death. His beloved forest should break its silence and offer a eulogy.

Her mood had lifted only when she returned to the house to find that David had produced another superb meal. After dinner they had settled companionably on the porch with Francis. Abby found it strange that, though she had known this man somewhat less than twenty-four hours, she felt very comfortable with him. Perhaps this had a lot to do with the fact that last night he had seen her at her worst—strung out, hysterical, weeping and out of control, all the things she never wanted to be. After that there could be no pretense, no image building, and certainly no presentation of a refined and finished self.

She recalled her thoughts when she walked out of the doctor's office after the presence of her disease had been confirmed. She'd realized then that she could never go back to being the person she had been before the diagnosis. The world as she knew it had been shattered, and along with it her self-image. Maybe she would never be able to put the pieces of herself back together. Maybe, like the Wanderer, the best she could hope for was simply to soldier on, like him keeping her own counsel and trying to do her best, whatever that was, to stand steadfast against the forces of fate and annihilation.

She shook her head in disgust. How lugubrious!

The ringing of the phone interrupted her gloomy meditation, and David glanced quizzically at her.

"I'll answer it," she told him. "It's probably my sister." But it was Sada Anand, to whom she immediately offered her condolences.

"Yes, it's an enormous loss for all of us," Sada Anand replied quietly. "I called to tell you that there will be a memorial service, or rather 'a celebration of Bob's life' at our home next Saturday, a week from today. Seven p.m. The professor's invited, too, if he's still here." Evidently Sada Anand had caught a glimpse of her neighbor coming to or going from the house. Or perhaps Lieutenant Henderson had said something. "And Francis, of course."

"Oh, Sada Anand, what can I do to help you?"

She hesitated for a moment before replying. "There is one thing. You've met Pam Haines?"

"Not yet, but I rather feel as if I know her."

"Could you call her about the memorial service? I've got the number here."

"Certainly."

As soon as she heard the phone click and got the dial tone, Abby called Pam.

"Yes, yes, I'll be there." The poor girl sounded as if she might break down and cry. Abby hated to end the conversation while Pam was in that state, so she chatted a little bit with her about Bob. When Pam sounded a little more together, Abby brought up the subject of One Universe.

"Bob was getting very interested in One Universe, wasn't he?"

"Oh, yes. He was working on a web site, and I know it would have been really awesome."

"I gather that he was good with computers."

"Very good. At least that's what people said."

"You know, I feel guilty because I've been so out of it lately, worrying about my own problems. I just haven't been. . . well, very focused. Do you think something had gone so wrong with Bob's life that it drove him back into drugs?"

"No!" Pam replied vehemently.

"That's what I think, too. But keep your ears open. If we could find out more about his activities before he died we might find a clue to help explain what happened. Let's get together and talk sometime." *And when you're feeling less heartsick, I'll ask you about the missing Alfa Romeo,* Abby added to herself. She gave Pam her telephone number.

"One more thing, Pam. Bob was a good person, and he liked you very much. I know his death must be extremely difficult for you, but hang onto that thought."

"Yeah, he was special," the girl replied in a muted, tear-filled voice.

Abby rejoined David and told him about Sada Anand's plans. "Thank goodness somebody will be doing something. I was definitely feeling the lack. Will you still be here for it?"

"I'd like to be. There's always plenty of work to do here, and the Khalsas sound like very nice people. Colorado can wait a few more days."

Belatedly it occurred to Abby that she was occupying this man's house. "Where will you stay?"

"Don't worry. As I said, I can always bunk with a colleague from the University."

She hadn't thought about the logistics. For some reason she had just taken David Neale's presence for granted. This was, after all, his home.

"Wouldn't it be easier for you if you stayed here?" she asked. Of course David Neale might be dangerous or quirky, which could amount to the same thing. You never knew in today's world. But with the Khalsas and Lieutenant Henderson, to say nothing of Becky, looking over his shoulder, what could he do? Of course she would lock her door. However, David didn't look like he was so desperate he would leap out of bed to try to seduce her, lock or no lock. In fact, even with the much improved hair, which he had actually noticed and commented favorably on, she thought that, seeing her in her present state, seduction would be the last thing on any man's mind. Also there were her vague and probably unfounded suspicions about Bob's death. Not that she *really* thought she might be in any danger, but for the time being it was nice to know that someone else would be around the house.

"It would be easier for me," David answered slowly. "But not necessary if I'm creating an inconvenience."

"I gather that you will be spending most of your time at the University."

"So true. I could give you a week's free rent."

"Just cook dinner." She thought back with pleasure to tonight's repast: chicken breasts sliced thin and marinated in soy sauce, then grilled with strips of red bell pepper over mesquite and served on curried rice with diced vegetables. David had complemented the main course with a green salad embellished with tomatoes, red onions and a touch of feta cheese, which he topped off with a light vinegar and oil dressing. So much better than anything she could have come up with! "I don't have the energy to fend much for myself in the kitchen, and I don't find eating alone in a restaurant particularly fun. How much Thai take-out can one person consume?"

"A deal," David laughed. "You've got yourself a deal."

* * *

Pam wasn't sure whether she felt better or worse after talking with Abby Taylor. She missed Bob so very much. Even hearing his name made her want to cry. But at least he hadn't dropped her. He *had* liked her. If she could believe Abby Taylor, he *had* cared about her.

Pam felt restless. Even without her roommates, the tiny shared quarters were closing in on her. She had to get out, *do something*. Well, she had been wanting to talk to Titus and now was as good a time as any. She was pretty sure where she'd find him.

Sure enough. She located Titus in the rundown bar he preferred. He sat alone reading what looked in the dim light suspiciously like a book of poetry. If that was the case, it was poetry in a most unlikely setting. Pam's eyes drifted from the scarred wooden floor to the high ceiling of pressed tin. She took in the decorations, a couple of animated neon beer signs together with a few posters, mostly advertising events that had happened long ago, taped to the yellowing once-ivory or even white walls. However, although the floor and walls might not be much, the ceiling with its intricate pattern was gloriously vintage and the bar that ran down one long side of the shoebox-shaped room was awesome indeed. It was a long bar of some well-polished dark wood so smooth and glowing that its surface could have been marble. Behind it was an elaborately carved back bar of a somewhat lighter colored wood inset with beveled mirrors clouded with age. She speculated that the bar and back bar were probably there at the end of the nineteenth century when cowboys rode in from the Hashknife outfit where they ran sixty thousand cows over two million acres of grassland. Or at least that's what they'd said on the special about Northern Arizona she'd seen on TV. But that was then and now was now. A television mounted on the wall at the far end of the bar and kept running nonstop grounded the bar's patrons firmly in the present.

Although it was Saturday night, the place wasn't doing a great deal of business. A few men watched sporting events on television, a fat business type with his well-rouged lady friend with a laquered coif tucked their ample stomachs in around a small square table, and a couple of cowboys at the opposite end of the bar from the television watchers each had a beer in hand and a foot on the rail. Pam had learned about cowboys that you could tell the real thing by looking at their hips. An old cowboy might grow a gut, but his hips remained narrow, his ass flat forever.

"Hi, Titus."

"Pam! But this is a strange place to be seeing our little Midwesterner. I hope you're not trying to cage a beer."

"No, no beer." As a matter of fact she wasn't of legal age, although in a place like this they were unlikely to card her unless she tried to order something.

"You've heard about Bob?" she asked as she sat down uninvited.

"Terrible news. Jesus, Mary, Joseph."

For a few moments they recalled good things about Bob and speculated on the manner of his death.

"You were working with him on some computer projects, weren't you?" Pam asked when the conversation started to lag.

"Oh, the web page he was designing was amazing."

"But there was more to it than that, wasn't there?" She was guessing, but the tiny start on Titus's part suggested she wasn't far off the mark. Considering the time Bob and Titus had spent together, there just had to have been more than the web page, she'd reasoned.

Titus turned his beer bottle around absently, then looked at her thoughtfully. "I guess it won't hurt to talk about it. I promised Bob I'd wouldn't say anything, but that was because he didn't want to be getting into any trouble."

"Whatever he was doing won't hurt him now," Pam responded sadly.

Titus took a long swig of beer. "I suppose there'd be no harm in telling you. Bob was doing some hacking, checking out that Pycenium Mine. Not changing anything, mind you. Just taking a look-see."

"He wasn't afraid of getting caught?" Pam's voice arced up, expressing her shock and surprise. And she'd been so sure Bob wouldn't try anything illegal.

"Evidently hackers don't look at what they're doing as being really wrong, at least if they don't make any changes. And they don't think they will ever get caught. Bob said somebody'd have to be top notch to catch up with him, although I got the impression he didn't think such a thing was really possible."

"But why? Why was he doing it?"

Titus stared up at the intricately patterned ceiling for a long moment or two.

"Lying in front of bulldozers, monkey wrenching, waving placards—that sort of thing gets people's attention, but only for awhile. Something like a hazardous waste spill hits them hard, but as you heard Peter Rivers say awhile back, it's fucking dangerous. On the other hand," a malicious glint appeared in his eye, "get any project wound up in U.S. government red tape, and everything grinds to a standstill. Maybe indefinitely."

Titus drank some more beer while Pam pondered what

he'd said.

"You've been reading up on the Mining Law?"

"I know something about it," she hedged.

"Then you probably know that to hold onto mining claims you have to do at least one hundred dollars worth of work on them a year—a significant amount back in the 1870s. Not much today, but now there's a hell of a lot of paperwork. Forms to fill out. Affidavits to sign. Christ only knows what all else. I don't know the ins and outs myself, but a friend of mine in the Sierra Club does."

Pam nodded. It made sense to her. So much of life evolved from forms. University classes, driving a car, taxes, getting a credit card. Probably you had to fill out a form to die, she thought with uncharacteristic black humor.

"The idea, a damned good one if I do say so myself, was to find out if the Pycenium had slipped up anywhere. Then point out where they had mucked up to whatever agency's supposed to be overseeing that area. For the most part Forest Service, I suppose. The Forest Service isn't very happy to have to deal with situations like the Pycenium in the first place. They don't like the destruction in the forest, and sometimes these mines end up blocking forest service roads, which is a real nuisance for their personnel. The mines can be a real pain in the ass. Also the Forest Service gets a lot of flak from the public. When people realize what's happening in 'their' forest, people start bitching, although there's not a damn thing Forest Service can do."

"And if the Pycenium missed a piece of paperwork?"

"The Forest Service or whoever ought to catch it. But sometimes they miss things, too. On the other hand, if we could point out anything that's been overlooked, they'd act. They'd have to. At the very least, you'd be looking at a snarl of red tape that could tie things up for a hell of a long time."

"So did Bob find anything?" Pam asked eagerly.

"He seemed pretty excited at the beginning of the week, only he wouldn't say anything definite. I 'liberated' some papers from the mine office during the demonstrations—and damn well managed to drop some of them! But Bob said what I gave him was a big help. Like an ass, I didn't make copies. No telling where they are now. And no telling where the information he dug up hacking has disappeared to. I'd sure like to see what got his interest up."

Titus finished his beer, then looked at Pam speculatively.

"Do you know that sister of Bob's?"

"I'm going to a celebration of Bob's life that she's planning."

"Do you think she'd be letting you look through his things? To look for records from the Pycenium and for disks."

"Disks?" Pam cocked her head.

"Now I know I'm not very knowledgeable about computers. After all, men got on for millennia without them and didn't feel the want so far as I can see. But today, as I understand it, if you're wanting to store information from one of the beasts, you do it on another computer or on disks more often than on paper—hard copy, they call it—which is really quite fine as far as I'm concerned because it's saving the trees."

"Trees?" Titus was off on one of his tangents and she wasn't quite sure she was following him.

"Paper is made from trees, Little One, or didn't you know that?"

"Yes, of course," Pam replied shortly. As a matter of fact, she wasn't "little." For all her sins, most especially a love of chocolate, she was definitely bigger than Titus.

"What disks are made of I don't know. Probably plastic like everything else today. But not from the Good Lord's growing things. Anyway, if Bob wanted to store his material and he didn't have a computer of his own, he'd be making disks, wouldn't he? Or would he be running hard copy so he wouldn't lose anything?"

"I honestly don't know," Pam answered, now following the drift of Titus's conversation. "Maybe both. But I doubt Sada Anand would feel comfortable having me scrounging through her dead brother's stuff. On the other hand, I think I know somebody she wouldn't object to." Well, she'd done her part. It looked like the ball would be in Abby Taylor's court now.

CHAPTER 9

Sunday morning at Macy's Coffee House and Bakery. Not a bad place to be, mused Abby. The traffic on the back street where the restaurant was located was minimal this early. A couple of blocks away the roar of Sante Fe Avenue, which for a way paralleled the railroad tracks, had softened to a gentle purr. The clear tones of a church bell rang through the still, sun-filled air.

While David went in to get them something to eat, Abby and Francis secured a sidewalk table and settled themselves comfortably. Dogs weren't allowed in the restaurant, but in any case it was far too pleasant to be indoors. Although the days were hotter now than promised by the Chamber of Commerce—up into the nineties, which was highly unusual for Flagstaff—mornings such as this were fresh and beautiful, a peaceful, gentle opening to the day.

Macy's had a friendly, casual college atmosphere with a heterogeneous collection of chairs and tables, and not too many of the latter so that any free space got taken, making it a nice way to meet new people. In this way Abby had made the acquaintance of a well-read, well-traveled woman from the French Department at the University, someone she had resolved to get to know better when things were less hectic, or she had more energy, or perhaps both. She really had isolated herself far too much, she admitted, and for that there was no excuse, since Flagstaff was not a difficult place to meet people with interests similar to her own.

Abby looked up from *The New York Times Book Review*. Oh, God, she thought with a sinking heart. One person in Flagstaff she had met and wasn't too sure she wanted to see, or at least not at present, was at hand. Undoubtedly he would bring up Bob, something she didn't want to think about now. The wound was still far too raw.

"Good morning, Miz Taylor."

"Good morning, Mr. Wilson."

He threw back his head and laughed.

"Okay, we've done the formalities. Can't we just play things California style? First names only? Real casual?"

"Yes, of course, Jim," she responded. California casual in keeping with his khaki shorts, Polo shirt and sandals. It was time, she told herself sternly, to get off her high horse. Jim Wilson was not really obnoxious or offensive—just a little too big, too handsome, too outgoing. How could anyone condemn a man for that? And probably none of this would have mattered in the slightest had "The Disease" not made her feel so vulnerable. She definitely didn't want to get involved with *anyone* just now, and particularly not someone stalked by Sorrell Lawrence, whom she had begun to think of as the leopard lady. On the other hand, she could at least be polite.

At that moment a low rumble from under the table suggested that someone else was skeptical of the interruption.

"Hush," Abby commanded.

"Will your dog allow me to sit down?"

"Of course. Go right ahead."

He joined her, removing his sunglasses and placing them before him on the table.

"Do you go everywhere with your little dog? Everywhere but cocktail parties, that is? And is your friend Robert Curtis in tow as well?" Jim asked a little too heartily. He was clearly trying very hard to be sociable, but a growl from Francis was enough to throw anyone off his stride, even a big, confident man like Jim Wilson.

"No, Bob isn't here."

"Oh? I haven't seen him lately. No more spying around the mine. Did he move on?"

"No," Abby replied, hoping to bring this conversation to a quick end. "He died."

"Died?" Wilson stared at her. "My God, he was young. An accident?"

"Yes." Abby saw no reason to elaborate.

"I'm sorry, I didn't know." Absently Jim ran a hand back over his head. Abby noticed that the gray touches at his temples set off his dark blond hair as effectively as if they'd been planned that way. What surely had been foreseen was the way the sea blue of his short-sleeve Polo shirt brought out the deep, marine blue of his eyes. "I've been out of touch with things in Flagstaff. Been down in Phoenix on business. Had you known him long? Was he a special friend?"

"I had only known him since earlier in the summer. He was staying with his sister and brother-in-law, who live next door to the house I've rented for the summer. But yes, he was a special friend." She smiled bleakly.

"Again, I'm very sorry."

A whistle bleated mournfully and they could hear a train chugging slowly along the Santa Fe tracks. Wilson let it pass before speaking again.

"Alice Olson mentioned that you're an English professor but not teaching now," he said, deftly changing the subject. "I think she said something about a leave of absence?"

"That's right. A leave of absence." Again she felt no need to add extra details. "How's the pumice?" she countered, effecting her own conversational redirection. David was certainly taking his time, she thought. He'd probably gotten deep in conversation with a colleague. That sort of thing happened at Macy's.

"Fine, thanks. Great business. We're thinking of expanding."

"What's pumice used for, besides stonewashing?" she asked curiously.

"As a matter of fact, only a proportionately small amount is used for stonewashing. That takes a special grade. The largest percentage of pumice is used for construction, especially for building materials like concrete blocks. With pumice you can manufacture a lighter block, one that's easier to handle and needs less additional support in multi-story buildings. Good thermal and insulating qualities, too."

"Oh?" She thought that if anybody could be said to wax eloquent about pumice, that somebody was certainly Jim Wilson.

"Pumice's also used in landscaping. Lightweight boulders, ground cover, and so forth. And for abrasives—cleaning products for grills, swimming pools, and that sort of thing. Oh, there're other uses, too, but construction is by far the most important. It accounts for about sixty percent of the market. Stonewashing is only about nine percent at best."

"And you are able to mine in the National Forest because of this 1872 Mining Law?"

Wilson gave her a quizzical look. "You've been doing your homework, haven't you? And you're right, but only because we're dealing with a special grade of pumice. The idea of the Mining Law was, and is, to encourage development of national resources, specifically the discovery and exploitation of valuable mineral deposits. 'Valuable' is the key word here. If the mineral isn't valuable then you can't stake claims under the Mining Law."

"Pumice is valuable? I mean, of course it's worth something or someone like you wouldn't mine it. But valuable like, say, gold or copper?"

"Our grade of pumice, pumice used for stonewashing, is. It's valuable because it's rare. The old law of supply and demand, you know." He smiled winningly, showing teeth as white and straight and even as Sorrell's. Did all Californians look like candidates for toothpaste ads? "Other pumice, like the pumice used for building materials, for example, falls under the 1955 Surface Resources Act along with minerals like rock and gravel. If you want to mine that sort of pumice you've got to buy the land, not claim it. And since a person, or in our case a company, couldn't buy land in a national forest, you're right about the Mining Law."

Abby had to admit that Jim Wilson could be affable when he wanted to be, or perhaps when not challenged and put on the defensive. To her surprise, he was refreshingly knowledgeable and straightforward in his answers.

"Why pumice to begin with? I mean, you didn't start out in mining. Did you go prospecting for it?"

"No," he laughed. "The days of the old prospector with his mule were pretty much over by the time they passed the Mining Law in 1872, although there've always been a few one-man, or one-woman, operations. In fact there are still enclaves in the mountains in California where some old-timers do just enough mining so they can hang onto the land and eke out a small living. But as for me, I started out in real estate development in California. Then the market slipped and I got caught. After that little fiasco, I thought I'd try something else for a change. By chance I met Shorty Dean. He's the one with the mining skills. I got the backers, worked on getting the necessary permits from the Forest Service, and now run the business end. It's. . . ."

"*Latte* and a sweet roll," David announced as he placed her food before Abby and then sat down himself with his own, more substantial breakfast. Today instead of howling critters, his tee shirt sported a peregrine falcon, great wings stretched out against a vivid aqua background. Beneath the falcon the shirt announced "San Pedro Riparian Area, Arizona Nature Conservancy." Abby thought that although the professor was undoubtedly an ardent conservationist, he certainly didn't favor the granola clothing so beloved of that species.

"David, this is Jim Wilson, the pumice miner I mentioned. Jim, meet David Neale, a member of the College of Forestry at the University. My landlord this summer."

The two men eyed each other curiously, even somewhat antagonistically, she wondered? Or was this just normal male testosterone? In any case, she had given them a topic of conversation in common. She ate her roll and drank her coffee as the air filled with references to "fugitive dust," environmental impact statements and particulates.

Then, excusing herself from the men, who were deep into a discussion of current U.S. Forest Service policy, she went in to buy some bakery goods for Pooh-Bear, as she had begun to think of the little girls, and their family. Though the Khalsas were vegetarians, they were one of the less extreme sorts and countenanced eggs, milk, cheese, butter, and other dairy products. Thus Abby felt safe in stocking up on an assortment of breads, rolls and cookies. She reasoned that Sada Anand could freeze some of them and have treats for the girls for the rest of the week. Also, much as she dreaded it, she could use the opportunity of delivering the goodies to ask Sada

Anand about following up on Pam's suggestion, made by phone at the crack of dawn that morning, to look at Bob's possessions in hopes that disks or something else that provided some insight into his snooping for One Universe might turn up.

* * *

Later, when she and Francis dropped the things by the Khalsas', she was glad she had made the effort to buy the bakery goods. Pooh and Bear drooped as if someone had pulled a plug and their usual vitality had drained out of them like used bathwater out of a tub. The sight of the treats and the chance to love Francis helped restore their spirits somewhat, although there was still a long way to go until they had returned to anything like normal. Abby speculated that the loss of their beloved uncle would always leave a large void in their lives.

As for Sada Anand, she looked tired and frail, as vulnerable as a delicate, attenuated icicle caught in the rays of the rising sun. Abby hesitated momentarily. Though she had experienced her own share of grief in her lifetime, she was never quite sure how to express her concern and caring when someone else was suffering, particularly someone as self-contained as the tall, slender woman in white standing before her. Then she embraced Sada Anand gently, physical actions sometimes speaking more clearly than words.

"I miss him so much," she heard Sada Anand whisper. "Our whole growing up was Bob and me against the world. We supported each other, always. Having him gone is like losing part of myself."

"I can only imagine, but I think I'd feel the same way if I lost Becca. She is so very much a part of my life."

"Oh, it's so awful." Sada Anand sighed, then rallied. "Come, let's have a cup of herbal tea. How about Red Zinger?"

Abby wasn't sure herbal tea was what she wanted after the *latte*, but there was nothing for it except to follow Sada Anand's lead.

"I had it so much easier than Bob," Sada Anand confided when they were seated with two steaming mugs of tea in the immaculately white kitchen, the girls and Francis in the backyard where Sada Anand could keep an eye on them. "Being a girl, no one had any great expectations for me. I floated through high school, floated through one of those two-year women's colleges, really glorified finishing schools, which still exist in some corners of the South. I guess I would have continued to float until a friend asked me what I was going to do when I graduated. Of course I didn't have the vaguest idea and asked her what she had in mind. Physics, she said. She had been accepted at MIT."

Sada Anand took a bracing swallow of tea. "Now I'm sure this doesn't sound strange to you, but to me at the time it was utterly unreal. Physics? MIT? The girl was bright, no doubt about it, also very popular and very attractive. I guess I'd assumed that she would do quality volunteer work, raise a family, maybe even run for the state legislature at some point down the road. But physics? All of a sudden a whole new world opened up."

"And you went for it?"

"Big time," she said, taking another swallow. "Our parents didn't care. Arizona State University? Acceptable. Nursing? Well, at least I'd know what to do when a kid, presumably mine, ran a fever. Becoming a Sikh? Not part of the game plan, but after all, Arizona is a long way from Florida. Poor Bob messed up on home turf. Unacceptable, but totally," she observed bitterly.

They reminisced about Bob, his potential, his talents. His expertise with the computer came up quite naturally and gave Abby the opportunity to ask about any traces he might have left about a project or projects for One Universe. Very gently, Abby raised the possibility that this might have something to do with his death, though as far as she could see any connection was tenuous at best.

"I would do almost anything to know more about why he died, and you're welcome to look at anything you want," Sada Anand told her. "But I should warn you, Lieutenant Henderson's people have already checked very thoroughly, everything from Bob's personal things to Soul Singh's computer. There was nothing there, nothing at all."

"Then there's no point in me going over the same ground twice." Abby felt greatly relieved not to have to paw through the possessions of a dead man, but she had followed up because she thought Pam's point about learning more of Bob's actions prior to his death had been a good one.

"Actually I really shouldn't say that nothing was there," Sada Anand corrected herself. "Bob had created a file on Soul Singh's computer about the forest—things he'd read, things he'd seen. He was so protective of it! Lieutenant Henderson said it looked like he'd been in a brawl shortly before he died." Sada Anand's long fingers played with the hem of the white tunic she wore over white slacks. "I'll just bet he ran across some of those guys he thought were so destructive!"

Again the idea of an accidental overdose flitted through Abby's mind and again she rejected it. Partiers, bikers, whatever, any of them might pummel Bob, but she didn't think they'd shoot him full of expensive drugs. Though such an act might have served as a warning, a severe beating would have done equally well, and the fact that Bob's body had been bruised prior to death suggested that someone had acted on that thought.

"Is there anything I can do to help you?" Abby asked when they'd finished the tea and conversation had frittered out.

"As a matter of fact, there is." Sada Anand left the room and returned with an armload of books. "Bob checked these out of the library. Would you be going that way next week? They're due on Tuesday, and I'm just not going to have much time."

"No problem. I'll take them on Wednesday on my way back from the nephrologist's. I think there's a day grace period, but one way or another, don't worry. I'll get them there."

* * *

Bob certainly had been doing a lot of reading and just the sort of thing she had expected, Abby thought as she put the books on the small table in the front hall of David Neale's home. *Fire on the Rim*, a book about fighting forest fires at the Grand Canyon, *The Mining Law: A Study in Perpetual Motion* by John D. Leshy, and *Golden Dreams, Poisoned Streams*, also on mining and put out by something called the Mineral Policy Center. There were two of David Neale's books as well. They were about ponderosa forests, most especially the effect on them of forest fires. Having not seen any of her landlord's writing—like many professors he probably kept that sort of thing at his office at the University—she turned to one of his books and was soon engrossed.

Not only was David's subject matter far more interesting than she had imagined, but he wrote beautifully. His theme was the interrelatedness of all the elements of the forest, the dynamic tensions that wove them together. Fires were an integral part of all this, both a cleansing and a chance for rebirth, especially since certain seeds required the intensity of a fire to germinate. He traced the plants as they returned to a burned area and described the gradual reintegration of the fauna in a manner that Abby felt sure was technically correct but was also accessible to the general reader. What a pleasure not to have to wade through academic verbiage!

"Are you taking up a new field of study? Don't tell me I've got some serious academic competition," David laughed when he returned home to find the pile of books in the hall, one of his own on top. The fact that it was Sunday had not deterred him from spending time at his office at the University.

"I'm quite satisfied with the Anglo-Saxons, thank you," Abby replied. "These are books Bob Curtis checked out of the library. It looks like he was doing just what I suggested, getting a bit of background on forests in this area and finding out something about you and your research."

"A good ploy," David admitted as he joined Abby in the living room. "All academics are suckers for someone who shows an informed interest in their particular area of expertise."

"You can now consider my interest somewhat informed. I've been reading this book of yours." She held it up for him to see the cover, gold lettering over a photograph of deep green ponderosas. "It's all very interesting but particularly the part about fire. Fire seems to be your specialty. You said your son was fighting fires on the Arizona Strip. He must have inherited your genes."

"Andrew?" David asked as he settled himself on the couch and stretched out his Levi legs. The great screech owl on his tee shirt looked ready to flap away. Abby had thought she'd accumulated an interesting collection of tee shirts over the years, but now she had to acknowledge that she was far outclassed. "I guess you could say that I shared my interests with him, but nothing through the genes since I'm not his natural father."

"Oh?"

"Nina was married briefly to a Sioux. She left him shortly after Andrew was born."

"And the tribe, or in this case tribes, let you keep him after his mother died?" Abby asked curiously. "I thought they vehemently opposed allowing one of their own to be raised outside their tradition."

"Tribe, singular. In a case like Andrew's, the parents have the right to decide on the child's tribe. Since the marriage was breaking up and Andrew was going with Nina, they declared him a Navajo. When Nina and I married, I legally adopted the child. However, if the Navajo Nation had thrown its weight against my custody, I can pretty well guess who would have won. But by the time Nina was killed the child's natural father had died. A swimming accident in some river where he shouldn't have been swimming," and wouldn't have been if he'd been sober, Abby thought she heard David add.

"I had already established a good relationship with her people. I respect their tradition, and they could see I had no intention of standing between Andrew and them." He reached over and turned on a lamp. The light was fading now and the lamp by which Abby had been reading left dark, shadowy pools in the corners of the room which the second light did not entirely dispel.

"They also recognized the fact that not only did I love Andrew, I could give him advantages here he couldn't get on the reservation. Fortunately, Flagstaff isn't all that far away. I made sure that while he was growing up he saw a lot of his mother's family. He spent extra time with them during summer vacation and always attended any ceremony or any other sort of gathering they suggested. He's absolutely bilingual, which is a great advantage for a kid no matter what the second language."

"And you read your Tony Hillerman?"

"And I read my Tony Hillerman." He grinned at her. "You know they use his books in some of the schools up on the Big

Reservation?"

"I heard that somewhere. And spending so much time up on the Navajo/Hopi Reservation is how you became sensitized to diabetes?" She remembered that one of the first things David had asked about when he knew her kidneys were failing was whether she had diabetes.

"Yes, it's rampant. And, you know, I still have no idea what your disease is, if you don't mind my asking?"

A polite phrase for him to add, but Abby much doubted David Neale would hesitate to ask most anything if it piqued his curiosity.

"It's called autosomal dominant polycystic kidney disease. Dreadfully cumbersome name, isn't it? It's generally referred to as PKD."

For a moment David's forehead creased in thought. "I've never heard of it," he admitted.

"Most people haven't. That's strange because, as the doctor who first diagnosed it told me, it's by far the most prevalent of any of the potentially life-threatening hereditary diseases. In fact, PKD affects more Americans than the combined number of those suffering from cystic fibrosis, sickle-cell anemia, muscular dystrophy, hemophilia, Downs syndrome and Huntington's disease. But there's been almost no publicity. You come across articles on all sorts of other diseases, often some pretty obscure ones that only affect a handful of people in the entire world. Yet nothing on PKD. I guess kidneys just aren't very glamorous!" Inadvertently she glanced down at the place where the catheter lay coiled like a slumbering serpent beneath her dress.

"So tell me about this autosomal dominant polycystic kidney disease. What is it and what does it do?"

"The first two words refer to its transmission. The disease is hereditary. Any child, male or female, with a PKD parent stands a fifty-fifty chance of inheriting it. The disease is absolutely politically correct," Abby added with a hard, dry little laugh that expressed not an iota of humor. "Not only is sex irrelevant, so too is skin color, ethnic background, sexual preference or any of the other factors some people use to discriminate against others." As when talking to Bob about dialysis, her voice slipped into the neutral mode, presenting the facts purged of all emotion.

"Should we all be so p.c."

"Really. The rest of the name is just what the words suggest— many cysts, specifically many cysts in the kidneys, although sometimes the liver is also affected. Thanks to a mis-programmed gene, cells pump too much fluid into tubes that are only the diameter of a hair. Cysts develop that eventually begin to clog the works and prevent natural kidney function. If the process goes far enough, the kidneys don't function at all."

David got up and went over to the sound system. That afternoon Abby had been listening to classical music on KNAU, but now what she considered one of Flagstaff's all-too-frequent talk shows had come on. Evidently David felt the same way. He turned on the CD player and the rich, liquid sound of Saint-Saëns filled the room.

"You say PKD is very common?" he asked when he had settled back on the couch.

"Very, although at this point it's impossible to come up with an exact body count since it's still so often misdiagnosed. But it's estimated that one in every four hundred to one thousand persons has it; perhaps twelve and a half million people are affected worldwide. But that's just a guess, definitely on the low side, because in some cases it never manifests itself. And even when it does, not all cases become as advanced as mine." Abby ran her fingers through her newly improved locks, a gesture that she would never have made with her old, more formal style. There were, she decided, definitely some advantages to short hair.

"Who had the disease in your family?"

"My father. Becky, my sister, doesn't have the disease, thank God, and obviously I do. We both could have had it, or neither one. There's no way to tell how it's going to play out."

"And your father?" he asked gingerly.

"It killed him."

At that moment the phone rang. Abby reached over and answered it while David wandered off in the direction of the kitchen, presumably to give her some privacy.

"Yes, Tuesday," repeated the cheerful voice of Alice Olson. Abby wasn't at all sure she wanted to take up Alice's invitation to lunch. Or rather to attend a luncheon, which somehow made it sound all that much worse. She had always been loath to interrupt her working day, preferring to have a quick bite in her office than to linger over a larger meal. No working day now, of course, but she felt so damned tired that the very thought of getting dressed to go out was daunting. Yet, what would she do if she didn't accept Alice's truly kind offer? She looked about her as if her landlord's well-filled bookshelves might offer inspiration, but they didn't. Yes, just what would she do? Sit in the house and sulk like a teenager who hadn't been asked out on a date? *Surely you can do better than that, Abby Taylor*, she admonished herself sternly.

For years she had thought about what she might do if only she had a bit more time—the books she wanted to read, the research she would like to tuck into, and the museums she looked forward to visiting with friends. Now she had plenty of time. No money worries, either, thanks to two of her former Vassar College classmates who had turned out to be financial wizards and over the years had coaxed a nice inheritance into something really substantial. Time and money, yes. But no drive, no energy, no will.

Well, maybe she still possessed a sliver of will. She automatically straightened her back in the armchair she had burrowed down into while talking to Alice. Once again she resolved not to let The Disease completely dominate her life. Luncheon with Alice and her cronies might not be anything like a priority, but she was going to go and damn well enjoy it.

"I would be delighted to join you, Alice. What time and where?"

"Oh, I'll pick you up about 11:30, because I'll need to be there a bit early to arrange the flowers."

"I can drive."

"No, I *insist* my dear."

"Won't it be out of your way?"

"Oh, no. I'm going into town for the flowers anyway." Alice swept over her objections. "Tell me, is there *anything* you shouldn't

169

eat? There will be only six of us, so we'll be ordering off the menu. But if you need something special prepared. . . ."

"No, I'll be fine. I just have to watch the salt, but that's not much of a problem in today's world." And any other modifications I can make on my own, she added to herself.

"Then I'll look forward to seeing you Tuesday. No need to dress up in anything fancy. I'll be wearing a skirt because pants don't seem to fit over the old hips so well any more," Alice admitted with a hearty chuckle. "But slacks will be fine if you prefer."

Abby, who would be in Empire-waist dresses that didn't rub the wound for some time, knew she didn't have much choice. Ah, well, one less decision to make.

* * *

Congressman Toby Barrett felt very pleased with himself as he headed toward Capitol Hill on a bright Monday morning. In fact, he was rather pleased with life in general. And that in spite of the weather. He knew that beyond the windows of his Lexus (a fortunate pre-"Great Betrayal" purchase, before that s.o.b. Foster Richmond had played havoc with his fortune) the air was already hot, sticky and polluted. Thank God for refrigeration. Barrett recalled that the British used to give their diplomats extra "hard duty" pay for their stay in Washington's semi-tropical climate. The humidity was what did it. It could easily be over ninety degrees in the shade, with ninety percent humidity, especially in those torrid days before the August recess. Even today the legislators and their staffs suffered when the HVAC systems couldn't cope with the press of humanity jammed into small cubicles.

He glanced beyond the usual snarl of traffic at the scenery. Earlier in the year the azaleas, magnolias, and other spring blossoms had budded pink and white and yellow. But now they had faded away and the capital's mature trees had leafed out rich, green, cloying, rather like the city itself. Too much of everything—wealth, power, intrigue, exotic food, liquor. The list ran on and on. Although it all looked great on the surface, after a while the excess became burdensome. It hemmed a man in, made it hard for him to breathe.

As he cursed the traffic he thought what a contrast this was to the drive he'd taken early this spring with his old high school buddy, his UCLA roommate and frat brother Gene Turney, in Gene's vintage Jag to check out the route for the Copper State 1000. The jet black XKSS had churned up Arizona Highway 666 with what seemed like a million miles of New Mexico floating green and blue off to the east and Christ only knew how many acres of Arizona undulating west like some great fathomless ocean as yet undiscovered by the Conquistadores or anyone else.

It wasn't that the Jag had actually been going that fast—not by present standards anyway. Back in the late Fifties the XKSS had been clocked at 144 mph, 0 to 70 mph in 7.5 seconds, and that under test conditions—nothing like ascending a steep, winding, two-lane mountain road with occasional traffic coming down the other way. But with the steady roar of the fine-tuned engine slipping into higher and lower cadences of sound as the gears moved up or down, the cool dry air riffling his hair which added to the illusion of speed, and the sensation of gliding over patches of shade like shallow ponds of dark water, then skimming smoothly out into the March sunlight again, it had seemed as if they were breaking the sound barrier.

As the Lexus, along with a herd of other vehicles, stalled at yet another stoplight Barrett contrasted his sensations of speed and freedom in the Jag, the world unfurling around him like a morning glory coming into bloom. A taste of raw power, that's what the Jag had really given him. What a feeling! The car, the day, the future Toby envisaged for himself, had all combined to give him a rush that had nothing to do with chemicals.

"What do you think about the Jag?" Gene had raised his voice to be heard over the roar.

"A goddamned miracle. Jesus, I can still remember reading about it in *Autocar* when I was a teenager. I wanted to drive a car like that even more than I wanted to explore what Cindy Schultz had under those pink panties of hers." The two shared high school as well as college memories.

"Quite a gal, our Cindy," Gene remembered.

"Something else," Barrett concurred. The memory of the

dark, moist mystery beneath the panties that she had finally permitted him to explore still stirred him. "But then so is your XKSS. As I said, a goddamned miracle."

"You know that this is one of the originals. Only sixteen were built before the factory burned and destroyed the body jigs. They made a few more later, but then switched over to the D-types."

"Beautiful, just beautiful. And that engine sounds as good as the day it was created."

When Gene had called him in Washington in January, Toby had jumped at the chance to come to Arizona the following spring. Life in Washington had lost its zest. It all seemed stale, spoiled, inconsequential, like Saturday night's street litter on a Sunday morning. Politics, an endless round of posturing and polemics. The monotonous committee meetings, prolix floor speeches with "extended remarks," tedious roll call votes, ubiquitous procedural delays. Although the office technology steadily improved, the demands escalated to match it. There was simply no way to respond satisfactorily to the thousands of phone calls, faxes, e-mails and letters containing trivial, mundane and sometimes quite touching pleas and requests. His staffers, from the dedicated to, he suspected, the duplicitous, from the selfless to the self-serving and solicitous, never seemed to be up to the task.

And always on the horizon yet another election. Every other goddamned year, for Christ's sake, which meant endless fund-raising endeavors. And speaking of money, the Great goddamned Betrayal had left him teetering, if not exactly on the edge of bankruptcy, at least on the brink of a lifestyle that left much to be desired. Oh, a congressman was entitled to generous retirement benefits, and eventually he could prostitute himself as a lobbyist. But this did not compare to having his own personal tidy fortune.

Gene's call had come at the end of a long, gray January day, the sky alternately pissing freezing rain and small, thin flecks of snow. As the traffic around him started to move sluggishly again, Barrett reflected that the capital was always either hot or cold. The damned place was no more temperate than its politics.

The day Gene had called proved damp and cold enough to

penetrate to the marrow. It had been a day so routine that for the life of him he couldn't recall the particulars, only that it had ended with another Washington reception and he'd had at least one too many martinis. By the time he got back to his place his head was already throbbing. And then Gene's cheery voice on the phone. "This spring, would you like to go with me to triple-check the route to be used for the Copper State? In April would you like to act as my co-driver in the event itself?" Would he ever! Not even the news that his nemesis Foster Richmond, with his new toy, the Alfa Romeo 6C 1750, planned to participate in the event had stopped Toby Barrett.

Yes, by God, he would go, he had gone, and it had changed his life. The memory gave him a glow, an enormous feeling of self-satisfaction that bolstered him even as he battled the District's traffic and considered the long, essentially tedious day stretching ahead of him.

* * *

Abby finally caught up with Pam by phone late Monday. "Bob's sister said that Lieutenant Henderson's people went through everything at the Khalsas' carefully. On the computer nothing but some notes on forests. David Neale, my landlord, who's here for a short while, checked his home computer just in case and, again, nothing. I don't know exactly what your friend Titus expected us to find, but it's not there."

"Titus isn't exactly my friend," Pam protested. "But he really cares about One Universe. He thought maybe Bob had found out something about the Pycenium, something that would get it tangled up in red rape and at least slow things down. He said it could be something really simple, just a form that hadn't been filled out."

"You haven't exactly said so, but I gather Bob was doing some hacking?"

"Yeah. But just a look-see. And he wasn't changing anything," Pam added defensively.

Abby was less than thrilled at the news. Again she gazed at her landlord's well-stocked library. Again it failed to give her inspiration.

"Well, Pam, if anything does turn up, which I doubt, I'll let you know. But in the meantime, there's something I want to ask you. Did

One Universe have *anything* to do with the theft of the Alfa Romeo?"

"No. 'Fraid not. We just used that for publicity."

I just hope you're not lying to me, Abby said to herself.

CHAPTER 10

"How's it going, my dear?" Alice asked when she had bundled Abby into her enormous automobile. "The dialysis? Or do you want to talk about it?"

"I really don't mind," Abby replied with what she hoped translated into an upbeat smile. She intended to live up to her resolve to go to the luncheon and damn well enjoy it. She meant to be a highly satisfactory guest as well. "I guess you could say it's going as well as could be expected."

Abby knew she would soon be getting used to the peculiar new sensations, the funny feel of the dialysate trickling into her peritoneal cavity and the relief to her overextended system when the dialysate, along with other accumulated liquid, flowed out. So far she had just practiced once with Lida, then left Frankenthaller's office "dry," that is without any dialysate in her. She would keep up this regime until she felt entirely comfortable with it.

"Anyway, it doesn't hurt," Abby added, trying to be more precise without going into any gory details. "What's hardest is the mental part, not the physical. Knowing that you've lost your independence, that you're dependent on an artificial process to go on living."

"Giving up independence is *dreadfully* hard, and I see it more and more often among people in my age group—although, of course, not because of kidneys. It's usually a matter of driving. A far cry from dialysis, I have to admit. But in Arizona, with so little public transportation, giving up your car means being *terribly* confined and, worst of all, being cut off from your friends," Alice observed as the huge car sailed past a still larger truck. The car made Abby feel as if she were being ferried through space in a cocoon that almost entirely insulated her from the world around. True, she could see beyond its confines. But she could hear nothing other than Alice's voice and the gentle purr of the air conditioning, smell nothing except the floral scent of Alice's perfume mixed with the rich odor of new leather, and feel nothing except its buttery softness. Her own Volvo had proved to be a good, reliable form of transportation; Alice's vehicle raised the idea of transport to an entirely new dimension.

"Daphne Goodson, the reason for this little impromptu luncheon, is going through that now. Her eyesight is dreadful, so she can't drive any longer. Of course, she can afford cabs, but we all want to have our own cars to go when and where the mood strikes us. I guess more than anything driving is a symbol of our independence."

That rang an all-too-familiar bell with Abby.

"Is Daphne from Flagstaff?"

"No, Scottsdale, or maybe it's Paradise Valley. The boundaries are terribly confusing. Sorrell Lawrence is trying to help her sell her big home down there and find a condominium. Or maybe a townhouse. Sorrell invited her up here to get out of the heat for a day or two. Sorrell *does* have her good points, you know, but still, she can be grating," Alice admitted.

Remembering Sorrell's peremptory claim on Jim Wilson and her insistence upon having her hair done *immediately*, Abby silently agreed.

While Alice carried on about the pros and cons of Sorrell Lawrence—a control freak but a very effective Realtor who got the job done—Abby let the words flow over her like the scenery flowing silently past beyond the windows. She'd already come to much the same conclusions. And, in any case, the Realtor, the leopard lady, had little to do with her own life.

Alice really had been kind to pick her up, Abby reflected. The luncheon was to be held at the clubhouse that was part of the exclusive and carefully planned development in which the Olsons lived, but Alice had come all the way into Flagstaff and, flowers or no flowers, had gone out of her way to get her. Abby resolved not to put her out again and to ask for a ride back with one of the other women.

Alice's car swept past the gatehouse. She drove along a forest-lined street until she reached the club house. There she parked, and Abby helped her carry in the flowers. A round table had been set up on a long, covered, but otherwise unenclosed veranda. Alice had brought her own colorful linen napkins, whose abstract pattern matched the flowers—pristine white, deep red, sparkling yellow, cool lavender and a touch of forest green, also the color of the tablecloth. She was still working with the waiter to get everything arranged to her satisfaction when one of the guests, a Gladys something or another, arrived, followed shortly by Martha Van Dyke. It did say something about tolerance or breeding, Abby thought, that the combination of Martha, given her strong opinions about the pumice mine, and Alice Olson, whose husband was a major investor in the Pycenium, was not immediately incendiary. Evidently Alice and Martha both were good friends and supporters of Daphne Goodson, whose needs had priority that day. Abby tried not to look at things from a sexist point of view, but there really was something admirable about the way women could rally around a friend in need without making an issue of it.

Daphne herself turned out to be a pert little old lady who seemed to be doing quite well except for her eyesight. She appeared with Sorrell, beautifully attired as usual, today in beige, raw silk pants with a batik print top in beige, brown and black. With a well-manicured hand resting lightly on Daphne's arm Sorrell guided her around obstacles without drawing attention to the problem. In her other hand Sorrell carried a vase of perfectly beautiful and extremely delicate lavender flowers.

"Oh, Alice, I see you already have flowers for the table," Sorrell said as she got Daphne seated. "I'll put these over here," she said, indicating a serving table, "and you can take them home later."

"They're *lovely,* Sorrel. They look like wildflowers."

"They are. From the forest."

"You shouldn't pick the flowers in the forest," Martha snapped. "What if everybody did that? They could no longer propagate."

"I only picked a few," Sorrell replied with a proud toss of her mane. Clearly the statement was not intended as an apology. "I think the forest can survive that."

"If everybody. . . ."

Alice cleared her throat. "Ladies, if you would please sit down. The waiter is bringing the menus, and he wants to know what you would like to drink."

"Some people never think that the rules apply to *them*," Abby heard Martha mutter, but the older woman didn't pursue the issue.

Given the potential strains at the table, the luncheon went off quite well in Abby's opinion. From beginning to end the focus was Daphne. Her friends clearly yet unobtrusively offered support as she dealt with her eyesight problem as well as her need to make a significant change in her lifestyle, yet another hurdle in the aging process. A recent widow, Daphne was finding the home she and her husband had loved too large and, even with good day help, too much trouble to care for. Sorrell was working with her to find something more practical and convenient, and clearly Sorrell had made up her mind precisely what Daphne ought to be looking for.

"No, you definitely don't want stairs, not even a single step leading down into a sunken living room. It's simply too easy to trip," Sorrell informed her client. "You do, however, want a little space to garden. You can put in a few rose bushes and have the pleasure of puttering around with them. And, Daphne dear, you *do not* want a pool. All these developments have a community pool one can use. It'll be heated all year around, and you won't have to bother with maintenance."

A bit later Abby overheard Sorrell tell Daphne, "No, that's simply too much space. Why bother to buy and maintain all that space when you can entertain at your country club? A smaller place is so much easier to shut up and leave during the summer when you go back east to see your children and grandchildren."

No pool, less space. Just the sorts of things that would lower the price tag and thus the commission. And here Abby had always thought that bright, aggressive Realtors were expected to go for the last farthing! Evidently Sorrell wanted everything to be right even more than she wanted the extra money—but right from whose perspective?

"A very controlling woman," pronounced Martha Van Dyke, who had agreed to take Abby home. "But not unethical, so far as I can see. She really needs greater scope. Although she's been successful here in Arizona, quite successful from what I've heard, I think she requires something more. A bigger project. Something she can mold her own way, be absolutely in control. Those Californians. . . ." Martha grimaced.

The car veered dangerously toward the center line, and a cement mixer coming in the opposite direction gave a warning toot. Abby's heart fluttered uncontrollably as she grabbed for the armrest, wishing that she were back in Alice's tranquil cocoon. It occurred to her that Californians were better not mentioned when Martha was at the wheel. She searched her mind for a less explosive topic.

"Tell me more about One Universe. I gather that you're very much involved."

Martha's lined but still attractive face brightened. "The idea of One Universe is the inter-connectedness of everything, organic and inorganic alike. Although that concept definitely stretches the limits of the ordinary person's imagination. Let's just say that human life is part of a complex web that encompasses everything from rocks and algae to those much maligned spotted owls."

Martha was now staying within the confines of her own lane. Abby made an encouraging sound.

"We humans tend to be very short sighted, which is to our own detriment," Martha observed tartly. "People will fight to make it possible for a corporation to build a plant that, in spite of all the precautions taken, could create substantive air pollution. But when some "radical" points this out, they insist that it's just this *one time*, that the powers-that-be are going to take all sorts of precautions, and besides, think of the jobs that will be created! Very nice indeed until little children start developing lung problems, only by then it's too late. Does the corporation do anything?" she demanded angrily, glancing over at Abby to make sure she had her complete attention. "'It would cost us too much money to clean things up,' they protest. 'We would have to close the plant, and then all these good people would lose their jobs.' A serious consideration, only none of this helps the children who can't breathe."

Abby realized that she had started to relax too soon. Martha whipped around a slow-moving, extremely ancient Buick and squeezed in between it and a delivery van with only inches to spare. Instinctively Abby reached for the armrest again, her heart once more at full flutter. At this rate she might not survive to worry about dialysis. But if something were to happen to her, what about Francis?

"Of course, today that example is somewhat outmoded, thank heavens, because people have awakened to the hazards air pollution poses to their health. In some ways we can, and are, doing a bit better. But that sort of thing happened often enough in the past, and happens today in other areas, most especially with commercial ventures threatening the purity of our water. I've got to say one thing for that pumice mine, at least it's not in a riparian area, so we don't have to worry about that sort of pollution."

"How did you happen to join One Universe?" Abby segued, hoping to avoid mention of Jim Wilson or any other Californian.

"I'm one of the founding members," Martha announced proudly.

"Oh? What motivated you?"

The car slowed as Martha no longer pushed the speed limit. "It's a personal thing."

"If you don't want to talk about it. . . ."

"No, that's all right. My husband, my late husband," she said with almost unendurable sadness in her voice, "came from a wealthy and influential newspaper family in the Midwest. Not long after we were married the family acquired a major newspaper in Phoenix and sent my husband, with me tagging along of course, out to manage it. I think the family actually bought the paper because of my husband, who had emphysema. This was the late Forties and Arizona was still a healing place, or at least for Donald it was. Like many of the tuberculosis victims who came west earlier in the century because they were told that Arizona was their last chance, he started to gain weight and feel better in the pure, dry air."

Martha's dark eyes seemed to be looking back at a past only

she could see, a past centered on a much-beloved husband who had gradually regained his health in the warm, dry desert.

"After awhile he could even play golf again," she continued with wonderment. "Instead of going from crisis to crisis we began living a very happy, normal life. Naturally, there were ups and downs, but that's only to be expected," she added with a short laugh. If nothing else, Martha was a realist, Abby surmised.

"We had a son. One of our sorrows was that we only managed the one child. However, he was, and is, everything we could have wanted. After college he married. He and his wife had a lovely daughter and their own precious little son. That little boy and his grandfather communicated in a very special way right from the very beginning. Not that Donald didn't love his granddaughter just as much, but he and the boy. . . . Well, you know how these things happen sometimes."

Abby nodded. She herself had had an especially beloved great aunt, so she understood how every now and then a young one and an old one would hit it off on some subliminal level, and what a great joy it could be to both of them.

There was a long pause. Martha seemed to be on automatic pilot, but at least she wasn't challenging any delivery vans or cement mixers. Abby didn't mind the hiatus. She felt herself beginning to tire. It would be good to get back to the professor's and curl up with a book and Francis.

"The child was playing near a river—not here, in the Midwest—and fell in," Martha said abruptly.

Abby started. Drowned, she thought with horror.

"No, he didn't drown," Martha added, as if reading her mind. "Although it might have been better if he had. The river was badly polluted. Our grandson got an untreatable infection. I don't want to go into the details, but it was a horrible way for anyone, especially a child, to die. The owners of the plant that was the principal polluter insisted that there was no cause and effect. But on investigation we discovered that our grandson wasn't the only one who had become ill, and even died, after contact with that water. Cause and effect or no cause and effect, we—the family, that is—got that water cleaned up," she announced grimly. "Donald lived to see the job mostly done. The doctors said he died of heart failure. I think he'd lost the will to live."

"I'm so very, very sorry." Those damned, inadequate words again, Abby reflected. Why with a language as rich and nuanced as English couldn't she do better?

"That left me to run the newspaper in Arizona, which I did," Martha continued briskly. "I didn't have the background Kate Graham had when she was put in a similar position with *The Washington Post*, and I was older than she was when the responsibility came—which has both its advantages and disadvantages. However, I muddled through, thank heavens with no major strikes or Watergates to contend with!"

"And One Universe?"

"For a long time I had been contemplating the contrast between the health offered by a relatively unpolluted environment and the disaster we bring on ourselves when we're careless or greedy or both. Did you know that there's a group that brings sick children from Chernobyl every year to Ireland, where the poor things improve markedly away from the aftermath of that radiation spill? Environment can kill, and it can cure—or at least help in a cure. That knowledge is what motivates me." She patted her cap of gleaming white hair and appeared to enter the present again.

A very motivated woman, Abby acknowledged. Would she engineer the theft of a vintage Alfa Romeo? Definitely, if she could make an environmental point. Moreover, this woman undoubtedly had the organizational skills to pull off such a theft. Would she commit murder? Abby stole a glance at the trim, fit older lady beside her. Perhaps, if given sufficient provocation. But Bob had been on her side. Hadn't he?

* * *

Toby Barrett glanced down at the day's lineup of activities his secretary had just handed him. Thank God it was Friday. The week had dragged on interminably, and today would mark a fitting end.

"Your legislative assistant will be here momentarily to brief you on this morning's sub-committee on Agriculture," his secretary told him cheerily, and then went on to review the high points, or to him probably the low points, of his day. But Barrett hardly paid attention to her as he thought about the sub-committee meeting, one of special concern to him since it affected some of his most influential constituents, the agricultural PACs. The meeting was intended to clarify some of the NAFTA protocols concerning the movement of oversized, unregulated tractor-trailers carrying produce from Sinaloa and Sonora, Mexico, into the U.S.

"Shit," he groaned *sotto voce* in frustration. *It isn't fair,* he thought. *All those cheap fruits and vegetables from south of the border, produced by growers who pay their people slave wages and have virtually no environmental regulations to contend with.* He knew they would cut right into the profits of his constituents and hence into *his*, Toby Barrett's, campaign contributions.

"And do you want me to reconfirm your luncheon plans with the congressman from Minnesota?" his secretary was asking.

"Yes, sure," he replied absently, focusing his eyes on a Roland Peterson painting from the late Fifties, a slightly abstracted version of canals and rich irrigated California agricultural land, the land that supported the PACs and hence him. And now competition from over the border threatened the PACs, most especially *those damned unregulated trucks.* But for all the stress that charged through his body like an electrical current at the very mention of those trucks, there existed some compensation. They had, after all, indirectly provided the inspiration for the brilliantly conceived disappearance of the Alfa Romeo.

"Anything more for now, Congressman?" the secretary concluded.

"No, that's fine." Barrett tried to calm the jumpy, hyped-up feeling in his stomach by studying the calming blue line of Peterson's canal, the bright green of a field about ready to be harvested, the soft brown of a field waiting to be planted. Only land, thank God. Not a truck, regulated or otherwise, in sight.

Then his mind shifted back to the Alfa Romeo. It had all begun with a man named Mohammed. Interesting how he'd met

Mohammed to begin with. It had been at one of those numberless Washington receptions. Some tedious embassy function, he recalled, probably sometime in February, because he'd already gotten Gene's invitation to participate in the Copper State 1000. Maybe he'd casually mentioned the event for lack of any other suitable subject of conversation and had expressed his eagerness to take part even though that s.o.b. Foster Richmond was going to be there with his ill-gotten Alfa Romeo. In any case, he and Mohammed started discussing classic cars. It soon became evident that Mohammed was an aficionado. Or so it seemed at the time. Actually the aficionado had turned out to be the man behind Mohammed, but Barrett hadn't discovered this until later.

By chance—really, no chance at all, he thought later—he kept running into Mohammed. Not all of his name but "our names are so long and cumbersome for your tongue. Just Mohammed will do quite nicely." Gradually, he was never sure quite how, it evolved that Mohammed's man wanted the Alfa Romeo. Money wasn't an issue. Barrett would be, and in fact already had been, richly rewarded. Mohammed had assured Toby that all he had to do was to plan. Everything would then be taken care of. No one would get hurt, or at least no more than a tiny bit of roughing up. Most assuredly no one would be killed or even badly injured.

Barrett paused abruptly in his musings. Where was his legislative assistant? Barrett rang his secretary.

"He's on his way, Congressman," she assured him, all sweetness and light.

He glanced at the stack of papers on his desk awaiting his signature and then his thoughts strayed back to the Alfa Romeo. Grab the sucker! Nothing could have pleased Barrett more after what that bastard Richmond had done to him, churning his account, taking his money, making him look like an imbecile. Knowing Foster, why had he ever been stupid enough to trust him? Foster Richmond had already been a spoiled mother's boy when they'd first met in Santa Barbara, Mrs. Richmond having deemed Connecticut winters far too cold for her delicate little darling. Delicate, hell! Foster may never have had much muscle, but he carried more weight than any other kid his age and was in the habit of quite literally squashing any opposition.

What Foster wanted, Foster took—from the treasured toy pistol of the Mexican gardener's son to candy from his classmates. He bullied the other kids and, thanks to the backup of his formidable mother, was even able to intimidate a number of teachers. He became notorious for cheating on tests. Not that Foster was dumb, just too lazy to study. But he did do his own work in math. From the beginning Foster had been a whiz at figures, and had later become a very successful stockbroker. And that, Barrett thought, was the only reason he could offer for his own monumental lapse of judgment. Well, now Foster was getting his own back, in spades.

The secretary announced the legislative assistant, who appeared breathless and with a large stack of papers in hand.

"Good morning, Congressman. I think we've got some good strategy worked out here."

Barrett nodded as the young man began his briefing. He wondered if his LA was nearly as clever as he himself was. His own planning had been brilliant. Mohammed had put his strategy into action and dealt competently with the messy details. Both had recognized that the car, once stolen, still had to be transported thousands of miles over land and water to the Middle East, remaining all the while out of sight and in pristine condition. Too bad it couldn't simply be containerized and shipped air freight on a regularly dispatched cargo plane! Then Barrett had thought of the chicken trucks.

"And the congressman from Minnesota?" the LA was asking.

"I think we've come close to reaching some sort of accord," Barrett responded absently.

Chicken trucks—the subject had come up as a humorous aside during an oversight committee meeting concerning NAFTA. Someone had remarked that the big stuff like drugs and the UDA's, undocumented aliens, didn't account for all the illegal commerce between Mexico and the United States. How about the chicken trucks? A question to which no one could reply because no one had the faintest idea what the man was talking about.

Toby and the others around the table had then learned that there was a brisk business between Arizona and the state of Sonora, Mexico, in produce being cleared out of American supermarkets because it was no longer at the peak of freshness. Instead of the produce being confined to the dumpster, a little money passed hands and it was loaded on trucks—ordinary old farm trucks, not the shiny new refrigerated monsters that had brought it up from Nogales.

The trucks whisked the aging produce back south over the border by night, through places like the almost invisibly small town of Lochiel, no longer an official port of entry but still a passage point for those in the know. Once in Mexico there were plenty of hungry people who would gladly pay for what the gringos would only have thrown away. A further irony was that much of the produce had been grown in their own country.

"So, if this is some sort of open secret, why doesn't someone do something about it?" a woman aide had asked aggressively.

"It may be technically illegal, but it's relatively harmless, and what with the drug traffic, illegal aliens, and God only knows what else, the Border Patrol has bigger problems to deal with. Given 1,936 miles of border and enough serious crime to cause real nightmares, who gives a damn about some aging chickens, maybe a bit of hamburger meat that has passed the 'sell by' date, or a few soggy old fruits and vegetables?" the chicken-truck expert had responded philosophically.

Yes, who would care? A chicken truck it would be, Barrett had thought with glee. Then down through Mexico. A little *mordida* passing under the table and that would be no problem. Down to Topolobampo, from which, carefully concealed by tomatoes grown in the fields of Sinaloa and sardines harvested from the Gulf of California, the car would be shipped by freighter to its new home in the Middle East. There it would be treated like a rare gem or a fine painting by a very wealthy and influential man—Barrett preferred to remain uncertain as to the person's identity or even the role he played in his country's elite—someone who wasn't any more particular than Foster Richmond how he got what he wanted. And to think that the guy had a whole country of his own in which to play with his new toy!

Toby pushed back a wave of envy. Well, he was getting what he wanted now, thanks to chicken trucks and ironically thanks also to those damned environmentalists at One Universe. He just hoped they'd continue to play the role he'd scripted for them. It wasn't much longer now.

* * *

"Abby, wake up, we're being evacuated."

As she struggled into consciousness, Abby peered around trying to figure out where she was and what was happening. Flagstaff. She was in Flagstaff. It was Friday night, or perhaps early Saturday morning, a week after she had returned from Phoenix to discover that Bob was dead. She had started dialysis, or at least practice dialysis. This much she patched together, but none of it explained what was happening now.

Strong hands shook her determinedly, but, her groggy brain told her, it couldn't be a very threatening somebody because Francis wasn't growling. In fact he, too, seemed intent on awakening her. And how could that be? Evidently she hadn't locked the bedroom door.

"Abby, damn it, get up!"

David, David Neale, her landlord.

A heavy, acrid odor permeated the room. Tears sprouted from her irritated eyes and she found it impossible to draw a deep breath. "What's going on?" she gasped.

"There's a forest fire. We've got to leave, *now*. Here's a duffel bag." He thrust the bag at her. "Put on some clothes and throw whatever else you need into it." She noticed that he had pulled on sandals, Levis, and another of his collection of tee shirts, this one ironically picturing a cool, blue-green waterfall with two deer drinking from the pond below. His hair was tousled, his face haggard.

"I'll put the leash on Francis. Right now it's calm out, but if the wind picks up, we could be in deep shit, so move it!"

Obediently she did as he ordered. She could hear the eerie ululation of sirens throbbing through the night and the plangent warning blasts from the emergency vehicles. Staccato reflections of flashing lights glanced off the blinds.

"Do you feel awake enough to drive?" David asked as she emerged from the bedroom.

"Yes, I think so."

"Good. I'll put these things of yours in your car and then you follow mine," he said, heading for the garage.

"Francis?" she looked about in alarm.

"Right here. I'll put him in with you."

"The Khalsas?"

"Awake and just about finished loading. I talked briefly to one of the firefighters who came to the door. They don't expect the fire to get this far, but they can't take any chances. Let's get going."

An excellent idea, Abby thought as she slid behind the wheel of the Volvo. She could barely breathe and poor Francis was making coughing, choking sounds. Fire personnel in full garb roamed the street, helping people put a few possessions in their vehicles, carrying children, even carrying the old woman from down the street who could walk perfectly well when she wanted to.

Although there were no flames to be seen, the red strobe lights from the emergency vehicles created the impression of an inferno. Heat, smoke, piercing shafts of light, a cacophony of sounds. Her nerve endings shrieked in protest. Grimly, Abby gripped the wheel and followed David.

As they got further from the forest, she saw a dull red glow behind her. She pictured all the forest creatures scurrying madly for a place of safety, all the tall, stately ponderosa pines consumed by the fire, and all those wonderful dells, cool and quiet, where Pooh-Bear loved to romp turned into a broiling hell. After tonight, David Neale was going to have to go a hell of a long way to convince her of the benefits of forest fires.

* * *

It took Abby a long time to settle down and get to sleep, though it was through no fault of the arrangements David's friends, the Carmichaels, made for her. They insisted that since their two daughters were at summer camp, accommodations for the refugees posed no problem. Abby was given a bed made up with brightly flowered yellow sheets and provided with enough stuffed animals to have populated the Serengeti. But the stuffed animals reminded her again of the denizens of the forest, the doe with her fawn, the delicate butterfly, the bouncing rabbits and the loquacious squirrels. How many of them outran the fire? The specter of their mad dash from the heat and the flames haunted her into the early morning hours, and when she did doze she had an awful nightmare.

With a mighty roar the flames chased Francis, who ran frantically through the forest. Then they pounced on him, and he disappeared in a broiling maelstrom of red and orange. Somehow at the same time the flames also engulfed David's home. The comfortable green house with its books and music and the stately spruce in front was no more.

A terrible leg cramp rocketed Abby back to consciousness. Just another sign of an unbalanced system, but it hurt like hell. At least, she thought as she massaged the knot in her leg, it had sprung her free from that terrible dream about Francis. With gratitude she looked at the little dog waiting patiently beside the bed for his good-morning petting.

Wrapping herself in a white terrycloth bathrobe, she wandered groggily kitchenward with Francis, his tags jangling, right behind.

When she saw David Neale her heart seemed to stop beating and her throat constricted painfully. "Your house. . ." She remembered the rest of her dream. "Did the fire. . ."

"It's fine."

With a sigh of relief she turned to Marybeth Carmichael, a small woman with a few extra pounds on her petite frame, strawberry blond hair, and a radiant smile. "Excuse me, but is your yard fenced? Can Francis go out?"

"Here, I'll give him a little walk," David offered. "Get yourself some coffee. Marybeth has made the real thing, and you look like you could use it."

"You really do something for a lady's ego," she shot back at him. But she knew he was right. From what she'd seen of herself in the patches of bedroom mirror not decorated with snapshots of pre-teen girls and rock stars, she looked almost as bad as one of the fire victims.

"Have they put the fire out?   Did it burn any homes?"

"It's virtually out, and it didn't get into any residential neighborhoods," David replied as he snapped on Francis's leash. "The wind didn't pick up, so they got it under control pretty quickly. They're still monitoring the area just in case.   But the fire remained localized, so there shouldn't be any problem.   I'll tell you more about it when I get back."

Marybeth, whose husband was off on some errand or other, provided Abby with a large, fluffy towel and a mug of coffee. Abby had showered, dressed, and finished her coffee before David and Francis returned. She was working on a piece of toast when Francis pranced in beside David, who led him to his water dish, from which the dog lapped greedily.

"Christ, but it's hot out there already. Almost twenty years in Flagstaff, and I've never known such a summer."

"Nearly as bad as Phoenix," Marybeth suggested.

"Oh, no, not *that* bad," David answered with a laugh.   "But still formidable for this elevation."

David sat down and accepted another cup of coffee.   He had traded his usual Levis for khaki shorts with which he wore a hot pink tee shirt advertising the Phoenix Zoo and featuring a disdainful camel.   He hadn't shaved yet and the shadow of an incipient beard blended with his skin, darkened by years in the intense sun of high elevations.   Abby noticed that the dark skin made his blue eyes look bluer, as blue and sparkling as the summer skies above the San Francisco Peaks. David Neale seemed to have spent as much of his life outside as possible. His body was that of someone who enjoyed active physical pursuits in the out-of-doors.   There was no evidence of the sort of muscles cultivated in a health club or gym, only the hard, lean form of a fit man who used his body constantly and as a matter of course.   He looked. . . *terrific*!

Abruptly Abby caught herself. *My God, I've been living with the man—rooming with him, whatever—for a week now and this is the first time I've really looked at him, except for a cursory inspection that first night when I discovered he didn't fit the picture I'd painted of him. Good Lord, have failing kidneys made me that blind and insensitive?* She felt her cheeks grow warm and glanced around to see if anyone else had noticed.

David turned to her. "They found your party boys. Three of them up from Phoenix, in theory for the summer session. Majoring in bimbos and booze, I'd say. The fire. . . ."

"Oh, no, they weren't. . . ." She'd wanted them disciplined, not dead.

"No. They weren't even hurt, although a little singeing might have taught them a good lesson. The only pain they're suffering is the direct result of their own actions, hangovers that would probably rate 7.8 on the Richter Scale. But it was just dumb luck that no breeze came up to turn the fire on them. They were so drunk they were going around in circles in the forest when some of the firefighters found them. And the firefighters got there so quickly only because the owl watchers alerted them."

Startled, Abby stared at him. "*Owl watchers*? Who are they and where do they come in?"

"You and Lieutenant Henderson both would like an answer to that question. I called him earlier this morning after I watched the news. He says those boys were damned lucky about the owl watchers, if that's what they really were. But to give them some credit, they were in an area where there are reputed to be a couple of Mexican spotted owls."

"So why shouldn't they be owl watchers?" asked Marybeth, sipping a steaming mug of coffee. "Or owl listeners. It would be awfully hard to see anything in that forest after dark."

"Henderson says he doesn't think the two who reported the fire could tell one end of an owl from the other. But he knows for sure they're members of One Universe. So what were they really doing wandering around Coconino National Forest in the middle of the night?"

"Thank God they were," Marybeth said over the lip of her coffee mug.

"And the party boys?" Abby asked.

"Evidently they're the ones everybody's been on the lookout for."

"Did they kill. . ." Abby found she couldn't finish the thought.

"They had some sort of run-in with Bob Curtis before he died. That's for sure. Hated his guts. But when it finally dawned on those idiots that they were in serious trouble, they had the sense to shut up. Their families are sending some big mucky-muck lawyer from Lewis and Roca up from the Valley."

Henderson was a pro, but he would be pitted against a pro, too. How long would it take before the lieutenant knew anything, Abby wondered. Days? Weeks? Surely no time in the immediate future. *Damn, damn, damn and double damn.* Abby could feel disappointment weighing her down like a boulder. She glanced up at the kitchen clock.

"Look at the time! I didn't realize it was so late. The Khalsas. . . . I want to help them get ready for Bob's memorial services, or celebration, or whatever it is this evening."

* * *

As it was, Abby need not have worried about the Khalsas. A large sign in their front yard announced that the celebration would be held the next day, Sunday, and at another location since the fire had left the air in the neighborhood acrid and almost unbreathable.

"Tomorrow evening," Abby mused aloud as they stood there rereading Sada Anand's message. She had a sense of letdown. Although it looked more and more as if the mystery of Bob's death, like the lesser mystery of the Alfa Romeo, would remain unsolved, at least she would feel somewhat better when his life had been celebrated, when some sort of resolution of that life had been achieved. Closure, they called it. *My parents, Mark, now Bob— too much closure,* she thought. *And with the dialysis, too much. . . what? Nothing. I'm empty inside, drained, as if my senses have all shut down. Perhaps it's a way my all-too-vulnerable self is protecting me? Other than a profound sadness for Bob, I don't feel anything. Why can't I open up to what's around me? It's as if there's plate glass between me and the rest of the world. See but not touch or be touched, like riding in the cocoon of Alice Olson's car.*

Why, I can't even begin to relate to David as a damned attractive man.

Francis coughed almost apologetically.

Abby reached down and gave him a reassuring pat. "The air is foul, isn't it?"

"Godawful," David agreed. "We ought to get out of here. Go someplace else for the night."

"But where? The Carmichaels were nice enough to put us up for one night, but it would be overkill to ask them for another. We could, of course, spend a night at Iron Springs with my sister."

"Let's leave that for another time. I've got a better idea. Have you ever been to Monument Valley?"

"John Wayne!" Abby's spirits soared. Just for a while she wanted to forget all about death, disease, and dialysis. She wanted to play the part of a carefree woman out on a lark with a fun, intelligent, good-looking man. She wanted to feel things, good things, to enjoy herself. "No, I've never been to Monument Valley, and yes, yes, yes, I want to go there," she told David with a broad smile. "I want to go there now."

CHAPTER 11

They were in luck. When David called Gouldings Lodge, which offered the only guest accommodations in Monument Valley, he discovered that they had just had a last-minute cancellation. Abby and David quickly threw some clean clothes and dog food into David's Bronco. Within a half an hour they were heading north from Flagstaff up Highway 89, busy on a Saturday morning with SUVs, trucks pulling boats up to Lake Powell, and a variety of touring vehicles. Big, expensive models that were really self-contained homes vied for road space with smaller ones sprouting bicycles like a cactus sprouts spines. Abby even spotted a converted bus, psychedelic designs still faintly visible, that had probably first seen service with the Flower Children. Along the way numerous stands selling Indian jewelry, rugs and trinkets did a thriving business.

Beyond the highway spread open, barren land like a partly used tub of margarine, naked in the harsh sunlight. Abby turned to look out the rear window, where she could see the San Francisco Peaks dominating the landscape as usual. The Peaks, always the Peaks, she mused.

"I think I'm beginning to understand why people around here, well. . . revere the San Francisco Peaks. They're more than magnificent. Just being there they're like a statement of the dignity and endurance of the land. What I can't believe is that pumice is so valuable that it gives the Pycenium a right to desecrate them," she observed thoughtfully. "Jim Wilson said that you can only stake claims on public land when you've found a valuable mineral, and that pumice for stonewashing qualifies. But what's the criterion for valuable?"

"Something called the 'Prudent Person' test," David explained. "If I remember correctly, the original law just called for a mineral to be profitable under current market conditions. Rather vague, isn't it?" He grinned at her, and for the first time in a long while a warm sense of happiness washed over her. She felt as if she had left dialysis and all the other problems associated with polycystic kidney disease at home with the boxes of dialysate stacked in her bedroom. Indubitably they were there, but there for later. For now she was free to enjoy. A forty-something woman playing hooky. Churning up the highway to who knew what adventure.

David ran a hand back over his thick dark hair with its shafts of gray. "Sometime in the 1890s the then Secretary of the Department of Interior, and don't ask me which one, declared that a mineral deposit was sufficiently valuable to fall under the mining law if a person of ordinary prudence would feel justified in the further expenditure of his labor and means in mining it."

"Speaking about vague!" Abby snorted in disgust. "What if a huge deposit of gold were found someplace in the world and gold on the world market fell to practically nothing? Or if the need for copper wiring was made practically obsolete because all transmissions were bounced off satellites or however they do it, and recycling took care of other copper needs? Or, better still, if we all stopped wearing stonewashed jeans?" Fat chance of that, she added to herself, but still, it was a logical consideration.

"I don't think they could do anything about claims already made and mines currently in operation. But the owners of those mines probably couldn't stake any more claims. In other words, they couldn't expand," David told her. "And they probably couldn't patent either, which I imagine they're anxious to do to circumvent the environmentalists."

Abby admired his strong, suntanned hands with a few tentacles of dark hair steady on the wheel. A good, reliable driver. A good person as well. He had been unfailingly kind to her since that first night when he had endured her hysterics and then not left her alone. Only she knew it wasn't goodness or kindness that presently teased her stomach and sent her heart on a spin.

"As a matter of fact, I've heard that the demand for stonewashing pumice has declined somewhat, though not enough to seriously harm Wilson's operation."

Changing the subject, David asked, "Would you like a cup of coffee at Cameron?"

"Sounds good to me."

Cameron turned out to be a busy roadway stop offering food, souvenirs and overnight accommodations, the outgrowth of a trading post founded in 1911 after a much-needed bridge had been built over the Little Colorado River. Although today a bridge hardly seemed necessary. Abby could spy not a single drop of water in the riverbed. Cars and campers crowded into the parking lot. What were obviously fairly new buildings signaled expansion. However, hints of the past remained in the older buildings, which were built of river rock and to Abby's eyes had a wonderfully antiquated appeal.

After Cameron they turned off on Highway 160, leaving behind much of the traffic. Abby noticed that green was almost entirely absent from the palette of the high plateau. The patches of pinyon and juniper were so dark as to appear black against the nearly colorless dry grasses. The snows of winter and the relentless summer sun had faded the dominant color, sienna, to a pale, sandy shade. Here and there a deep arroyo sliced the land, ready to broil with reddish-brown water when the rains came, the rocks and boulders strewn along its bottom testifying to the potential force of the water. But now the arroyos, like the Little Colorado, were dry, the land, desiccated. Abby wondered how anything could ever survive in such an arid world.

"You mentioned that the demand for stonewashing pumice has diminished?" she asked David, recalling their pre-Cameron discussion. "As far as I can see stonewashed clothes seem to be as popular as ever."

"So true, but I've heard there's been a drop in demand for the pumice because the industry's developed a new chemical process that uses less of it. However, whatever happens, Wilson and his investors should come out in great shape. It's not as if they've purchased a lot of exotic equipment and built a huge processing plant. What do they have? Some earthmovers, sheds and an office, which is really just a double-wide?"

Abby nodded.

"All of which could be sold off and moved. They've already claimed well over two hundred acres, so there's a lot there to work with even if something went wrong and they couldn't claim more. As for patenting? Well, only a part of that has been patented as far as I know. But so far they seem to have done fine without more patenting, though they do want to get it."

They drove on for a while in silence. In spite of the starkness of the terrain, Abby found herself responding instinctively to the openness and to the minimalist beauty of it all—the great, impossibly blue arc of the sky, the sharp, clean lines of the land, the crisp black shadows. Signs of habitation were limited to the occasional hogan, from time to time a manufactured home, but usually something far more modest, including the traditional round hogans of rough wood and sod. Towns like Red Lake and Cow Springs slipped by, so tiny as to be almost invisible. The only place of any size through which they passed was Kayenta, where they picked up some soft drinks and sandwiches.

When the great red rock formations of Monument Valley began to appear, Abby felt as if they had entered another world, perhaps even been beamed onto another planet. "Just like the movies!" she breathed softly. But in fact it was far better.

Here before her stretched a land as vast and uncluttered, as dramatic in form, and as sweeping in vista and vivid in color as ever it had appeared on celluloid. A unique, unexpected world where thin spires of red rock shot up into the cloudless sky and huge sandstone battleships steamed forever across the flat, sandy surface of the land. A world like none other.

And yet, thanks to all the times it had been filmed, it was strangely familiar. Abby could imagine herself riding in a stagecoach along with John Wayne, or maybe jogging behind Forrest Gump. However, while actors and plots might change, the scenery remained the same—just as it had been for millennia.

"God, but it's beautiful," she whispered reverently.

David pulled over, stopped the car, and all three got out, Francis's nose twitching eagerly. The silence was overwhelming. It was silence not as a complete absence of sound but rather that of a vast land filled only with the gentle whisper of soft wind through dry grasses and the drone of insects half-dazed by the sun—a muted chord on the outer edge of the perceived decibel range. Abby experienced a moment of pure pleasure: the near silence, the hot spicy smell of high summer, the warm sun on her face, the caress of the light breeze. *This is what's been missing*, she thought. Ever since the diagnosis, she had been running, always running, running as if that were the only way to survive. Never able to relax enough just to be, to embrace the moment whatever might lie beyond. Walling herself up so she wouldn't fall apart. Terrified of being so vulnerable. Trying to be strong, but strong like the concrete walls of a prison, rigid, inflexible, unfeeling. That might be survival, but surely not life.

She turned to David, this man who'd somehow sensed needs she hadn't even known existed. "Thank you," she said quietly as she laid a hand on his warm, bare arm. "Thank you so very much for bringing me here."

* * *

"You brought your laptop? A computer to Monument Valley? Are you compulsive or what?" David asked in surprise. He had showered and changed into a tee shirt with a Bengal tiger prowling through a chartreuse jungle. Abby thought it fortunate for David that formal dress did not seem to be part of the northern Arizona lifestyle.

They sat on a porch at Gouldings watching the shadows cast by the spires and rock monuments lengthen steadily out across the plateau. A quiet time as the day slid silently away.

"As a matter of fact, I am a bit compulsive," Abby admitted. "However, the laptop is just one of those things. An accident. I put it in the duffel when we took off for the Carmichaels' last night and I didn't repack the duffel today. Just took out dirty clothes and added fresh ones."

"So what are you going to do with it now?"

"I hope to put down some of my impressions. I don't want to lose today." She gazed at the great red rock formations turned redder still by the setting sun, their knife-edged black shadows reaching further and further toward the east, where a few small, puffy clouds reflected the last blush of the dying day.

She glanced over at David, leaning back in the chair, legs stretched out in front of him, waiting, listening. Waiting for her to explain further, she knew instinctively. Abby loathed sharing her deepest feelings. She had bottled them up within herself for so long. Even Becky had been privy to only part of them. But if she and David were ever to become more than passing friends—*and did he want this as much as she was beginning to want it*, she wondered?—then the situation called for more openness. She summoned up her courage.

"Being diagnosed with that damned multisyllable disease—well, it knocked me end on end." She searched for a simile. "Like racing down a ski slope, hitting an unexpected hillock and suddenly finding yourself on your butt in the cold, wet snow. What now? How do I deal with this? Those are the questions. Only it's not like skiing where you can pick up your aching body and injured pride and make for the lodge and a hot fire." She shivered, but not at the thought of the snow.

"It's like lying there in the snow when it's getting dark and not even knowing the direction of the lodge." Her voice trembled, and she tried to hold it steady.

The first star of the night popped out of the darkening sky. Abby knew she should wish, *star light, star bright. . .* but she wasn't even sure where to begin.

"No, it's worse. It's Stephen King. The lodge is lost, or it isn't there at all, and you aren't really you. I mean, who're *you*, David Neale?" She turned and stared directly at him.

He checked to make sure that this was not a rhetorical question. Evidently what he saw convinced him that she was serious. "Well, I suppose you can say I'm a member of the College of Forestry at NAU, a professor, the father of a fine son, the author of several books about forests, a backpacker. . . Any number of things."

"See," she said defiantly, as if he had proved her point. "All things you do—teaching, writing, fathering, backpacking, whatever. And if you'd asked me the same question even a year ago I would have said that I teach Old English at Vassar College. That was my identity." The lump in her throat had gotten so big she could hardly force out the words. "Now I'm not really anything. Not a teacher, a skier, a backpacker—well, maybe a walker. But you get the idea," she concluded bitterly, gripping the laptop fiercely as if somehow it might try to get away from her.

"Abby," David shifted his chair closer to hers and rubbed a hand in gentle circles on her back. Francis, who, with the black tip of his nose rotating as if on a ball bearing, had been watching a couple of feral-looking dogs sniffing beyond the porch, trotted over and laid his head on her knee. "Abby, give yourself a chance. Some space, some time. . . ."

"I refuse to be just somebody who's sick!" she broke in angrily. "Also I've gone on living while too many people have died." Her parents, Mark, now Bob—the tears welled up within her, a tidal wave flowing across the sands of the desert. "I've got to do *something* to justify being here on this earth." And something besides mindless running, she added to herself.

David continued to massage her back as she broke into dry heaves. Francis licked her hand. Gradually she began to regain control of herself.

"Abby, a hell of a lot has happened to you lately," David told her in a low, soft voice. "Don't push it. As I said, give it time. Nina's dying wasn't the same sort of thing at all, but I felt as if my whole world had lost its center, gone black. No path. I know just what you mean about the lost lodge." He sighed. "But you're going to have to stumble around for awhile. I know you want to be strong, organized, get it all worked out, go on like nothing's happened, only real life doesn't work that way." With a finger he wiped a tear from under each eye. "Don't be so hard on yourself. Don't be so concerned about being strong all the time. There's an old saying, Chinese I suppose, that the tree that bends survives the storm."

Stars sparkled all across the sky now, a dizzying array of celestial lights. Around them answering electric lights came on inside. A long silence. Francis returned to observing the local dogs.

"So what are you going to say about today?" David asked at last, with much of the old warmth and humor back in his voice.

"I put a few thoughts down earlier," Abby answered tentatively, reaching for her reading glasses. "If I can just remember what I put it under." She pulled up a list of files.

"I must not be thinking very clearly. Here's a file I don't remember at all—*Francis*." Her voice lifted with surprise. "I've got the records of all his shots in hard copy. Why would I also put them on the computer?"

"Why don't you look and see?"

"But David," she said as the file came up on the monitor, "this doesn't have anything to do with Francis. It looks like some rather complicated accounting." She handed the laptop over to him.

His brow furrowed as he studied the file. "It does indeed."

A feeling, somewhere between fear and excitement, welled up in her. "And Bob is the *only* one who could have put it there. He had access to the house while caring for Francis. I never thought to check the laptop! I haven't been using it lately. It was put away in the corner of my closet." She tried to control a sudden surge of anger. Damn, she hated the idea of anyone, even Bob, rummaging through her things. But evidently that's what he'd done. Nothing else made sense.

"These figures don't mean anything to me." David shook his head. "But they might to Lieutenant Henderson. We'll have to contact him as soon as we get back to Flagstaff."

* * *

Another day, and another sunset blazed across the western sky. Deep purple clouds lined with gold streaked the horizon, and below them the sun's great orange globe pulsated with burning gases as it sank into the green-black forest. A night worthy of the funeral pyre of an Anglo-Saxon king, Abby reflected.

If Bob Curtis had been such a king, or equally a great warrior, those assembled would have vaunted his valor in battle and recalled his many venturous deeds. As far as she was concerned, Bob *had* been a warrior, ever ready to oppose whatever foe threatened the forest. But under Sada Anand's gentle guidance tonight's remembrance was more restrained. Bob received praise for his patient and loving care of Pooh-Bear rather than his willingness to take on careless college boys. He was lauded for his general helpfulness to all who knew him rather than his aggressive challenge to tattooed motorbikers. And he was remembered for his interest in returning to college rather than his active curiosity about pumice mining on the slopes of the San Francisco Peaks.

As darkness descended and the thousands of shimmering stars pricked the night sky, they all quaffed not the heady mead of old England but fresh fruit concoctions, strictly non-alcoholic. All that is but Francis, who had been especially invited and was the object of a particularly enthusiastic love-in by Pooh-Bear.

"Bob would have approved," Abby told David as they drove home. She herself felt considerably better. Although the question of his death remained, at least his life had been duly celebrated. At last she had been able to say goodby.

Sada Anand and Soul Singh planned to sprinkle his ashes in the forest so that Bob would forever rest in the place he had come to love. That, too, struck Abby with a satisfying sense of rightness. But, oh, she wished she could have known Bob longer, and had the opportunity to see him take his life in hand. With all that had been resolved that evening, Bob's life would still be a door left ever so slightly ajar.

* * *

When Abby and David got out of the Bronco a low, ominous sound rumbled from deep within Francis's throat. As they opened the back door his muzzle creased, drawing up the skin to show his fangs. Then he flung himself into the house ahead of them barking madly. The light that David had turned on abruptly went out and for a short time all was confusion. Something heavy grazed the side of Abby's head and she reeled around the kitchen trying to get her bearings. Further into the house a yell and a curse suggested that Francis had clamped those sharp teeth of his down on someone's anatomy, while a sharp yelp seemed to indicate that someone had kicked back. A door slammed followed by wild barking. From the dining area came the thump of solid flesh connecting with solid flesh and the gasps and oaths of two men locked in combat. Then another, more decisive thump, the sound of running feet and the front door opening, and finally silence.

Abby got her wits back together and turned on the lights. Her head ached and she still felt unstable, but everything seemed to be intact. She found David groaning on the floor beside the dining room table. He raised himself up on one elbow. His hair was tousled, blood dripped from his nose, and his left eye could have used an application of steak had there been any in the house. However, nothing appeared to be broken. Francis continued to bark frantically somewhere in the front of the house.

"Oh, shit," David exclaimed as he staggered to his feet and viewed the wreckage of his living room. Books lay strewn about the floor, chair cushions were gutted, and what seemed to be acres of red plaid upholstery had been wantonly destroyed. "So the bastards wanted the television and the computer equipment, but why trash the whole place?" shouted David as he kicked a cushion, which belched forth a cloud of small white feathers.

"Oh, David," Abby moaned as she collapsed on the violated couch. "I'm so sorry! They've absolutely ruined everything." She looked around in horror. "Your books. . . " She picked up one with a split spine and held it closely, like a child in need of comfort. "All that Royal Stewart. . . ."

"Christ, that's no loss," he responded with disgust. "I never liked it anyway. The work of an old girlfriend. After Nina's death I put all our Navajo rugs and other special things into storage. I couldn't bear looking at them. Later, much later, I acquired this girlfriend who decided I needed a new image. Scottish laird or some such concoction. She found the furniture at a going-out-of-business sale." He shook his head. "At least I didn't invest a lot of money. When she and I parted ways, I never got around to doing anything about it."

Abby burst out laughing hysterically. And to think, she'd based her image of this man on furniture he hadn't even chosen! Oh, she was really losing it.

"So what's so funny?" David demanded crossly.

Between gales of laughter mixed with tears she tried to explain. Eventually he got the point and joined in.

"You know," he told her, sitting down beside her and throwing an arm around her shoulder, "this is the first time I've ever heard you laugh. I mean really laugh, not just a small, polite sound. Jesus, what a mess, but it may be worth it." Cupping her chin in his hand, he gave her a long, questioning look.

A tentative knock at the half-open door and then Sada Anand came in.

"Oh, no, not you, too!" she gasped, putting a hand to her chest. "I thought our place was bad, but nothing like this. They stole Soul Singh's computer, and his backup disks if you can believe it, but that's as far as they got. This is absolutely awful!"

"We'd better call the police," David said in a tired voice. "Hell, as a law-abiding citizen, I've seen more of the authorities the last ten days than in the last ten years, probably than in my whole life."

"You should call the city police, of course. But I think you should also contact the Sheriff's office and leave a message for Lieutenant Henderson," Abby suggested as she got up to find and liberate Francis. She remembered telling Becky that Flagstaff was hardly the crime capital of the West. In spite of what had happened tonight she'd stick with that assessment. No way was this an ordinary crime or act of random violence.

* * *

What would have happened if Sada Anand had not come over when she did? Abby wondered as she brushed her hair the next morning. The face that looked back at her from the mirror blushed like a teenager on her first date. Good God, she thought as she put the brush down with a resounding thwack. What was going on? She had dialysis to worry about. Her disease, the Alfa Romeo. And then last night's break-in. No time, she cautioned herself, to be getting involved with any man, even someone as sympathetic and supportive as the professor. Later, yes, she prayed, later. But not quite now. *Uh oh*, she hesitated and then consulted the wide hazel eyes in the mirror, *is the concrete wall going up again?*

Abby heard the doorbell ring, then the deep bass of Lieutenant

Henderson's voice, and she went to join the men. Fortunately David's coffee paraphernalia had remained unscathed. They settled around the dining room table, another survivor, with steaming mugs.

"You and the Khalsas both? That doesn't strike me as accidental," the lieutenant snorted. "Do you have any idea what they could have been after? Anything else unusual happen lately?"

"Yes," Abby and David chorused.

"We were going to show you anyway." She got her laptop and brought up the *Francis* file.

"Interesting," Henderson murmured as he gazed at the monitor. "Can you print it out?"

"They got all the other computer equipment," David replied tersely. "I don't even have a spare disk."

"How come they didn't get this?"

"It was still in the car," Abby explained and added a few words about their impromptu trip. "We were running late coming back, so we came into the house just long enough to freshen up a bit and give Francis some dinner. We left everything in the Bronco. No temptation that way to do any unpacking and run still later."

"So this may well have been what the thieves were after. The file, that is. Which is why they took your computer," the big man inclined his head at David, "also the Khalsas'. The printers and the televisions were just to make it look like your usual burglary. But why they pulled books down and slashed furniture. . . ."

"Maybe they had an aversion to Royal Stewart," Abby suggested, and she and David exchanged a knowing smile.

"I'm glad you two can find something to smile about." He gazed around at the room, which had a long way to go before it would be entirely habitable again. Fingerprint powder dusted by the officers who had answered the 911 call added to the bleak impression of general destruction. Abby, following his glance, decided that in the light of day the scene looked even worse than it had the night before. And there was nothing pretty about David's battered face, either. His nose had swollen and his left eye matched the nightscape that served as the background for the bat taking flight across a gibbous moon on today's tee shirt.

"Fortunately almost all the files that were here were also on my computer at the University," David told Henderson philosophically. "Everything was insured. I just wish they hadn't roughed up the books the way they did," he added angrily, pounding his right fist into his left hand. "But the upholstery's no loss. It was scheduled for a change anyway."

"I guess they thought something might be hidden in or behind the books. Maybe a disk? A disk would also have fit in a chair cushion," Abby mused.

"Could be," the lieutenant agreed. "May I take your laptop and get this file printed?"

"Of course. There's nothing I really need on it for now. But as for the file, as you've seen, there doesn't seem to be much there. It could be the accounting for almost any business, legal or otherwise."

"Even drug runners have to keep records," the lieutenant observed.

Abby grimaced but kept her mouth shut. Bob *wasn't* guilty either of taking drugs or selling them. Surely something would turn up to prove his innocence.

* * *

After the lieutenant had left, Abby prepared to go off for another dialysis training session while David, assisted by two athletic-looking graduate students, prepared to deal with the house. Abby agreed they should just tape up the cushions until David returned from his backpacking trip, at which point he had decided he would retrieve the rugs and other things that had long been stored and do some serious redecorating.

David had put off his hiking trip until Friday. By then the house would be in decent order again. Life, Abby decided, was easing back to normal, that is, if anything about her present lifestyle could be considered "normal." She wasn't sure whether to be glad or sorry about David's leaving. Her thoughts were in turmoil, as confused as many a freshman's first essay exam. She reminded herself sternly that for the present she needed to focus entirely on the dialysis. On the other hand. . . .

The phone rang. When she answered her eyebrows lifted in

surprise. A call from Jim Wilson was something she hadn't expected.

"Alice said you'd had a burglary. Is that true?"

How Alice did get around, Abby marveled. This morning she had left a message on Becky's answering machine—heaven help her if her sister found out about the burglary from some other source—mentioning the disturbance but keeping her version very low key. Becky must have called Alice and Alice had told Jim.

"Some damage. Some losses."

"Anything I can do to help?"

She weighed his words and the sound of his voice for a hint of a hidden agenda but could detect none. "That's a kind offer, but I can't think of a thing."

"Perhaps you'd like to join me for dinner sometime next week? Something casual? Get your mind off other things."

Two men showing interest? And she'd never felt more off-balance and less attractive in her life. Of course given the proprietary attitude of Sorrell Lawrence, any involvement with Jim was highly problematical. But she did enjoy his company. That brief conversation at Macy's had, after a rocky beginning, been very pleasant. And with the prospect of David leaving, the aloneness she had formerly found comforting suddenly did not seem so appealing.

"Could we talk about it next week? I'm just not up to par at this moment."

"Alice told me about the dialysis." Jim sounded embarrassed, as were so many men at the mention of illness, but also genuinely concerned. "Do you have to go through this regime indefinitely? Do you ever just feel like taking a day off?"

"Even if you feel like it, you don't. Not if you want to keep living." A ring of bitterness crept into her voice.

"God, what an awful thought! Tied to a machine. How long would a person last without it?"

"Well, I don't use a machine. There are other ways to go about it. As for time, I don't know. A few days, I suppose. Perhaps a little more. It would all depend on the individual and the circumstances. But without dialysis eventually a person would go into a coma, and die." Abby felt no need to explain that this wasn't exactly true in her case because as yet she still had some kidney function left. The important point was that dialysis was a life-support system and had to be respected as such, not something you didn't do because you didn't feel in the mood some days, like fixing up your hair or taking a walk.

* * *

By late Wednesday David and the graduate students had the house clean and back in order. It positively gleamed with polish and the effects of vigorous scrubbing. Abby felt shamed into doing something about her own things, which, fortunately, had escaped the worst of the tossing. She took everything out of the closet she was using, vacuumed the floor thoroughly, washed things that probably didn't need it, and checked all of her clothes to see if they needed a button reinforced or could use ironing. Every drawer in the chest of drawers got a similar treatment. Afterward Francis got a vigorous brushing, and she checked in the accordion file she used for records to make sure he wasn't missing any shots or vaccinations. There a surprise awaited her.

"See." She showed the sheets of paper she had found to David. "They look a lot like what was in my laptop, only my impression is that some of the figures are a bit different. But I would need to see the computer figures again to be sure."

"Again filed under Francis?"

"Yes. They were along with his medical records in my accordion file."

"And the thieves didn't get them?" he asked, taking the papers from her hand and examining them carefully.

"When you came back and took over the front bedroom, which is where I was keeping things like this until then, I shoved the file under the bureau in the master bedroom. There's the right sized space, and it was out of the way. I guess they just didn't see it, or maybe we arrived back before they could get that far. Actually they would have had to move the bureau or to reach under it to have found the file. A good, out-of-the-way place to keep it, but not exactly a hiding place, either. I think they must have assumed what they wanted was cleverly hidden."

"*The Purloined Letter*?"

"Not quite," she admitted. "But since it wasn't really hidden they didn't find it either. Can you drop it by for the lieutenant on your way to the university tomorrow?" Did they dare hope the figures would reveal anything?

"No problem about the lieutenant. And I'll pick up your laptop while I'm at it."

* * *

The lieutenant reported back almost immediately. His expert thought that the printout had been fashioned to make it look like whatever business they were dealing with was more profitable than it actually was. The computer figures were probably altered for the printout, then presumably altered back on the computer program.

"Maybe someone like Jim Wilson's trying to fool his investors?" Abby asked David when he returned from the university that evening and they had settled on the back porch to avoid the depressing sight of taped cushions.

"I've been asking around about Jim Wilson, and he'd have to be pretty clever to be putting one over on his investors. Especially with Shorty Dean on the scene. A rough diamond, but very sharp. Of course they could be in a deal together."

"No, I just don't see it that way," Abby replied thoughtfully. "While I don't pretend to have any special insight I do, or did, deal with all sorts of people day to day. In a situation like that after awhile anyone who pays any attention gets a sense of who's playing loose with the truth and who isn't. Jim Wilson may be movie star handsome. . . ."

"Oh?" David interrupted her with a raised eyebrow.

Abby ignored the implied question. "But I don't think he's either a pathological liar or a great but as yet undiscovered actor. When I talked to him at Macy's he seemed to be genuinely pleased with how the pumice business is going. I may be all wrong, of course, but it's hard for me to believe he's cooking the books to impress his investors. Maybe, just maybe, we'll know by the time you emerge from the Rockies."

* * *

David Neale, resplendent in a fuchsia tee shirt with a gila monster scrambling across it, packed his gear and headed off the next morning bound for Colorado. Abby took Francis and Pooh-Bear on a short forest walk, but somehow her heart wasn't in it. The dialysis was going well, and physically she was doing better. Emotionally, however, she felt flat, empty, without effervescence, like a carbonated drink left open too long on a warm day.

By Saturday morning she was positively restless. After the flurry of activity during the preceding week, the house was clean and her wardrobe was in as good a shape as it was ever likely to be. What now? She couldn't even take Pooh-Bear on an extended forest walk because they were getting ready to go with their parents to Kendrick Peak on a camping expedition.

"Well, friend," she said, looking at Francis. "It's just you and me."

Francis gazed at her quizzically.

"All right, you and *I*, but must we be so grammatical?"

Francis didn't appear to be any more enlightened. However, when she reached for the leash that, in his mind at least, clarified things. Leash meant walk, and walk meant squirrels and wonderful smells and lots and lots of trees to receive his special attentions. He chased his non-existent tail in tight circles to express his enthusiasm.

"Lots of water, Francis, if you're going to get full enjoyment out of those trees," Abby told him. She pulled out not one, but two of the water containers she kept in the freezer about a third full of frozen water, and filled them the rest of the way with tap water. Then she settled them in her day pack against a nylon jacket she carried for padding. Today she certainly didn't need even a light jacket for anything but padding. Where were these famous summer storms everyone talked about? Every day seemed hotter than the last, and the only thing resembling a cloud she'd seen were those dramatic purple and gold banners that unfurled along the horizon at sunset.

After a moment's thought she added some dog cookies, a wedge of hard cheese, some bread and an apple. Her potassium still posed no problem, thank heaven.

The day was even hotter than she'd realized. She and Francis soldiered doggedly on, Abby, at least, moving on auto-pilot. Not until Francis began to lag noticeably did she think to slip her backpack off and pull out the little tin measuring cup she carried there. She filled it with water for Francis, who greedily replenished his tree-marking capacity.

She had not consciously headed for the Pycenium, but suddenly there it lay before them. To her surprise, no one seemed to be around.

Well, she thought, lunch time Saturday on a *very* hot summer day. The men had probably gone to get a burger and a cold beer, or maybe they had quit for the day. But surely someone must have stayed around to keep an eye on things. Jim had mentioned guards, only she didn't see them. Moreover, she realized that she seriously needed to use the toilet. She headed for the trailer that served as an office. The door was unlocked, so she walked in. She called out. No one replied. But there, thank God, was the toilet, door partly open so she couldn't miss it. Her nose wrinkled. Not very clean, but adequate.

As she prepared to make her way out of the trailer Shorty Dean appeared at the open door.

"So, another goddamned snooper." Francis lunged forward and Abby only barely succeeded in leashing him in before he took a large hunk out of Shorty's leg, which was clearly what the little dog had in mind. Dean had a choice word or two to say about Francis, including an accurate comment about his ancestry. Then, with an obvious effort, Dean pulled himself together.

"Sorry, Dr. Taylor. I don't much like dogs. Never have. They don't like me neither."

Francis rumbled ominously.

"I can see that Jim's not here, so we were just going anyway." Only an implied lie, she salved her conscience.

"No, don't go. It's a hot day. Can't I give you something to drink? A beer, maybe?"

"No, thank you. Is Jim due back soon?" She ought to say something to Jim Wilson now that she was here. Why, she wondered, had she wandered so far and in this particular direction?

"Yeah." Shorty glanced at his watch. "Maybe ten minutes or so."

"Well. . . ."

"A soft drink, maybe? Think we've got one or two of them around here."

Abby felt very tired. The heat had taken more out of her than she realized. It would be good to sit down a few minutes before heading back.

"That would be nice." She tried her best to sound pleasant.

"While I'm getting it, would you mind, ma'am, putting your little dog outside? There's not much room in here and he acts like he don't like me."

A confirming rumble came from Francis.

She took the dog out and, with a silent apology, slipped his leash over a snag under a scraggly, undernourished jack pine which provided some shade. In any case, she wouldn't be long. She checked her watch. If Jim didn't appear in ten minutes, she and Francis were out of here.

She gave Francis a reassuring pat and then stepped back into the trailer. Shorty Dean handed her the soft drink which he had opened for her. She glanced at the name on the can. It was a brand she didn't know, but at least it was cold. The trailer had a small refrigerator in the corner. Dean pulled out a beer for himself. He clicked on a fan which stirred the tepid air. However, there was no air conditioning. Most summers no one in Flagstaff needed refrigeration, she'd repeatedly been told. So how had she managed to pick one of the hottest summers on record? Beginner's luck, she supposed.

"Where is everyone?" she asked.

"We don't usually work after noon on Saturdays, 'specially if it's this hot." She could smell a faint reek of sweat from his skin. He took off his hat and with the back of his arm wiped beads of sweat from his hair line.

"But the guards?"

"One's sick. The other had some business in Phoenix, so I'm here for the time being."

There was a long moment of silence.

"Do you come from this area originally?" Abby asked for lack of anything better to say.

"Down round Bisbee."

"Have you always been in mining?"

"Mostly mining; some cattle, some cotton. Didn't much take to the cattle or cotton."

"Is mining pumice difficult?"

"Naw. You've got to get rid of the trees and stuff. Then you strip off the overburden, rocks and dirt mostly, with a bulldozer. When you get down to the deposit, you use a front-end loader to take the pumice to where it's separated by grades. I guess you know we're after the right grade for stonewashing. The other stuff we try to sell for gardening and construction. The stonewashing pumice is what counts. That's where the money is."

"And?"

"That's about it. Dig it up, sort it out, haul it off. Oh, and keep it dry. Not that this summer there's been much problem on that score," he snorted.

"No, I imagine there hasn't." So hot, so dry, she thought and took another sip of the soft drink. The drink tasted pretty awful. This was one brand that, if she ever ran across it, she would never buy. "It doesn't sound as if you're very impressed with the pumice."

"It makes money." He shrugged. "But who could be impressed with this little bit of cat scratching? Ever seen the Lavender Pit?"

She shook her head.

"Now there's a real open pit mine. They've taken almost four hundred million tons of ore and waste out of that dude. Seen the open pit mine at Morenci?"

Again she shook her head.

"Bigger than twenty-seven football fields put end-to-end. Ate up the whole town. Had to move it."

"The town?" she asked, incredulously.

"Yep, they moved the whole darned town. Built a new one. Back about '69."

"Mmmm." What could she possibly say to that?

"So what do you do for Jim Wilson?" she asked instead of trying to pursue the fate of the moving Morenci.

"Well. . . ."

She saw him debate with himself about how honest to be—pride versus keeping a low profile, she'd bet. "Jim's got good ideas. And he can get people interested and that sort of thing. But the day-to-day stuff. . . ."

"So you run the actual mining operation?"

"And keep the books. Went back to school. Studied computers and some bookkeeping at the community college. Man needs a tad more education than he used to."

This was certainly a sentiment with which she agreed wholeheartedly, but when she tried to nod agreement her head felt very heavy. She decided this was the last time she and Francis would walk so far in the heat.

"You're right, of course," she said, rather groggily to her own ears. "Education *is* important. Did you find it difficult to go back to college, as an adult that is?"

"Most of the people in these 'continuing education' courses, so they call them, have been around a bit. It was kind of strange at first, being in a classroom again like I was a kid. But it meant a lot more money and steadier work, and the computer part came easy. Teacher said I was a natural."

"And the books?"

"I just log in the basics. We've got a gal over in California—a genuine Certified Public Accountant—who gets everything prettied up for the tax people."

And do you make any significant changes while you're at it, Abby wondered? So many potentially interesting things to ask, so much she would like to know, only she found herself unable to articulate the most basic question. Her mind wandered. The heat, the close air, the soporific drone of the fan. She felt herself drifting off through space.

Later, she had no idea how much later, Abby came to partial consciousness as angry voices argued over her head.

"You can't kill the dog. It's *got* to look natural." Abby recognized Sorrell Lawrence's strident voice, and a chill ran through her despite the heat. What the devil was she doing here?

"Keep your pants on and don't be so damned hoity-toity, Miz Know-it-all California." Shorty Dean—she'd know that nasal twang anywhere. "I'd love to wring that dog's neck, but ain't about to touch a hair of his ugly hide. It'll look natural all right. Look, she goes walking. The day's hot. Too hot for her in the shape she's in. She collapses. Misses a couple of those dialysis sessions Jim was telling me about. Becomes disoriented. Can't get back. So who's going to look for her? That Neale fellow took off for Colorado yesterday to hike or something, and I heard her sister's over in Prescott."

"What happens if she doesn't get the dialysis?"

"From what she told Jim, pretty soon she goes into a coma and that's that."

"It's too bad but sometimes things happen that way." Sorrell sounded no more concerned than if she'd been discussing a new hairstyle. In fact, less. "We're not actually killing her, just letting nature take its course. But the dog would never leave her. I don't care if he did take a chunk out of your leg when you drugged Bob Curtis and had another try when you and your buddy were ransacking her place the other night. If she's found without the dog there are going to be too many questions."

"I told you lady, I'm not messing with the mutt."

Abby wanted to move, to scream, to go at them with fists and nails, but she couldn't even manage opening her eyes. She drifted off again. When she came to again, heart hammering in her chest,

Sorrell and Shorty were still arguing above her prone body as if she had already died. The trailer's indoor-outdoor carpeting felt hard and scratchy against her cheek, and was probably filthy as well, but she couldn't seem to open her eyes to find out.

"What's Jim going to think when he finds out. . . ."

"He's not going to find out," Sorrell hissed. "Any more than he really knows what really happened to Bob Curtis. Jim may suspect, but he doesn't *know* anything. And we're going to keep it that way."

"Yeah, well, so long as I get my money," Shorty responded sullenly.

"Don't worry about that," Sorrell's voice reassured him soothingly. "I suppose it's too bad Curtis had to die. But how long would he have stayed off the drugs anyway? He was a loser. You just speeded up the inevitable." Abby would have bet anything that the bitch accompanied her words with a shrug and a nonchalant toss of her palomino mane.

"Bob Curtis was one thing. This gal's another." Shorty lowered his voice. "Jim seems kind of sweet on her."

"Tough luck," Sorrell snapped. "Like Bob Curtis, she found out too much."

What am I supposed to have found out? Abby wondered. *Just because Shorty found me in the office, he thinks I was snooping.* She wanted to protest she didn't *know* anything, but even if in her present groggy, confused state she could have managed to say something, she realized it wouldn't do her a damn bit of good.

"Anyway, sooner or later she'd be dead from the kidneys. You can't tell me that this dialysis thing can go on indefinitely. Very unnatural," Sorrell observed with disdain.

I am not going to die, not when I'm just beginning to figure out how to live, Abby screamed in her head. Then again she lost consciousness.

At some point something filtered through about spotted owls, night time, and someone—was it Titus or Bob?—spying.

"Yeah, that Curtis sure was one hell of a hacker," Abby heard Shorty saying when the fog again rolled back sufficiently to make sense of the words overhead. His voice brimmed with admiration. "I mean, it had to be him. None of those other tree hugger types have the skills. I'll bet he got hold of that special software program— the Security Administrator Tool for Analyzing Networks. SATAN. With something like that, breaking into our computer would of been child's play. Anyway, you're right. It sure was lucky I got that baby rigged so I can tell when somebody's been messing with it. Course Curtis couldn't have proved a thing."

"Doesn't matter." A moment of comparative silence, the only sound that of someone moving around. "No, no ropes, Shorty," Sorrell commanded. "Just one rope burn. . . ."

"Okay, okay. I guess she's not about ready to give us any trouble. About Curtis. . . ."

"With what he got together along with the financial records that slimy backwoods bastard Titus stole, they would have figured out enough to make a good case to the Department of Interior's Board of Land Appeals. No more claims. No patents." The usually unruffled Sorrell sounded uncharacteristically strung out. "For *my* development. . . . Only two hundred some acres claimed and not by any means all of that patented! I've *got* to have at least five hundred acres for anything first class, and more would be better."

Shit, Abby swore to herself, *shit, shit, shit*. Bob had died, she might soon die, so this aggressive, domineering bitch could get her own real estate development?

* * *

Abby hovered between painful consciousness and the moments of reprieve when her mind slipped away to an infinitely dark, infinitely quiet place. Once she heard Francis barking furiously, then yelping with pain. And again she slipped away.

She came back to the present in darkness. Panic swept over her like a cold wind. As a babe she had been born from darkness into light. Now she felt she was slipping inexorably back into the primal darkness again. Not a gentle journey. Her head ached violently, her body was an alien thing—violated by the now useless mechanisms of life. Her abdomen felt distended, the unexcreted fluids that dialysis could have removed pressing heavily upon her.

217

She was trapped. Trapped by the sickness of her body, trapped by the lightless, almost airless place of confinement. Perhaps after all death would be a blessed release.

Desperately she fought the panic as well as the waves of nausea that assailed her. Neither hysteria nor vomiting would be the least bit of help, she reminded herself grimly. Nor would the tears she struggled against with equal resolve. But the loneliness, the sense of loss and isolation, almost overwhelmed her.

Her limbs were cramped, but when she tried to move, slowly and tentatively, she realized that she wasn't bound or fettered in any way. When she finally managed to open her eyes, she discovered that in fact she wasn't entirely alone for there, beside her, was Francis. In the dim light she could see that someone had muzzled him with a heavy piece of rubber. When Francis saw her eyes open he fought, as he must have fought before, trying desperately to tear off the offending object.

"Just a minute, old boy," she told him in a creaky voice that sounded not at all like her own.

Abby looked around her. They were in some sort of metal storage shed. Only a little murky light trickled in from an air vent above. She patted Francis reassuringly and felt around them. Her hand encountered something. Her pack! At least they hadn't taken her pack. Although she hadn't been hiking, as opposed to walking, since she moved to Arizona, it still contained her emergency kit, including the scissors she kept on hand to cut a piece of moleskin when she got a blister or to trim an Ace bandage to size in the unhappy event of a sprained ankle. And maybe also her Swiss Army knife, she thought with a tingle of anticipation. She reached in the front compartment and her fingers encountered the tiny emergency flashlight she always carried. Miracle of miracles, the batteries still worked.

It took the knife, which she did find, to set Francis free. Once the dog had been relieved of the cruel muzzle and given water, only a little so he didn't throw up, she checked hopefully to find out what else might be in the pack.

Not much, but the roll call was comforting. Compass, Ace

bandage, and the little kit from which she had extracted the knife and scissors. The kit also held a fine-tooth comb to remove cholla cactus chunks from the unwary hiker, tweezers to extract cactus spines, matches, a mirror to signal with, a whistle, moleskin, Band-Aids, aspirin and some heavy-duty pain pills in case she was seriously injured. Rummaging around she also found antihistamines in the event of bee stings and finally some rubber bands and safety pins, both of which she had included on general principles. The routine inventory kept at bay, at least temporarily, the panic that threatened to engulf her.

The shed had no windows, only the air vent, and when she struggled to her feet and tried the door it was, as she had assumed, locked from outside. Probably a padlock, she thought, heaviness settling into her limbs. She vaguely remembered seeing two such sheds at the mine, both of them locked in that fashion. Not that there was much to steal in this one, nothing more than a pile of screens probably used to separate the stonewashing pumice from the other grades.

God, but it was hot and stuffy! For a minute she simply sat and suffered.

She remembered Sorrell, or maybe it had been Shorty Dean, saying something about letting nature take its course. And it would, only not as they'd envisioned. They didn't realize that she was not as yet entirely dependent on the dialysis. The kidney problem wouldn't kill her, certainly not in the time frame they could count on. No, the kidneys wouldn't do her in; the real threat was dehydration.

She looked at her watch. Late Saturday afternoon. David Neale was long gone, she thought with a pang. The Khalsas wouldn't be back until Sunday evening, and they probably wouldn't notice her absence until Monday at the earliest, if then. Becky had her hands full at Iron Springs. She might call Sunday afternoon, but she wouldn't really start to worry until Monday. And Monday was Becky's book club, so she wouldn't begin to panic until Monday afternoon at the earliest. Surely the men wouldn't be working at the mine on Sunday, and Dean would think of some good excuse to keep them off the job until he was sure she was dead or at the very least in a coma. Terror trickled into her limbs like an icy cold injection.

Thank God she had packed extra water. However, Francis and she had already used a fair amount of it on their walk to the mine, and there was no chance that what was left would take them through the weekend. Not with this heat.

Until that moment she'd been too much occupied with examining the situation to take in its gravity. All of a sudden the full horror of it hit her. She and Francis were going to die like forest animals caught in one of those awful, sadistic traps. Or like that poor, unfortunate homeless man who had recently fallen into an old mine shaft. What a dreadful way to go, slowly, painfully, knowing each moment what lay ahead. Too awful to take in! Well, at least Francis was spared the knowledge of approaching death, but she was sure he must sense her utter despair. She turned off the flashlight. Might as well save the batteries, although for what she couldn't say. Weeping softly she gathered Francis in her arms.

* * *

David Neale tried to suppress the concerns that nagged at him all the way across the Big Reservation. The burglary. Abby. The dialysis. Bob Curtis and all the unanswered questions. Then Abby again. Always back to Abby.

He had spent Friday night and part of Saturday with Nina's family in Chinle. On the road again he drove hard up 191 and then east on 160, hoping to get well into Colorado before he quit for the night. But he decided to stop for a stretch at Four Corners, where many Indians, some of them Navajos he knew, had booths displaying crafts for sale. There he ran across an uncle of Nina's and spent much longer talking with him than he'd anticipated. As he was about to depart, the old man, his dark face as scored and abraded as the barren land, looked at him shrewdly. "I dunno what it is, but sumthin's going on with you. You're worried, worried way down deep."

David felt chagrined. Evidently all those worries that had plagued him as he drove across the reservation showed on his face.

He had thought himself a little more subtle than that.

"You tell me you're go'n on a fine backpacking expedition. A man can walk away a lot of things. But this time it won't work, I think. I think what's bother'n you is going to keep on bother'n you because you're a man with unfinished business."

* * *

The Khalsas had reached the camping ground at Mt. Kendrick, set up their tent and had everything in order, when Bear started to vomit violently.

"She's never been sick like this before in her life," a very worried Sada Anand told her husband. "It can't have been anything she ate or Pooh would be just as sick. You know they share everything."

Soul Singh placed Sat the cat, who had insisted on coming along despite the animal's usual reservations about any travel by car, in the little girl's arms and then felt Bear's head.

"You feel, Sada Anand, but it seems to me like she's burning up with fever."

Bear buried her face in the cat's fur.

Somehow Sada Anand located the child's forehead. Soul Singh had been right. The child was on fire.

"Williams or Flagstaff?" she asked.

"Flag. They have the hospital and you know the people."

* * *

Abby came back to consciousness again and wished she hadn't. Once more despair and panic threatened to engulf her.

With a great effort of will, she tried to pull herself together. At least the storage shed was much cooler. So much cooler that, shocked, she realized that she was actually shivering, and cuddled Francis all that much closer.

She gave them both a drink of water. One thing she had learned hiking was not to conserve water past a reasonable point, even when running out on the desert. Too many people had been found dead with canteens or bottles still a third or so full. A person needed water to think clearly and deal with a situation. Dehydration muddled the brain.

A wind had begun to worry the shed. A flash of light lit the storage area through the air vent and was almost immediately followed by a huge clap of thunder. The much-vaunted monsoons were on their way! Not that it would do Francis and her any good, Abby reflected bitterly. Not trapped in a waterproof storage shed.

She slipped on the nylon jacket she'd used for padding in her backpack, gave Francis a couple of dog bones she found in her pack, and munched pensively on a bit of overripe cheese. She remembered reading somewhere that someone in danger of dehydration should avoid food. Was it that food took water to digest? Well, she wasn't sure about that, and in spite of everything her stomach growled.

Abby heard the wind pick up, the trees sigh and groan, the metal sides of the building shudder. Then she realized that she was also hearing a faint, alien sound, something that had nothing to do with the coming storm or the creaky storage shed. The sound grew steadily louder until she recognized it as a harsh roar—the sound of motorbikes. Never had a loud, grating noise been so welcome to her ears.

Seconds later the roar ceased and she heard voices.

"Ya' think we could get into one of them fuckers? That rain's coming fast."

"Rain, shit." A pounding began as if the shed and its surroundings had come under siege. "It's hail. It's going to take the fucking finish right off the fucking bikes!"

For a moment Abby was too shocked at the idea of rescue to react. Then, trembling, she reached into her pack and brought out her whistle. She blew it frantically and Francis, who seemed to sense the urgency of the situation, barked like a creature possessed.

"Son of a bitch, there's something in there. A dog. Maybe trapped."

"A dog blowing a fucking whistle?"

"Help," Abby screamed. "Please help me."

Abby heard the resounding sound of metal on metal, the sound, she hoped, of the padlock being knocked off by an iron bar. Then two wet, tattooed figures appeared wheeling their motorbikes. Her knights in shining armor actually wore black, sleeveless tee shirts, skin-tight Levis, and black simulated leather boots. But to her they couldn't have looked better if they'd been turned out in full suits of brightly polished mail.

Abby barely had time to take in the unlikely nature of her rescuers, when they heard gunshots cutting sharply through the clatter of hail.

"My God," Abby breathed. "Are they shooting at you or at me?"

* * *

"What?" Henderson roared into the phone. "Oh, damn. I'll be right there."

There, he thought, went a promising evening, and made a brief apology to the lady veterinarian who had treated Francis so kindly.

"A crazy situation," he told her as he straightened his shirt. "We got an SOS from One Universe via cell phone. They say they are doing pitched battle with someone, identity unclear, in Coconino National Forest next to the spotted owl habitat. Something about stealing or maybe kidnapping. But I just can't believe the owls are in danger, even if they are rare. How would you get hold of one of them in the first place? And what would you do with one if you got it? I'd say the whole thing was a farce except that the dispatcher says she clearly heard gunfire in the background and that the person who called sounded damned scared."

* * *

Henderson looked down at Abby in amazement and she looked up at the big man looming over her with equal surprise. "How did you get here so quickly?" she asked.

Gradually the firing had become more sporadic, finally ceasing altogether. Abby had then convinced one of her tattooed rescuers—either Seth or Dan, she couldn't tell them apart—to slosh through the rain, break into the trailer, and call the lieutenant. This took the knight errant as little time as if the door had been left standing invitingly open. Clearly these boys' education had been broad and varied and definitely on the wrong side of the law.

"I was already heading this way," the lieutenant explained.

"Oh?"

"It's the damnedest story, but I guess we've got a minute before the ambulance gets here to take you to the hospital."

"I don't need an ambulance," Abby argued as she tried to rise from her sitting position in the shed. The world whirled around her and she abruptly sat down again.

"Well, you're getting one anyway. Also we've got an injured member of One Universe."

"What happened?"

The lieutenant squatted down beside her, his square face almost on her level. "Do you know, or know of, Martha Van Dyke, a leader in One Universe?"

"I do indeed. Quite a committed woman."

"Which is putting it mildly. It seems that about two weeks ago Mrs. Van Dyke and a friend came out to check on the owl habitat. They wanted to see how close the pumice mining was getting, if the dust was causing a problem, and so forth. Mrs. Van Dyke's dog went after a rabbit and chased it into a drift, a more or less horizontal mining tunnel. I gather that the dog's collar hung up on something. Anyway, nothing for it but Martha Van Dyke goes into the drift to set the dog free, and lo and behold, there is a large and very carefully wrapped object which turns out on closer inspection to be the missing 1929 Alfa Romeo."

"The stolen car!" Abby shrieked like a teenager who's been told her favorite rock star is coming to town.

"That's right. Manna from heaven, she decided, and began to consider how to exploit the situation. That woman is nothing if not clever. When she reported her find to a few select members of One Universe, they were afraid that someone might come to retrieve the car before they could perfect a plan and put it into action. One Universe members started taking turns watching the area. Everyone except for Titus, Peter Rivers, and Linda Wallace were told that someone was threatening to wipe out the owls and their habitat, which would have eliminated one impediment to the expansion of the mine. The owls needed protection. As a matter of fact, the 'owl watchers'—owl watchers, now give me a break—who reported the forest fire undoubtedly thought they were caring for their feathered friends."

"The gunfire tonight?" Abby demanded eagerly.

"Someone came for the car."

"Who?"

He shrugged his broad shoulders. "We may never know. Current speculations include everything from Mexicans to Iranians. In any case, they got more than they bargained for. Titus and Peter Rivers were on duty tonight. You know, Saturday night and the young 'owl watchers,'" the lieutenant grimaced, "had better things to do. Titus and Peter served in Nam and know their stuff. Both were armed. Fortunately they weren't shooting to kill, just to frighten the other guys off. And whoever it was wasn't interested in a pitched battle. Titus got a bullet in his arm, but as far as we know that was the only casualty."

"So you've got the car?" Abby asked incredulously. *Oh, Becca, just wait till you hear this!*

"Yes, and all the law enforcement personnel in Coconino County will undoubtedly be rejoicing."

They didn't even begin to know about rejoicing, she thought with a feeling of elation that transcended dizziness, nausea, cramped muscles and probably a whole lot of other aches and pains that hadn't had a chance to surface yet.

"What will they do about Martha Van Dyke and One Universe?"

"Not a goddamn thing, if I have anything to say about it. They should have reported the discovery of stolen property, but why make an issue of it? And those kids who were 'owl watching' last week did make sure the fire was caught early on. No, I would say One Universe has done more good than harm. Best to let the whole thing drop."

* * *

The nursing floor supervisor took one look at the hospital room and appeared about to explode when Lieutenant Henderson escorted her out into the hall. What the big man said could not be heard, but the supervisor did not return and the nurse who came in a bit later to check Abby made no comment on the number of after-hours visitors.

All parties had converged on the hospital at approximately the same time. Members of One Universe had come to offer Titus moral support. The lieutenant, with Francis, and the bikers, Seth and Dan, had followed the ambulance bearing a reluctant Titus and a still more reluctant Abby.

Not realizing that David Neale had left for his camping trip, Henderson had asked the dispatcher to call the house, where she reached a puzzled Neale, who had just returned and was wondering where his renter had gone. The dispatcher had also reached Dr. Frankenthaller, who was fortunately in Flagstaff and not Phoenix for the weekend. The Khalsas got the news of Abby's arrival through the hospital grapevine, as their pediatrician was examining Bear, who, in the way of children, was soon recuperating as quickly and inexplicably as she had become ill. All of them, except One Universe and Dr. Frankenthaller, who had left after examining Abby and assuring her that she was doing remarkably well, now crowded into her hospital room.

"Why in the hell did this Sorrell person and Shorty Dean try to kill you?" David Neale snarled with a palpable rage that extinguished all signs of his usual casual good humor.

"Shorty found me at the mine's office. I guess he thought I'd come to snoop and worried that I might have seen something that proved that the Pycenium's financial statement made the mine look more lucrative than it actually is," Abby answered wearily.

"Somebody's trying to cheat the investors?" asked Soul Singh.

"Not the investors. The government."

"Taxes?"

"No, the United States Department of the Interior."

"What?" Soul Singh looked puzzled.

"Sorrell Lawrence is a woman obsessed," said Abby, shaking her head at the memory of someone ready to write off any death that suited her purposes as simply inevitable. Bob would get back into drugs; Abby herself would succumb to her kidney problems. So why not simply hasten the process?

"The Realtor who rented you the house?" Sada Anand made the connection.

"Yes, although house renting isn't her usual thing. She normally deals in first-class residential properties. She's making *a*

226

lot of money, but she's out for more than that. She wants to be in charge of her own development, a top-of-the-line planned community, probably gated. I suppose with a golf course, the whole thing. Only as everyone knows, there's precious little private land around Flagstaff." She recalled the crowded feeling that first day when she had passed under I-40 into Flagstaff's main commercial area, her amazement at Sorrell's little copse in the center of the city, and Jim Wilson's explanation of how the land had been acquired for a development as expansive as the one in which the Olsons had built their large, elegant home.

Abby glanced about her, and smiled to herself. If only she could command such consummate attention when she lectured on the Anglo-Saxons! Except for Francis and Pooh-Bear, the three cuddling together contentedly in a corner—thank God the nursing supervisor hadn't realized what was under the blanket—those present were following her every word.

"Almost all the land is federal. Mostly Coconino National Forest." Lord knew she'd spent enough time walking in it. People here took it for granted. Even the desk clerk at the resort had commented on the number of forest roads.

"I think I should back up a minute." Abby rubbed her temples, hoping she was making some sense. Her head ached like hell.

"When Sorrell first came to Arizona she re-established contact with someone she'd known back in California, Jim Wilson, who was now mining pumice. In the National Forest no less. This ignited a lot of controversy. Native Americans, environmentalists, just a whole lot of ordinary people were up in arms. But nobody could do anything about the mine because it's quite legal under the 1872 Mining Law, which says that anyone can mine on public lands, federal lands that is, unless the land is specifically withdrawn from mining exploration." David nodded and all her listeners looked thoughtful.

"Not only that, after the miner or company or whatever has put in a certain amount of work on the mine over a given period of time, he or it can patent the land, which is just another way of saying 'buy' it. In the case of the Pycenium, for the princely sum of two fifty an acre." Abby laughed caustically and then wished she hadn't. The laugh did nothing for her headache.

"But the Pycenium is in the middle of Coconino National Forest," Soul Singh objected.

"No matter. Whatever else you may say about Sorrell, she's smart and does her homework. I discovered from one of the books Bob had checked out of the library that there are plenty of precedents both in California and in Arizona, and probably other places too, where mining claims have been patented and then later developed. Especially for summer homes, but also for more substantial developments." Abby reached for the glass on the bedside table and took a long swallow of water.

"The investors in the Pycenium wanted to patent anyway so they could avoid the environmentalists, whose hands are tied once something becomes private land. I imagine that Sorrell and Jim had some arrangement by which, once the pumice was depleted, she could get hold of those patents and, voilà, she's on her way to her own development, world class, et cetera."

"But to fall under the Mining Law the mineral has to be valuable." David seemed to know exactly where she was heading. "Stonewashing pumice is considered to be sufficiently valuable. However, thanks to new techniques the market has been falling. Not disastrously, but perhaps enough to subject new claims to a challenge or to jeopardize the patenting process."

"Exactly. And Sorrell, along with her henchman Shorty Dean, couldn't afford to take any chances," Abby finished his thought. "And even if the patenting process were to go like a breeze, the acreage claimed to date isn't enough for the sort of statement Sorrell has in mind. So, with some fancy bookkeeping—two sets of books, I imagine—they made it look like the mine was more profitable than it is."

"Bob?" Sada Anand asked tenuously.

"Bob hacked into Pycenium's computer and found one set of figures. Titus, who had probably been watching the mine all along, stole some others in hard copy. I don't know how Shorty guessed about Bob. Maybe he had some way of tracing the hacker or maybe he figured Bob was the only person associated with One Universe who had the skills. I have a vague recollection of hearing something like that when I was about ninety percent out of it."

"They killed Bob?" Sada Anand's voice was choked with rage.

"I think your first guess was right. He just wanted to see the forest creatures at twilight. Maybe check on the owls. Remember, this was before Martha Van Dyke discovered the Alfa Romeo, so no 'watchers' were in place. Anyway, Shorty must have spotted Bob and thought that he, like Titus, was snooping, trying to get more data to substantiate the double bookkeeping. So yes," Abby replied gently. "It was Shorty who was responsible." She just couldn't say the "k" word. "Backed by Sorrell, though whether she was actually there or not, I don't know." She skipped the part about Bob's expendability.

Sada Anand nodded briefly. Her paramount question answered, she retreated far, far into herself. So much pain, Abby reflected. Just as in the case of polycystic kidney disease, it wasn't just one person. The victim's fate was like a stone tossed into still water, creating ever-widening ripples.

"Francis?"

On hearing Abby utter his name, a wet black nose appeared from the blankets with which Pooh and Bear had made him a nest in the corner. Some wriggling and muzzle, head, and long ears followed.

"You know," she said to the room at large, "he tried to save me, just as he did Bob. A small animal, perhaps, but a very brave guy."

* * *

The Khalsas slipped away with Pooh-Bear and Francis, the latter discreetly wrapped up in a blanket like a baby. Lieutenant Henderson went off with a sheepish yet curiously elated Seth and Dan to retrieve their motorbikes, after first assuring the young men that, for the time being at least, they were on the right side of the law—undoubtedly a new if not unique experience for the two of them.

Abby leaned back against the pillow. Though intellectually she grasped what had happened, emotionally she had a lot of catching up to do. She hurt, she ached, she felt like a pile of doggy-do. Yet inside she nourished a warm glow. Tomorrow first thing, for it was far too late tonight, she would call Iron Springs and share with Becky the news about the Alfa Romeo. Not that its discovery could be chalked up to her own perspicacity or ingenuity, but that didn't matter. The car's discovery would take the heat off Charles, which was for now all that was important.

Meanwhile she was safe and sound and reasonably healthy. The law in its cumbersome way would deal with Sorrell Lawrence and Shorty Dean in due time. Yet she still felt confused, disoriented. She closed her eyes and dozed for a few minutes. When she opened them again, only David was there. Like the first time she met him, he looked tired and was unshaven. He even wore Levis, scuffed jogging shoes and a tee shirt sporting snow-speckled wolves, only tonight the shirt showed two wolves nuzzling. David reached out and took her hand.

"What happened to Colorado and the hiking?" she asked.

He explained about meeting up with Nina's uncle at Four Corners.

"Are the Navajos like the Celts? Do they have the gift of second sight?"

"No," David laughed. "He's a wise old man, but I don't think his comments had anything to do with second sight or ESP or anything like that."

"But. . ."

"He knew I was worried about something. It must have showed on my face."

"So he's a good people watcher?"

"The best, I'd say. And his theory is that I am a man with some unfinished business." He looked at her with an intensity that made the horrors earlier in the day recede, to be replaced by a warm glow. "And you, Abby, what do you say to that?"

She reached over and squeezed one of those strong, reassuring hands she had admired on the drive to Monument Valley. "A very wise old man."

230

* * *

When Toby Barrett opened *The Washington Post* and saw Albert Foster Richmond's fat, triumphant face staring up at him, he thought he would be sick. *Son of a bitch*, he swore as he skimmed the story; they'd found the Alfa Romeo after all. His guardians, the spotted owls whose presence ought to have kept everyone away, had proved instead to be magnets for those bastards from One Universe.

With disgust he perused the rest of the article. No one had been caught. Not that it would have made any difference to him if someone had because, except for feeding some very interesting ideas to Mohammed, he himself had never been personally involved. Mohammed had come up with the actor who resembled Foster Richmond and the luscious blonde. Mohammed had orchestrated the attack on Foster's mechanics in New York. A prosecutor might argue that money had exchanged hands between Mohammed and the congressman. But by this time any evidence of such a transaction had long since disappeared. That money was so well laundered that God himself couldn't find it.

No, Barrett knew he was in no jeopardy from the law or from Mohammed's backer, for whom he had done all that he had promised. However, he mused, there might be worse fates than being prosecuted or even dodging a would-be assassin. Seeing Richmond's self-satisfied grin splashed across the page was certainly one of them. All his joy had evaporated; all his happiness had turned to bile; his one moment of victory had been canceled out forever. Toby Barrett did something he had not done since he was a child. He put his head down on his arms and cried.

THE POLYCYSTIC KIDNEY DISEASE FOUNDATION

Polycystic kidney disease (PKD) is the most common of all the life-threatening hereditary diseases. It affects more Americans than the combined number of those suffering from cystic fibrosis, sickle-cell anemia, muscular dystrophy, hemophilia, Downs syndrome and Huntington's disease.

"Polycystic" literally means *many cysts*. These cysts grow in the kidneys, and sometimes the liver, of the person suffering from PKD, hindering the kidney's ability to do what it was intended to do (filter toxins from the bloodstream). In most cases PKD results in end stage renal disease, requiring dialysis or kidney transplantation for survival.

The PKD Foundation is the only organization, worldwide, solely devoted to programs of PKD research, patient education, public awareness, and advocacy for the nearly thirteen million people who have PKD. Over the past twenty years the Foundation has won the respect and involvement of the leading research scientists and medical clinicians throughout North America and beyond, funding 232 grants amounting to $9.89 million. It has emerged as the single most influential catalyst in causing expanded public and private investments in PKD research.

Today PKD, once viewed as hopelessly incurable, is seen in a new light as researchers explore therapies to slow and eventually stop the progression of this disease. Such successes grew from very modest beginnings. When, some twenty-five years ago, my father, Joseph H. Bruening, Kansas City business man and civic leader, discovered that my mother and I both had PKD, he immediately began to try to find out more about the disease. But, in his own words, "There was nowhere for us to turn for hope, encouragement, or even basic information."

By chance he came across a newspaper article about a Jared J.

Grantham, MD, Professor of Internal Medicine and Director of the Division of Nephrology and Hypertension at the University of Kansas Medical Center. Dr. Grantham was doing research in PKD, but having great difficulty awakening any interest among others in his field and even less in securing funding. As my father says, "At that point I made the decision to devote my time, energy, and money to research toward finding a treatment and cure for this devastating disease. I sold the family business and quickly enlisted Dr. Grantham's help. Together, in 1982, we formed the PKD Foundation."

The PKD Foundation grew slowly at first, then picked up momentum as more and more people concerned about the disease recognized the value of the scientific research that the Foundation was funding. At last victims of PKD and their families discovered that there was a place to turn to for information, encouragement, and hope. Yet, in spite of the enthusiastic response of the medical community and of those affected by the disease, PKD still received relatively little recognition from the general public.

Worn down by PKD, my mother died in 1989. A little more than two months later I had a kidney transplant, which turned my life around. A successful transplant is truly like being reborn. And, having been granted the gift of renewed life, I needed to do something to prove myself worthy of it. As an Arizona Press Woman since 1964, I had often tried to publish articles about PKD, but no one had showed any interest. Let's face it, I told myself, kidneys just aren't glamorous. A new approach seemed called for. Thus, after many struggles, *To Live or Die in Arizona* was born. My hope is that it will served to acquaint more people with PKD and to raise some much needed funds for the PKD Foundation and the Arizona Kidney Foundation. *Elizabeth Bruening Lewis, Phoenix, AZ, 2002*

The PKD Foundation: Kansas City, Missouri: 816-931-8655;
Information 800-PKD-CURE (753-2873)
pdkcure@pdkcure.org; www.pkdcure.org
The PKD Foundation is a 501(c)(3), 509(a)(1) public charity.

THE ARIZONA KIDNEY FOUNDATION

Currently, more than 5,500 Arizonans receive dialysis treatments at centers throughout the state. Another 1,000 patients use hemodialysis or peritoneal dialysis at home. One of the primary goals of the Arizona Kidney Foundation (AKF), an affiliate of the National Kidney Foundation, Inc., is to bring hope and help to these victims of end stage renal disease and their families.

My first encounter with the AKF at work happened when I visited my mother during dialysis sessions at a clinic in Scottsdale. A clean, shiny van with big windows would draw up in front of the clinic. The driver would get out, produce a footstool, and carefully help each of his passengers alight. His passengers were residents of the Salt River Indian Reservation, which at that time did not yet have a dialysis center. Nor did these patients have facilities for home dialysis. By providing the van with the helpful driver, the AKF was making it possible for them to receive their life-sustaining treatments.

Later, I happened across a far more dramatic example of what the AKF does as a matter of course. Recuperating from my kidney transplant, I met a woman on the same floor of the hospital whose life had been shattered by end stage renal disease. Upon hearing the diagnosis, her husband had left her with two small children and precious little in the way of funds. She was utterly desperate when the AKF stepped in. The Foundation sustained her throughout dialysis with much-needed emotional and financial support, including vouchers for food and dietary supplements. Then, having helped her find temporary care for the children, they got her down from her home up along the Colorado River to Phoenix for a transplant. Undoubtedly the Foundation subsequently helped her obtain the medications necessary for transplants, since the AKF is as concerned with giving aid to transplant patients as it is in assisting those undergoing dialysis. With tears in her eyes the woman said, "I would have died without the Arizona Kidney Foundation. And what would have happened to my kids?"

Nor does AKF's mission end here. Beyond patient aid, to which sixty-seven percent of its proceeds are directed, the AKF funds research directed toward moving kidney disease from treatment to cure, as well as toward improving the current course of treatment. The Foundation also encourages education for patients, professionals, and the public concerning the more recent developments in kidney disease prevention, treatment, and cure. And finally, the Arizona Kidney Foundation encourages support of organ donation. The need is acute. In the year 2000, about 150 kidney transplants were performed in Arizona. However, more than 50,000 individuals remained on the national waiting list for an organ transplant, including 586 Arizonans awaiting a kidney donation. *Elizabeth Bruening Lewis, Phoenix, AZ, 2002*

The Arizona Kidney Foundation: Phoenix: 602-840-1644; Tucson: 520-882-7640; www.AZKIDNEY.org; Organ Donor Information 1-888-840-ERMA (5762)
The Arizona Kidney Foundation is a 501(c)(3), 509(a)(1) public charity.

ABOUT THE AUTHOR

Elizabeth Bruening Lewis, Ph.D., has had a double career as a journalist and a cultural historian. Dr. Lewis holds a B.A. in philosophy from Vassar College, an M.A. in philosophy from Arizona State University, and a Ph.D. in medieval history from Georgetown University. She combined these two interests when she wrote *The Power of Sacred Images: A Guide to the Treasures of Early Christian Art*, an introduction to early Christian art and its period for the general reader. It won first place in the country in its category, religion and spirituality, in the National Federation of Press Women's 1998 communications contest. Presently she is finishing up a work on the Dark Ages, again for the general reading public. She is also an adjunct faculty member at the Frank Lloyd Wright School of Architecture in Scottsdale, Arizona.

Beyond history, Dr. Lewis's primary interest is the environment.

She served for ten years on the board of trustees of the Arizona Chapter of the Nature Conservancy and is a member of the Mineral Policy Center and of Law in the Public Interest. Her husband and she have spent many happy days hiking the mountains, canyons, and deserts of their beloved Arizona. They have a grown son and daughter and a Pembroke Welsh corgi.

Order Form

To Live or Die in Arizona is available for purchase through the PKD Foundation or the Arizona Kidney Foundation. The Foundation from which the book is purchased receives 100% of the sales price to be used to accomplish its respective mission. Price: $11.95 each plus shipping $3.50. Total $15.45.

Method of payment: ☐ Check made payable to either organization below. Or one of these credit cards:
☐ VISA ☐ MasterCard ☐ Discover ☐ American Express

_____

Credit Card Account Number

_____   _____

Signature   *Expiration Date*

Ordered by:

Name: _____

Street: _____

City/State/Zip _____

Daytime Phone (   ) _____

Ship To: *(if different from ordered by)*

_____

_____

_____

☐ **PKD FOUNDATION**
4901Main Street, Suite 201
Kansas City, MO 64112-2634
816.931.2600 1-800-755.2873
wwwpkdcure.org

☐ **ARIZONA KIDNEY FOUNDATION**
4203 East Indian School Rd., Suite 140
Phoenix, AZ 85018-5341
620.840.1644
www.azkidney.org